David McMullon now works as a commercial airline pilot, a boyhood dream, after leaving the RAF. He is happily married to Jill and has three sons but is pursuing compensation from the RAF over the effects of Gulf War Syndrome which he believes led to the loss of his baby daughter.

CHINOOK!

The Special Forces Flight in War and Peace

by David McMullon

POCKET BOOKS

LONDON · SYDNEY · NEW YORK · TOKYO · SINGAPORE · TORONTO

First published in Great Britain by Simon & Schuster UK Ltd, 1998
This edition first published by Pocket Books, 1999
An imprint of Simon & Schuster UK Ltd
A Viacom Company

1 3 5 7 9 10 8 6 4 2

Simon & Schuster UK Ltd
Africa House
64-78 Kingsway
London WC2B 6AH

Simon & Schuster Australia
Sydney

A CIP catalogue record for this book is available from the British Library

ISBN 0-671-01599-0

Printed and bound in Great Britain by Caledonian International Book
Manufacturing

To Jill, Andrew, Christopher, Alexander
and to the memory of Jenny.

CONTENTS

Acknowledgements		ix
Chapter 1:	Body Bags	1
Chapter 2:	Dreams of Flight	7
Chapter 3:	You're in the RAF Now	23
Chapter 4:	Chinook	39
Chapter 5:	Combat-Ready	59
Chapter 6:	Operational Action	77
Chapter 7:	Squadron Duties	99
Chapter 8:	Lockerbie	111
Chapter 9:	Snow and Sand	129
Chapter 10:	Exercise Cock-up	145
Chapter 11:	Welcome to Saudi	155
Chapter 12:	Bravo Four Zero	171
Chapter 13:	Lock-On	181
Chapter 14:	Kuwait at Last	191
Chapter 15:	Post-Gulf Disorder	207
Chapter 16:	Time to Go	223
Chapter 17:	The Mull of Kintyre	231
Glossary		249
Picture Permissions		253
Index		255

ACKNOWLEDGEMENTS

I would like to thank the following:

Robin Eggar who most skilfully helped me put my experiences into words, for all his hard work and the valuable time he spent with me on this project.

Roger Houghton, my agent, for his support and direction.

Martin Fletcher, Jacquie Clare, Katharine Young, and the team at Simon and Schuster for their professional expertise and commitment.

Andrew Fairfield for his support.

CHAPTER 1

BODY BAGS

I'd never seen a dead body before. Behind me were thirty cardboard boxes, neatly piled and stowed, secured by the cargo net.

We flew on in silence, interrupted only by the navigation calls. Flying in weather God had forsaken. Alone with our thoughts and our cargo. No idle chatter, no jokes, just business. No radar where we were heading. So we studied the map minutely, called out every landmark. Especially the wires.

My door was open. Now we were at low level I couldn't afford any extra refraction from the perspex. Not in those conditions. Outside was only driving, freezing rain. Storm clouds forced us lower and lower. The ground slid past us at 170 miles an hour.

My world was two-dimensional, a flat, ghost world in different shades of green. But I could see in the dark.

A town was coming, a blur in the far distance. If I took off my night-vision goggles, I could see its orange lights reflected on the cloud. But if I did that I couldn't see the wires the map insisted ran along the ridge of the next hill.

Bob wasn't wearing NVGs. He might have been the designated commander of the Chinook but he wasn't SF Flight. He hadn't got the same experience at NVG flying as

1

John, and if you're not used to them the NVGs give you a very false sense of security. It's not reality that you're seeing.

Bob studied the 1/4 map (one quarter million scale) too but he couldn't see it as well as I could. Bill was in his place at the back, just a shape behind the boxes. I could see his face staring out of his bubble. He was bound to be scratching his arse, this Jack the Lad, dreaming of the party we'd left far behind.

'Two miles ahead – I have a large village just right of the nose,' I called over the intercom. 'We need to be a quarter of a mile left of the road junction on a heading of two nine zero. Half a mile from the junction is rising ground and on top is a large set of wires, closing from four o'clock.'

I stared out the door. Visual contact was what mattered now. It was raining so hard I believed it was never going to stop. The wind and the aircraft's forward momentum were sucking the water back into the door. My right arm was soaked right through to the skin.

'I can see the wires,' John called. Good. So we were not going to hit them. I could study the map again.

We knew where we were going but we had no idea what we'd find when we got there. It wasn't a need-to-know mission. Nobody knew what had happened. Whatever it was, it was serious enough to fuck up Christmas.

I glanced back at the boxes we'd taken on board at Leeming. I knew what was inside them. Heavy-duty black plastic bags, two metres long with a giant zip running from sole to skull. Body bags.

I could still hear the voice that came over the intercom: 'We still don't know the full extent of the situation,' it clipped. 'However, the information we do have is that you won't need the medics any more.'

Half an hour to our destination. Time stretched like elastic. Aside from navigation instructions the only sounds I heard were the constants, the Chinook sounds you never escape. The high-pitched whine of the gearboxes. The thuck of the rotors overhead. The familiar, sickly, sweet smell of oil and warmed-up hydraulic fluids. All four of us were looking outside of the aircraft, constantly scanning the horizon.

'What the fuck—' John was a fraction ahead of the skipper.

Coming over the high ground, we all saw it. A queue of light. The fog lights and brake lights of thousands of station- ary cars. Bumper to bumper, stretching for fifteen miles along the motorway. Through the NVGs all the reds blurred into one long line of bright-green fire.

I flipped the goggles up, didn't need them any more. Now I could see the car lights distinctly, despite the pour- ing rain distorting and splashing everything. All aiming north. We didn't need a map now. Not with that blood-red arrow pointing straight at the heart of Lockerbie.

Just before we got to Lockerbie the red lights began to fade away, as if their job were done. We followed the road into town, goggles up. Circling right. Suddenly, out of the right-hand side of the aircraft, I saw flames, flashing blue lights, movement. There was a moment of silence

'Fucking hell,' said John.

'What is it? What can you see?' That was Bob, unsighted in the left-hand seat. If he could have jumped out of his seat he would. His head stared forward, jerked sideways, then back, desperate to catch a glimpse.

'Jesus Christ,' I said, 'look at that. It's a big one.'

I realised it was a passenger jet. Suddenly the huge dark cloud of uncertainty that had been hanging over me for nearly three hours lifted. I understood what I was about to see. This wasn't a Piper Cherokee that had taken the roof off a pub.

CHINOOK!

It was far worse than anything we had imagined.

The fuselage was the first thing I saw. A section of the passenger cabin seventy feet long. A quarter of a jumbo jet, but no cockpit, no tail and no wings. It had gouged a huge hole thirty feet deep, taken out two houses completely, right down to the foundations. There was debris all across the road and up the side of the hill. It was as if some angry giant had taken a boiled egg, laid it on its side and tried to slice it in half. But, unable to do it smoothly and evenly, in a rage he had torn the top half off. I saw the row of little windows, then a gap where the fuselage has been torn, then more windows, a jagged rip all the way down. All surrounded by a ring of flame. It was still burning, fire engines around it. The fuel had sunk into the ground and kept the fire alive.

But our priority was landing, not gawping. I identified the landing site, called out, 'Flashing lights down on the field at two o'clock.' Two search–and–rescue helicopters were already parked on the school playing field. We straightened up to come into the landing site and there, lying in the middle of the road, was an engine. Embedded seven feet down into the tarmac. I saw the compressor blades, the engine mount with all the cable lines and the hydraulic mounts dangling out of the top.

We snapped into our tasks for landing. I leaned out of the door, looked for any obstructions as we came round, then talked Bob down.

'Forward thirty, forward forty and right. Height is good. Telephone wires to cross. Continue forward twenty, clear the wires, twenty descending fifteen, ten.' I talked down the hover until we were a few feet above the grass, lowered the step on the door, checked underneath to make sure there was nothing sticking up to penetrate the fuselage. Shut down.

One of the search–and–rescue blokes came over to tell us

4

we were meeting at the hall. When we got off the aircraft we couldn't see the flames but we could see the reflection flickering in the sky, bits of ash floating up in the air. Coming off a Chinook you can usually smell only hydraulic and turbine fuels, but, as we walked towards the hall, the smell of the fire increased.

It was still burning fiercely, high temperatures and bright flames created by the magnesium alloy and aluminium from the aircraft fuselage. You can't put that out with normal water, but the fire engines were there valiantly trying to hose it all down. I smelled exhaust fumes from all the ambulances, fire engines and police cars milling around. There were sirens going off everywhere. When one stopped another started. There was noise everywhere. Constant, unrelenting noise.

But the flames were silent.

CHAPTER 2

DREAMS OF FLIGHT

Less than five years earlier I had been pushing my mum's Mini down the street trying to jump-start it so I wouldn't be late for work again. The battery was shot, the exhaust was gone and it stank rigid of petrol. Mum's car never had any petrol in it so I had to get up early to siphon fuel out of my dad's car (he used to think he was getting ten miles to the gallon and was forever taking it back to the garage to complain). Overhead I heard the sound of an aircraft. Without looking up I knew it was a Jet Provost Mark 3, one of the RAF trainers that used to come up from the training grounds and bash round Newcastle.

Lucky bastards, I thought. Imagine doing that for a living, instead of working in a bank.

I was so obsessed with flying that if I heard an aircraft overhead I could tell you the make, the model, even the part numbers on its engine. I was working at the Trustee Savings Bank in Whitley Bay ten miles away, dressed in a suit, bored out of my mind, pushing banknotes over the counter. All I thought about was flying. I had a private pilot's licence – a PPL – and a third share in an old biplane

7

that had nearly bankrupted me. It was cheaper to buy fuel at the garage, so I'd always carry a five-gallon petrol can in the car.

Some people fall in love with music. Some people fall in love with cars. Some people fall in love with tanks and guns. I fell in love with aeroplanes.

When I was a kid I never wanted to do anything else other than fly aeroplanes. I have never ever lost that love of aviation: I am still as enthusiastic today as I was then. My mother's brother used to be a technician in the RAF and worked on Lightnings. When I was nine I went to see him and he let me sit in an aircraft. It was the first time I had seen a plane close up and it really meant something to me. I will always remember sitting in that Lightning. It was just a single-seater rocket really, but it was the fighter of its era. Not a good plane now, but it could climb for fifty or sixty thousand feet at two and a half times the speed of sound, though it had about ten minutes' fuel endurance. From that moment on aeroplanes were the thing for me. I'd spend hours building model aeroplanes, and get a bollocking from my parents as they saw my plastic masterpieces being hurled out the window with their tails on fire, with me pretending that they had been shot down.

At that age, of course, I didn't have the thrill of actual flying, but simply sitting in a machine that could lift off the ground was enough. It's very difficult to put into words the feeling that this machine can do something that you as a mere mortal can never do, yet you have control over it. I can still recall the smell of that Lightning, the feel of the cockpit, the dials and knobs and levers on the instrument panel, the atmosphere, the size, the shapes and the sound.

The greatest music to my ears will always be the sound of the Merlin engine that powered the Spitfire, or the twin engines of the Mosquito. It sent ripples down my spine when I heard it back then. It still does today. My only wish was to be able to fly something like that.

At the beginning it was the concept of the machine. Later on it was the concept of flying. At that stage I loved the models but I always assumed there would never ever be any possibility of my flying. I just assumed it was another dimension I'd never be capable of, the sort of thing only extremely gifted and superior people would be able to do.

I don't know why I thought that. Later on I learned that anybody could learn to fly and get a licence if they really wanted to. I came across complete idiots who had managed to get themselves airborne when they shouldn't have been allowed to paddle a plastic duck.

My father had quite a profitable business. He was a self-employed credit trader. Before the era of credit cards he would walk into shops and get accounts at every one. Then he used to give orders to customers and they would pay him back with a percentage of interest. Dad was a very keen jazz musician – he'd probably have been professional if he hadn't had to support his family. He used to play trumpet in Louis Armstrong's backing band when he came over. Now that he's retired, he plays and writes arrangements for his own band, and goes to and performs at jazz festivals.

I was born on 1 February 1962. My brother Peter is two years older than I am. To the day. It's some sort of family trait as my great-grandmother and my great-great-grandfather were also born on 1 February. Peter and I had a cheery upbringing, in a small estate just outside North Shields in Tyne and Wear. It was a three-bedroomed house, nothing flash, but we always had two cars, motorbikes as teenagers, nice holidays. We both went to a private day school and got a good education.

Unfortunately I came out of school with just one A level

and five Os. Perhaps if I'd tried harder I could have got into university. It didn't happen so, just like Peter, I drifted off to the TSB, working to earn more money to get bigger motorbikes. By the time I was seventeen, I had switched my aircraft obsession over to motorbikes. They were within my reach, certainly fast enough. Sometimes they even left the ground. I loved the image, the thrill of speed, controlling the machine, the usual silly teenage things. I even picked up a couple of endorsements for speeding.

I lasted three years at the bank. It was the most boring bloody job in the world, sitting behind the glass – 'Can I have ten pounds out?' – watching all the pretty girls walk in, hiding from all the nasty old buggers. It wasn't for me. I didn't fit the image very well. The branch manager knew I wasn't future management material. He used to get mad at me for wheel-spinning my bike in the yard.

In a moment of insanity, with a few other bank employees in tow, I agreed to go on a parachute course to raise money for a local charity. We went down to Sunderland Airport – now it's got a Japanese car factory on top of it – and signed up for the course. While I was there I saw a leaflet advertising flying lessons for £15.

Suddenly all the things I had loved about aeroplanes came flooding back. I thought, Well if I just get off the ground and touch the controls, I'll have finally done that. So I did that flight in a Cessna 150. The instructor let me do the very first take-off, the actual heaving of the stick back at the point of take-off. Feeling this thing become light, getting airborne, biting into the airflow, was an absolutely amazing feeling.

Before we were five minutes into the air I knew that, no matter what happened, no matter what I had to sell, I had to get my own licence to fly this thing. When I came back down to earth I ran into the bank manager to get a loan. I sold my motorbike and all my possessions and worked over-time. Every time I wasn't at the bank I was at the airfield working and getting rides, getting involved, not just in the flying but the social side of the club as well. In 1982 it cost about £38 to £40 an hour for the forty hours' tuition. So it cost me nearly two and a half grand by the time I'd bought all my materials – rulers, pencils, instruction books and so on.

My first lesson was with a chap called Tom Watson, who remained my main instructor for most of my training. Tom had little hair, and talked in a very fast northern accent. After a briefing his usual words of encouragement were 'Go and start the fucker up, then.'

Tom was a long-term private pilot who had trained for his PPL at Sunderland and had progressed over the years to become an instructor. It always astonished me how he could look so casual, uninterested in his own safety when I was fly-ing the aeroplane. (It was only years later when I was an instructor myself that I realised that he was probably terrified and ready to pounce on the controls in a split second. A calm instructor gives a student more confidence.) As time drew near to my dreaded first solo flight, I spent every spare minute, and every weekend, at the airfield.

Tom was an assistant flying instructor, who was not quali-fied to send a student off for his first solo flight, so I was introduced to the chief flying instructor, John Corlett. John was only about five foot four and I am six foot two, so the two of us walking out to the aeroplane must have been an amusing sight. John was an excellent instructor and within a few circuits had me almost believing that I could fly this machine. Unfortunately, towards the end of the lesson, the winds had started to increase and were out of limits for students to fly solo.

'If the winds had dropped off,' he said, 'you could have

gone off there, Dave. But don't worry: you're booked in tomorrow and we'll get you off then.' My heart pounded at the thought of someone actually thinking I could get this piece of metal into the air and back down again in one piece.

The next day arrived and I saw that John was not there. Bollocks! I thought. Now I can't go solo.

'Hello, Dave,' said a voice in polished Geordie. I turned around to see the virtually bald head and healthy greying beard that belonged to Terry Dixon, a part-time instructor with the club. 'John can't make it today so I'll be flying with you.'

That was great. At least I might get the solo in. He discussed all sorts of emergencies with me and said I might get one or two on the way around the circuit. Normally that meant I might get one or two minutes of flying without emergencies! When he told me the engine was on fire just after we started to taxi, I knew it was going to be a hard flight.

'OK, Dave, that's fine. Let's continue on the circuit now.'

I eased the control column back and the Cessna smoothly left the ground in a gentle climb. It was going well, until the loud noise normally generated by the engine was no longer there. Terry had closed the throttle to simulate the engine failure. Without realising it, I was already going through the drills, the most important one of which was lowering the nose to maintain the glide speed of 60 m.p.h. and deciding which field I was going to land in. At about fifty feet off the ground I thought Terry actually wanted me to land in the field, until he said, 'OK, just climb away.'

We bottomed out at about twenty feet as I pushed the throttle fully forward and climbed away from the field. We did two more circuits – packed with more emergencies – then landed and taxied to the end of the runway. Terry opened his door, and said, 'Right, Dave, take off, fly one circuit, and land. Enjoy yourself. You've got no problems at all.'

He informed air-traffic control that a first solo flight was about to depart. This had the immediate and rather disconcerting effect of attracting the fire crew out of their crewroom and into their fire engines, on standby for any fuck-up I might make.

The right-hand door of the Cessna slammed shut as Terry disappeared off into the distance. Suddenly the empty space next to me seemed strange and silent. I felt very alone. 'Golf Juliet Uniform, cleared for take-off. Surface wind zero seven zero degrees, fourteen knots.' Air traffic's clearance came through and already I was opening up the throttle.

'Focus straight ahead towards the end of the runway. Keep straight with the rudder pedals. Check that enough power is being developed, and check that the speed is increasing.' I could hear these words buzzing in the back of my mind as I completed each action. Within seconds I was in the air, and the first thing that I noticed was how much more quickly it climbed with the weight of only one person in. 'Five hundred feet, check right, left, and start a climbing turn to the left.' I mumbled the instructions to myself, 'One thousand feet, lower the nose to the horizon and allow the speed to build up to ninety miles per hour, then reduce the revs per minute to two thousand three hundred for the cruise power, and finally trim.' Looking over my left shoulder, I could see the familiar sight of the runway in the correct position, so I turned left again to a downwind position.

I was by myself in an aeroplane.

'Golf Juliet Uniform, you're cleared to final number one.' ATC were keeping a watchful eye on me. At the end of the downwind leg I turned left again towards the runway and started the descent. 'Carb heat out,' I chanted, 'power back to seventeen hundred revs per minute. Let the speed come back to eighty miles per hour. Lower the flaps to twenty degrees and lower the nose to capture seventy miles per hour for the approach.'

It always seemed strange that speed was controlled by the altitude of the aircraft and rate of descent was controlled by the power. At 500 feet I made another left turn on to final approach. Once lined up on the runway, I had to concentrate on keeping the speed at seventy m.p.h. and controlling the rate of descent with the power to maintain the correct glide. The very important last ten feet were soon with me. 'Don't fuck it up,' I prayed.

At about the height of a man above the ground, I gently raised the nose to fly level, and smoothly closed the throttle. Without power the aeroplane then started sinking towards the ground. I continued to raise the nose to cushion the landing. The tyres touched the ground and did not even bounce back up into the air again.

'Congratulations, Golf Juliet Uniform. Well done, a nice landing.' I heard ATC breathe a sigh of relief in my cans. The firemen, disappointed at no blood, climbed down from their vehicles and made their way back into the crewroom.

I was earning about £400 a month. I was absolutely strapped. I spent six months' wages on getting my PPL. I didn't pay board to my parents while I was doing it. I paid off the loan for that and then got another one for £1,500 to buy a third share in a home-built two-seater biplane.

The Turner Special was named after its designer and builder, Chris Turner. It was of a basic wooden construction, with the fuselage shrouded in a very thin plywood. The wings were covered in a thin fabric, but they got their strength from the wooden main spars and ribs forming the shape of the wings, and the box section of the fuselage.

There were two seats, with the pilot's seat – as with most biplanes – at the rear. The cockpit had only the most basic of instruments in it; there was no battery on the aircraft, and all starts were by hand swinging. Unlike the Cessna, it did not have a nose wheel that was steered by the use of rudder pedals, nor did it have the view over the nose that the Cessna had. On the ground it was impossible to see over the nose, so you had to look down the side of the aircraft. Since it did not have brakes or a steerable nose wheel, the only way of steering it on the ground was to use bursts of power so that the slipstream from the propeller had enough effect on the rudder to turn it. If it drifted left or right on the runway, it had to be caught quickly with a combination of rudder and power to stop it from ground-looping.

It was great, exhilarating, fantastic fun, and as close to pure flying as you could get. Comparing it with the Cessna is like comparing a Mini Metro with an original open-top Jag with spoke wheels and no syncromesh gearboxes. Much more difficult to drive, but far more satisfying and fun. The Turner was more difficult to fly than most other light aircraft but it was an excellent trainer because, if you didn't do things correctly, it wouldn't do bugger all you wanted it to.

The feeling and sensations you get when flying in an open-cockpit biplane are fantastic, and unforgettable. On a summer's evening with calm clear skies, the feeling was one of complete freedom. At times I acquired the ability to sense every single small movement of the aeroplane as it floated through the air. Almost as if I were a bird. The sound of the airflow whistling through the flying wires, and the occasional blast of warmth from the heated air blown back over the engine – these all helped to give me aching cheek muscles. And that was due to the amount of smiling that was involved.

The view from the cockpit took some getting used to. I

had a square picture of the world looking forward through the box section of the wing strut supports, interrupted by the blur of the spinning propeller. On each side the distant horizon was trapped between the upper and lower wing. I built up hours in that, flying upside down, doing aerobatics. After 150 hours' flying I was getting a bit cocky, thinking I was Red One in the Red Arrows.

The most fun I had was after the airfield closed. Les Richardson, a former Lancaster bomber pilot who flew a similar biplane, would drag his aeroplane out of the hangar with the tail resting on his shoulder. Les was in his sixties but in his head he was still a kid flying bombing raid after bombing raid over Germany. The thrill of flying had never left him. He had a clipped grey moustache and wore a pair of John Lennon spectacles. On a cold day his head would be lost in the huge sheepskin collar of an old flying jacket that had apparently been used as an engine-oil filter for the last fifty years. He'd call, 'See you up there for a hoy-round, Dave.' With the challenge laid down I'd get airborne first, climb away at sixty knots in a tight left turn. Peering out of the goggles perched on top of my oxygen mask, I'd see Les taxiing out past the clubhouse that was attached to the side of the hangar.

Time for a beat-up, I thought. With throttle wide open I entered a shallow dive, the flying wires and engine revs howling as the speed increased: eighty, ninety, a hundred knots through four hundred feet. Then I went into a ninety-degree left bank, descending round the back of the hangar. I'd line up with the gap between the clubhouse and Les still taxiing out. Airspeed one hundred and ten knots. Height five feet.

Bill Eskdaile was standing outside the clubhouse. He raised his beer glass in salute. Bill could always be seen either in the bar or thrashing past the clubhouse at equally low level in his French-designed Jodel two-seater. When I landed he would start telling me how I was too high on my beat-up and that if he had known that it was going to be so high he would have brought his binoculars. Naturally when he had attempted a similar approach I would offer him oxygen in case the air was too thin at the high altitude he was flying. The club was full of characters who all added to the atmosphere of the place. Everyone loved aeroplanes, talking about them, being around them, and they loved flying them.

Just inches behind Les's tail I pulled the stick hard back and sank back into the seat under three and a half Gs of pressure. I pulled up at 400 feet, released the back pressure on the stick as the speed bled off, added more rudder pressure to balance the aircraft, did a sixty-degree bank to the left and looked back over my shoulder. The muscles in my cheeks were really aching. Next time over the circuit, Les was climbing out towards me. Time for more fun.

We would do nose-to-tail chases about fifty feet above the deck. If we ever saw a car driving across the taxiway it was hawk-and-chicken time. We'd immediately dive down, come straight at him and try to get him to swerve off the tarmac. I had a fantastic time, just like a teenage tearaway in a TR7.

I lived to fly but inside I knew a beat-up old biplane wasn't enough.

Driving to work that morning, I could still hear the Jet Provost whirring inside my head. I got to thinking: I can fly a plane as a private pilot. So why the hell don't I join the RAF – and get paid for it? I assumed I'd be able to pull the same stunts in a jet fighter – just a hell of a lot faster.

On my lunch break the following day I went down to the careers office and said I wanted to fly jets – Tornadoes or

Lightnings. So did everybody else. I did all the various tests and questionnaires and they sent me off to Biggin Hill for aircrew selection. I was already twenty so I was an old man to be joining the forces. They prefer people at eighteen.

I had my doubts but my girlfriend Jill convinced me to follow my heart. Until I met her I was more interested in aeroplanes and going for a thrash round on my motorbike than in girls. Being a late developer, as far as members of the opposite sex were concerned, it never occurred to me that wearing leathers and riding bikes might attract the girls. Not that my leathers had a chance to work on Jill. The first time I met her I was boozing down a pub. She was going out with a friend of mine, and I made such an impression she thought I was forty-five. Actually as she's two years older than me, I was a toyboy. Somehow she's always looked years younger than I do. She still does.

She worked in the building society down the street from my bank. Christ only knows what she saw in me. It wasn't the case that our eyes met and that was it. There was no fluttering of eyelids over the table. I sent her a birthday card for her twenty-first. We liked each other as friends and it grew from there. When I went to pick her up on my old 750 c.c. motorcycle her father, a Master Mariner who had retired from the Merchant Navy and become a river pilot on the Blyth, used to sit in his chair with his newspaper up, ignoring me in my leathers. If I came to pick her up in a car the paper would be put down and he'd chat away to me. I can't blame him, if it was my daughter being taken out on this huge motorcycle by a teenage bloke I would probably do the same.

Once we'd been going out for a while, we realised we'd be together for as long as we could be. It wasn't a question of 'If I do this, will you be with me?' – it was more a question of 'When?' She knew I hated the bank and wouldn't have been able to stick that. She was with me when I signed up for my parachute jump and my first flying lesson. She didn't like flying, still doesn't – she's only been up with me once or twice – yet she has supported me in everything I have ever done. Even when everything was geared to joining the RAF, leaving home – and possibly her.

At Biggin Hill I was put through all the usual medicals so they could check to make sure I had two eyes, two arms and two feet. Then I sat through the standard interview with Mr Nice and Mr Nasty. Family, education, other interests, all that sort of thing. Then Mr Nasty butted in and started grilling me about the RAF – 'Why do you want to join?' – trying to catch me out. Throughout the interview, sitting in the background, writing down notes on my reactions to things, was a third man, a psychologist.

Anyway, I passed that part and went on to aptitude tests to see what I was best suited for. Everybody did all the tests for pilot, navigator, air-traffic controller, fighter controller, loadmaster, flight engineer, and air electronics operator, regardless of the position applied for. The pilot tests involved a number of coordination exercises involving moving a dot around a screen using rudder pedals and a joy-stick. There were also hundreds of maths-type questions and interpretation of aircraft instruments. I failed fighter control, which I wasn't worried about. Who wants to be stuck in a hole underground, looking at radar screens? Then there were loads of leadership exercises, swinging round hangars on ropes directing teams, transporting a bin lid containing six tons of make-believe gelignite over a patch of straw you couldn't touch and a weird and wonderful assault course.

I thought I'd done pretty well – but then I got a letter saying they couldn't accept me for pilot training. However, they did suggest I reapply in six months. Alternatively, they would accept me for NCO aircrew entry immediately. My reaction was shock and horror because I didn't know what NCO entry was. I'd only ever seen myself flying a big rockety jet. That morning I was worse than ever at my job and at lunch break I went back down to the careers office.

'Six months, eh?' said the careers officer, a six-and-a-half-foot squadron leader navigator who seemed to be a reasonable bloke, keen to get any of the aircrew applicants through. Apparently, talking to some other non-aircrew applicants who went through the same office, he was a bit of a bastard and gave them a hard time. I had none of that, just helpful advice on the selection, and the advice he gave me for the first part of my training was: 'Make sure you're fucking fit. If you're not you'll drop out or be in constant pain for two months.' (Unfortunately, I fell into the 'constant pain for two months' category.)

'If they want you to come back,' he continued, 'then you must have been very close to the mark. Usually the letter you get is to reapply in another two years. Look, Dave, you've got two choices. If you reapply for pilot training you have a good chance of making it, but the thing against you is your age. If you fail next time you may have passed the civilian age limit for getting in as a pilot, which is twenty-two. But if you go in for aircrew training after a year you can remuster and transfer over for pilot training.'

The careers officer explained what aircrew training involved and that I could become a loadmaster either in a Hercules – which sounded like becoming an air stewardess – or on helicopters. I hadn't thought about helicopters before but the idea of working on search-and-rescue helicopters was very appealing. I could imagine myself as a romantic hero dangling from a rope plucking drowning sailors from the frozen wastes of the North Sea. I also knew the only person I'd be hanging if I stayed at the bank was myself. I knew I had to be in an aeroplane, no matter what.

Jill was delighted for me. My parents were not so enthusiastic. I've never shown emotions easily: whenever my mother would come to the door to kiss goodbye, I'd run away. Now she was terrified at the idea of her little boy dangling on the end of ropes, with the sea crashing away inches below his boots. She didn't like losing me to the services or my being away from home.

I did. I was nearly twenty-two. It was time to leave home. So I decided to sign up with the option of transferring to pilot training later.

However, for the first fifteen months of my time in the RAF, flying never entered the equation. The only time my feet left the ground was when I was jumping.

CHAPTER 3

YOU'RE IN THE RAF NOW

'Hands up any aircrew here,' bellowed the drill sergeant. It was my first morning at RAF Swinderby. Three blokes shot their arms up. I kept mine down.

'I know there are four of you,' the DS screamed. 'Where's McMullon?'

'Here, Sergeant,' I gulped.

'Why didn't you fucking answer when I called?'

'Sorry, Sergeant,' I muttered, thinking to myself, Jesus Christ what have I let myself in for this time?

'You will be sorry. It's taken me fourteen years to get these three stripes you see on my arm. It'll take you lot fourteen weeks – so you'd better be bloody good. Now move your bloody arses. You're in the airforce now.'

I'd kept my hand down because I'd been warned by the careers office to expect a bucketload of extra shit because I was aircrew. After fourteen weeks' basic training I would be a sergeant, accorded all the privileges, messing facilities and pay that went with that rank. Drill instructors could take anywhere from fifteen to eighteen years to get to the same point. They weren't very happy about this. In return they tried to make our lives extra miserable.

Nothing too drastic, but if someone was going to be picked on we knew it was going to be us. It was usually just a bit of extra bullshit like making us run round the yard three times with a chair above our heads. On every inspection it was guaranteed that four bed packs would be thrown out of the window and the only people who had to go on extra duties because something had not been cleaned were the aircrew. We did have a tougher time but it was just playing a game. You play it their way until you get through the training.

Sometimes aircrew do manage to get their own back. It backfired on one particular drill sergeant who came to RAF Odiham later. He'd never been posted to a Chinook squadron before, and the first time I saw him there I decided: Right, you twat, now for a dose of something you might recognise. Before we took him out flying I let our crew know how 'pleasant' he'd been during basic training. So we lowered the back ramp, to make him more comfortable, tied him to the harness and let the pilots run through their repertoire of sickening stunts. We gave him a hell of a time. At one point we even pretended he was falling out.

Because I was slightly older they made me senior man in the flight. I was very big and pretty muscular so there was never any question of physical intimidation or unnecessary bullying. I never even saw anything that might cause an outsider to raise an eyebrow. OK, the RAF regiment NCOs in charge of training might occasionally give someone a clip across the back of the head or make us do a bunch of press-ups, but we expected that. A few blokes started whingeing and were PVRed. That's RAF speak for being given premature voluntary retirement. I had expected it to be a whole lot worse, that I'd go in there and be crawling across the floor trying to keep up with the pace.

I was expecting to be chopped at any stage. But actually Swinderby was just weeks of polishing floors, polishing windows, making beds and learning to march – left, right, left, right – without falling over. We had to run everywhere, do fitness training that consisted mainly of PTIs hurling abuse at you – the usual stuff.

I did lose half a stone in weight and become reasonably fit. Running was a problem because I'm so flat-footed. I was never a racehorse – more of a carthorse. On the track the lowest time I ever got down to over a mile and a half was ten minutes, ten seconds. But as soon as I packed weights on my back, got the poles and the stretcher rigs and started running up and down the Yorkshire Dales, I was out at the front. I had one speed – McMullon pace – whether I was going up or down, on the track, or on the grass.

As soon as we graduated from Swinderby the aircrew cadets were whisked away for seven weeks of special training at RAF Finningley. Officially it was called the AAITC (Airman Aircrew Initial Training Course). There were about fifteen on my ITC, with five of us going for loadmaster. The idea was to apply as much pressure as they could. They were beasting the hell out of us, applying mental and physical pressure from dawn till dusk – and beyond. By the time I had finished all the tasks I was lucky to fall into bed by one in the morning.

Up to this point I'd always thought that they were scraping the bottom of the barrel to get to me and I was bound to be kicked out. I knew my weakness was speed but the PTIs used to push us so far that, regardless of your fitness level, you were pushed beyond it. I'd never seen how people can crumble under physical pressure before. It was all to do with self-discipline even when you were physically exhausted, and knackered. Did you still have the drive and determination to get the task done and think with a clear head? Quite often the fittest people would have a problem with this since they had never been put in a situation of such physical exhaustion and asked to complete the various tasks. The slow, flat-footed, lazy bastards like me were used to being completely shagged and just got on with it. People showed themselves up in various ways.

I'd run around and get to a certain stage of exhaustion, whereupon I'd throw up, enduring the PTIs screaming abuse at me and all my ancestors. Then I'd get my breath back and carry on again. There were people collapsing in tears and I thought, Well he'll be out tomorrow; but it never happened.

Those of us who survived the beasting were awarded their three stripes (aircrew sergeants were distinguished from ground crew by the addition of a small eagle at the top of the stripes). Following 'graduation' all the aircrew were sent to the various training centres for their different professions, still at Finningley, but in a different part of the camp. Loadmaster Training Squadron was a large building divided up into classrooms, offices and a training area with a mock-up of aircraft floors. Our living accommodation changed from the barracks block to the Gate House – the old married quarters –with three aircrew sergeants to a house. It was the perfect place for a perpetual piss-up.

We were supposed to bond together as a team but there were always a few blokes who were interested only in their own personal tasks. They couldn't give a shit about anybody else and they were the ones who caused problems throughout. It shocked me that they didn't get chopped. In fact only two people did, though there were three men I was gobsmacked to see were even there, and a fourth right on the border. The ones who are still in the air force still have the same character defects as they did on that course.

One bloke known as Bugs – because he had huge front teeth – managed to fail a navigation test even though I had stolen the exam paper and given him all the questions and the answers. He was extremely immature, a complete wimp and a tosser, one of those who would always perform in front of instructors and officers. But he wasn't a team man. If he was on our team he would be puffing and panting at the back, playing the slow, whimpering, exhausted act, the one who needed chivvying along. But, if he was in charge or the DS came around the corner, guess who would be running at the front wearing underpants on the outside of his trousers. He did know how to play the system – or perhaps it was just that the system tried to get people through. Even though he failed the exam he was recoursed. He played sick, claimed he had glandular fever, which he actually got the week after.

Nicking the exam papers was easy. Now, when I look back, I reckon it was expected, part of our initiative training. But you had to do it, otherwise there was no drinking time, and downtown Doncaster on Thursday nights would never have been the same. The training day was from nine to five, then all the instructors went home. We got some scran at the mess and because we were such good little boys who wanted to do extra studying at night we'd sign the keys out, break open the filing cabinet and unearth the exam papers.

One exam was plotting a navigation route. So we got the maps out, planed the route, put all the answers down, made a couple of intentional mistakes so it didn't look like we'd get a hundred per cent, then hid these maps underneath the new maps. While Bugs crashed and burned I got ninety-seven per cent, Bruce Laycock managed only ninety-six per cent and George Darcy a whopping ninety-eight per cent.

Bruce and I got on well together, but he did tend to take life too seriously, and needed to chill out a bit. He was heavily into polishing and ironing, while I preferred to spend that time usefully in the pub. My closest mates were Justin Maccasey and Dave Clarke, who were both on the AAITC behind mine. The three of us just clicked. We were inseparable going through training – the Three Musketeers.

Justin Maccasey was the most extrovert character I'd ever known, really fit and outgoing. Like me, he just wanted to fly, whatever the cost. Originally he'd been accepted for pilot training but he got chopped and remustered as a navigator, then he got chopped again. Basically his bar bill outstripped his payslip by fifty per cent each month and he wasn't following the officer party line. So he resigned from the air force and came back in to do loadmaster training and went through the same course. He always said he found it more demanding than Cranwell, where he had twice the time to learn the same stuff.

At Finningley the air engineers and air electronic operators spent the entire year there, while the loadmaster – or loadies – disappeared off on different courses around the country, so we were occasionally seen as outsiders. We would return there for ritual bollockings and to be reminded that we were still under their training wing, and as such could expect our testicles to be crushed in a vice at any time.

One such return coincided with the infamous Gate House festival, which involved loud music, large quantities of ale and young ladies visiting from Doncaster. I met up with Dave Clarke, who had been held back on F Troop – normally the last place you stay prior to being booted out of the RAF. Dave had broken the nose of one of his colleagues in the course of a private conversation he was having with him for being a tosser. The staff had found out about it and they were both suspended from training. (Fortunately, someone had some sense and released them back to training later on.)

The festival had a huge barbecue going, just under the nose of a Vulcan bomber aircraft that was rusting away on the site. After enquiring if we could consume some of the goods we were told to piss off. Dave and I thought the only solution to the problem was to climb on top of the Vulcan's nose and piss on the barbecue from fifteen feet above. Nobody saw us doing it and everyone continued eating, though there were a few complaints that the food tasted too salty.

The same night Justin ended up being chased around Gate House by another student, wielding a large knife and wearing only his underpants. Apparently Justin had fancied this guy's girlfriend, and climbed up the drainpipe to watch them on the job and see if she was any good. The problem was he couldn't resist making comments from the window ledge.

By the end of the night the party was getting well out of hand. The noise was incredible, the barbecue, which had survived its watering, was now a raging inferno threatening to set alight the Vulcan. This danger to the camp's safety coupled with seminaked females wandering about somehow attracted the attention of the RAF police. Led by the SWO (Station Warrant Officer), they were seen stampeding towards our party, looking as if they wanted to lock up every single aircrew they could find. Everyone dived for cover. I shoved myself out of sight behind a serviceable hedge only to hear a familiar voice growl, 'Watch where you're standing, Mac.'

I turned to see Andy Hardcastle squatting out of sight

behind me. Andy, one of the flight commanders on the AAITC, had appeared at the festival earlier embracing a large bottle of Grouse whisky. He was a popular bloke who, while he brayed the shit out of you in training, maintained the respect of his flight. We managed to slip away unseen.

The next day all the aircrew were given a huge bollocking – the usual threats of suspension, and waffle that this kind of behaviour was 'totally unbecoming of a senior NCO in today's RAF'. I could hardly keep a straight face because the bloke giving out all this was Andy Hardcastle. He glanced over to me and tried to put his killing face on. Somehow he couldn't hide the 'that was a fucking good party' look in his eyes.

After we got our three stripes the pay was quite reasonable. I was earning £600 a month – fifty per cent more than at the bank. Before being whisked away on our various courses, we stayed on for another five weeks doing general courses. 'This is an aeroplane.' 'This is an airfield.' Useful stuff like that. But they still wouldn't let us in a plane.

At the Loadmaster squadron we were due to be streamed on to helicopters or fixed-wing aircraft. I was praying for helicopters and, rather than waiting to find out, we decided to borrow the training-school keys to see what we might find in the filing cabinets. We were delving around the office when George Darcy suddenly announced, 'Fucking hell, I've been chopped.' He'd found a photo with a big red cross through his face. He had to go in the next day, stand there, look shocked and upset, pretending he didn't know about it. It turned out he was being recoursed.

We were then whisked away to Halton for a fortnight's first-aid course, which included watching autopsies and going to simulated crashes. (Later on we had to do a week with the ambulance crews in Basingstoke. I'd thought flying low level in helicopters was exciting but doing seventy-five knots through the centre of town is better.) Halton was a really tough assignment. Unfortunately, all the messes were full and we were billeted in the local nurses' home. If a girl walks past in a towel in an all-male block everyone hangs out of the doors. Well the reverse was true here. I was a sex object for the first and only time in my life. Not that any of us took advantage of it!

We passed that and went to Brize Norton to do the parachute course. Fortunately, as we were NCOs, we were fallen out before the bullshit started and we realised for the first time they didn't class us as trainee idiots any more. We learned how to fall properly and how important it is to get your parachute harness properly stuffed into the crack of your groin, how to make sure your bollocks were hanging down in the middle. There was a forty-foot tower, christened the Nutcracker, that helped reinforce the lesson. You jumped out with a parachute harness attached to a cable and were in free fall for about a second, and then it locked up like a bungee without any spring. If your harness wasn't properly adjusted it hurt – really, really hurt – and there were some very pale faces coming down. Naturally, the instructors deliberately put a few harnesses on back to front, which made a few people feel very sick.

The course culminated in a balloon jump, which scared the shit out of me, even though I'd already done a parachute jump. We went up to 800 feet in a basket with five jumpers plus an instructor. As the highest rank there I had to jump out first. People looked the size of an Action Man but, because there was no engine noise and the air was completely still, you could hear them talking on the ground. When you jump from the balloon you fall 200 feet in three seconds before the canopy opens because the air is still, and you have to fall away before the airflow takes effect. In a plane there is forward motion and air speed so the canopy opens immediately.

The instructor said, 'If you don't want to feel the sensation of falling just look down. It isn't so bad.' Lying bastard. The sensation of falling was horrendous. I stepped out of this thing with my bollocks hanging out of my mouth because they were desperate to stay in the basket. I looked up very quickly to see if my chute had opened. At 800 feet you haven't a lot of time if things go wrong. I saw it sag in after the initial airflow and thought, Shit. I had the reserve handle half out in my hand when I realised that this was normal and the parachute was a healthy one. I was still trying to stick the handle back in again when I hit the ground like a ton of shit.

I still hadn't started training for the job I was supposed to do and I felt that as soon as I did they would see how much of a pillock I was and throw me out. Although the reports I was getting were very good, I thought I was dodging the axe.

Eventually I was transferred to Shawbury, the helicopter training base, near Shrewsbury. We were due to be teamed up with the pilots, who had just come out of basic flying training. My first evening at Shawbury I went into the Sergeants' Mess for a drink and this hairy old warrant officer with a patch over one eye, ribbons of medals over his chest, took one look at me and snarled, 'I don't like the look of you. I'm going to make sure you are fucking chopped.'

Christ, I thought. That's me gone.

By the end of the week I realised it was just Spike Edwards's sense of humour. He started to wind his neck in and then if you got drunk at the bar with him you were best mates. (Throughout the forces the people who have the biggest problems socially are those who never drink, who stay in and study all night.) Spike was a real character. He had seen it all and done a bit more. He was flying in an air display in a Whirlwind that had a control box malfunction. It crashed. Spike bit his tongue off in the crash and was actually certified dead. So he got his death certificate and tried to claim on his life insurance. It always pissed him off that they wouldn't cough up. As a result of the crash, while he could see out of both eyes, there was something wrong with the coordination. He had to wear a patch to focus.

On the Friday after doing all the paperwork they let us climb all over this Wessex helicopter (after thirteen months in the RAF). I was actually sitting in an aircraft. The old excitement, that feeling of being nine years old, came flooding back. It gave me such a morale boost that when we started the course on Monday the usual ground school stuff – how many generators it had got, how many pistons, the limitations of the aircraft – seemed really exciting.

The RAF used Gazelles and Wessex helicopters for training. The Wessex has twin engines and a bulbous nose, and the cabin will hold twelve to fourteen troops depending on weight load. It's ideal for training because it's a very strong helicopter, built like a brick shithouse – you can throw it on the ground. At the time it was used as a support helicopter for the Army in Northern Ireland and Cyprus. Now they also use Pumas, which are more agile with a bigger cabin that can hold about eighteen people. The RAF also fly Sea Kings, but only in a search-and-rescue role.

Sitting in the open door of a helicopter for the first time with this huge beast whirling above my head was a parallel sensation to my first flight. The feeling was fantastic. I knew that this was what I wanted to do.

Initially, all they did was get you to speak to the pilot above you. All I saw were a pair of legs and his heels. I'd never see his face except on the ground. Although they were officers and we were NCOs there was never any problem. In the air it was all first-name terms.

Pilots had already spent sixty hours on Gazelles, a small army helicopter, effectively learning to fly again, how to hover, how to land, how to turn, emergencies, how to fly into confined areas. Then they were put into a more complicated scenario. Not only did they have to fly the Wessex, a more complex helicopter with two engines, but they were no longer the masters of their own destiny. They had to deal with a disembodied voice in the headphones – a crewman. High up on the priority list was teaching everybody to be multicrew. You will never fly a helicopter in the RAF without it being multicrew. So it's pointless being the ace-of-the-base pilot if the bloke in the back can't communicate with you. There is no way you can operate the aircraft to its maximum ability without the crew doing the job properly and absolute coordination between front and back ends.

It was difficult for the pilots. Suddenly, from having to do everything, the pressure was taken away. It was difficult to share the workload and trust the other chap to do his part. Once they got used to it and started coordinating as a crew, the aircraft started working far better. By the end of the course the idea was that pilot and crew operated almost as one mind. Everyone on the course would bend over backwards to help each other out. We all started the course as a team, and we all wanted to finish it that way. Sometimes, if either the pilot or the crewman was having a hard day, the other would be working twice as hard to help him out. Doing it in such a way that it would not be obvious to the instructors and look bad on the student's performance.

Naturally none of this fooled the instructors, but they were pleased at the efforts of the students to help each other and get the job done as a team. These, of course, were the seeds that they wanted to see grow. They formed the basics for future training on larger helicopters and the more demanding tasks when we went operational.

The basic crewman's course was for people who had never flown before. Starting with, 'This is a map'. How to navigate, fuel planning, radios. You had to become very efficient, to be able to do all the basic tasks without thinking.

We learned all about the theory of flight and how gyroscopes work. I got very confused when I learned that anything that is spinning round will not react to the application of any force until it has spun through ninety degrees. It makes no difference to the bloke flying it at all but the concept does make people scratch their heads. It might also explain why helicopter pilots tend to walk straight into walls when they've had a few drinks.

Most people got through eventually, though some of our guys got recoursed. Two pilots got chopped completely. They might have been able to get the aircraft to do what they wanted after another ten to twenty hours' flying, but the cost was deemed to be too high. Halfway through the course I felt I could really do this. It was the first time.

Then Justin killed himself.

I'd gone up north on an exercise and had a good time drinking all night and thrashing around in the daylight. Justin had gone off to Salisbury Plain to work with the Army on a Wessex. There was an announcement that Sergeant Justin Maccasey had been found dead in his car at the weekend.

Immediately Dave Clarke and I snapped a look at each other. The three of us had been inseparable. Only the week before we had been out on the piss and then gone on for a Chinese takeaway. Suddenly Justin, after getting some lip from the bloke in the queue in front of him, stuffed his hand down the back of the bloke's trousers, grabbed hold of his underpants and ripped them off up through the back of this guy's trousers, taking half his bollocks with them. The bloke turned around ready for a punch-up, only for Justin to spew his guts out all over him. The bloke gave up and ran out, closely followed by us. We were all banned from the Chinese for life. Not that it affected Justin now.

Now he was gone. Dead. It was a huge shock. The first of my friends to die. When I had left him he had been talking about marrying his girlfriend. Instead he went home, stuck the hose pipe round his exhaust and the other end in the car window. Then he turned on the ignition and started the engine.

Everything was going so well and suddenly my best friend had killed himself. How could he do that? He was very into reading Freud and writing poetry – one of the last things he wrote was, 'it feels strange that now I am a man I must die'. Special Branch came in and interviewed us all, asked stupid questions like 'Did he have a drug problem?' But none of us ever fathomed out why he did it.

I went to his funeral. At the wake afterwards one of the course commanders at Finningley went up to his mother asking for his uniform and watch and stuff to take back to put back in stores. Flight Lieutenant Bloody Sensitive.

Justin's death cast a huge shadow over the remainder of the course. But in the end all we could do was have a few drinks in his memory and carry on. At the end of the course the big thing was which helicopter you were going to go on to. You didn't get awarded the Spanner of Honour or even the ceremonial pickled egg for coming top, but you did usually get your choice of posting.

Everyone wanted to go on to Pumas. They operated with one pilot and one crewman so you did lots of flying. There was only one Puma spot available and Bruce Laycock was sent on it. I was really pissed off because I knew I'd done better than he had on the course.

Then the OC said, 'Right, Dave, stay behind. I want a word with you.' My heart sank. I thought I'd screwed up somewhere.

'You're a guinea pig,' he told me. 'You're not going on Pumas because you're going on to Chinooks and then straight on to the SF Flight.'

I'd never heard of it. To me it was just a Chinook and it wouldn't be so much fun. The Puma was a sports car while the Chinook was a double-decker bus. I was destined to be a bus conductor.

CHAPTER 4

CHINOOK

'How the hell does that get off the ground?' That was all I could gasp the first time I saw a Chinook. It was 14 October 1985. I had been in the RAF for sixteen months.

I was used to the Wessex. I thought that was a big helicopter, but this was an immense beast. It was – and still is to this day – a staggering size. After the other helicopters I'd flown in, it was like stepping from a small yacht on to the *QE2*. The aircraft is ninety-nine feet long tip to tip, almost twenty feet high and sixty feet wide, while the width of the blade is over three foot. The Mark 1 weighs twenty-three tons and can lift a ten-ton load – and in Vietnam, when the Americans were evacuating Saigon, they managed to pack in up to 120 bodies.

From the outside the Chinook looks the same as it has since Boeing started making them in 1966. Inside it is now very different. The Mark 2 aircraft, which was introduced after I left the RAF, is packed with all sorts of high-tech electronic gizmos. The name, Chinook, is taken from the warm wind that blows off the Rockies to the Pacific coast. The name sounds much more romantic than the CH-47, which is what they call it in the States. They used to call it 'Big Windy', which might be more appropriate. It is a noisy, lumbering beast.

CHINOOK!

The cabin, which was to become my second home for the next six years, was long enough to park two Range Rovers inside. For the first time I could walk upright. All the red canvas seats – the aircraft could carry fifty-four troops wearing seat belts – were folded out of the way. Every two feet down the cabin was a row of rings, each ring capable of supporting up to 5,000 lb which were used to tie vehicles down with quick-release straps. I walked the length of the cabin, fifteen paces to the hydraulic ramp beneath the aft engine. I stood there and stared up into this maze of hydraulic pipes. It looked like a load of knitting wool spun all around the place. A couple of them were leaking. The crewman's view was that, if there was no oil leaking out of it, it had no oil in it.

Once upon a time the ramp floor had been the same grey colour as the rest of the cabin but by now it was covered in oil spills and patches of hardened hydraulic fluid. In flight, once the engines were running and the gearboxes were up to temperature, a warm stuffy atmosphere pervaded the ramp area. That cloying smell of oil and hydraulic fluids mixed was unique to the Chinook. As was the sound. The constant high-pitched whine of the gearboxes overhead always managed to cut through and ignore any soundproofing. If the pilots suddenly applied the power and the helicopter started to climb the crew felt it instantly. I soon learned to trust my body. The pit of my stomach would lift off even before the intensity of the whine increased.

Each crew member in the cabin was connected to the intercom via a long lead with an 'interrupter switch', which allowed you to listen all the time. If you wanted to speak the switch had to be depressed. The noise inside a Chinook was so loud that if everyone had an open mike all the gearbox and engine noises would be amplified, which made conversation all but impossible. Occasionally a bellow of 'hot mike' would be heard over the intercom, which meant someone had left his switch open.

The Chinook is a big and capable machine but because it is bigger more things can go wrong. It requires more servicing time. Often the crew will be the only people around to sort the aircraft out so the crewmen had to have engineering training. After three months I was supposed to be qualified to do an online service on these things. I just stood in the back looking up at that gigantic web of hydraulic pipes, studded with dials everywhere, thinking, No chance.

To historians a torque is a necklace, a decoration worn by ancient Britons. To engineers and mechanics torque is a twisting effort applied to an object that makes the object turn about its axis of rotation. To a helicopter crew torque, created by the application or reduction of power, is a problem that has to be constantly dealt with. In a conventional helicopter as the power is increased and the rotor creates the lift to heave the machine off the ground, the fuselage tries to spin around in the opposite direction to the rotor. The tail rotor is used to counter this effect, and is controlled through pedals next to each foot. If the tail rotor stops rotating because it has been damaged, the aircraft fuselage will immediately spin around under the blade to compensate. If that happens the consequences are invariably fatal.

The Chinook is a tandem-rotor, heavy-lift helicopter, which means it has two sets of rotor blades, mounted on the forward and aft pylons. Twin gearboxes cause the blades to rotate in different directions so each torque cancels out the other. However, as both heads are moving in opposite directions, the aircraft still twists. If the pilot puts on a lot of power you can see a series of wrinkles forming down both sides of the aircraft. The fuselage is made of flexible material, a light aluminium structure (which helps in keeping the weight down), riveted on to various frames, which form the shape of the fuselage. This gives it strength, and the ability to flex slightly without causing damage – although it was the norm to find cracks in the skin of the fuselage.

The aircraft is powered by two Lycoming T–55–L712 turbine jet engines, situated just below the aft rotor. Until I started flying in Chinooks I shared the popular misconception that each engine powers one set of rotors, but as the aircraft cannot fly unless both rotors are working one engine can power both sets of blades.

At the end of the hot section on each engine is a power turbine that spins round like hell under this blast of jet power. A shaft taken off the end of that turbine runs back to the nose gearbox at the front of the engine. From the gearbox that power is turned ninety degrees into the combining gearbox, which is housed in the pylon section just above the rear ventilation. The combining gearbox is only a bit bigger than a human head and one of the three most important things on the aircraft. The other two are the forward gearbox and the aft gearbox. A midair failure of any of these results in your loved ones having to choose the finish on your pine overcoat.

At this point you have power but nothing to actually turn the rotor blades. Once again the drive direction is turned through ninety degrees and runs along tiny aluminium synchronising shafts – about two millimetres thick – to the fore and aft gearboxes. The rotors are synchronised to go in different directions at a different angle so they don't crash into each other. In order that the aircraft can maintain a level platform when flying forward, the front rotors are angled forward at six degrees, the rear set at four degrees.

Although the synchronising shafts look incredibly flimsy they're not. I've never heard of one breaking. Problems are usually caused by the thrust bearings in the gearbox. There are large splines in the gearbox and the ends of the shafts also have splines so they can slot in together. In one case I witnessed at Odiham the female end of the spline had been fitted incorrectly. It engaged but not fully. On the ground everything was fine but once you lifted under power there was a lot of strain on the spline because it hadn't fully engaged. So it sheared off. This immediately desynchronised the rotor blades, which promptly hit each other.

I was watching this particular Chinook. It went into a hover, then the caption XMSN CHIP DET flashed up on the instrument panel. Which in plain English means 'A piece of metal has been detected in one of the gearboxes. LAND NOW OR YOU WILL DIE.' As they landed the whole forward gearbox and rotor blades tore off and cartwheeled across the airfield. It wrote off five cars and a few buildings. God knows how nobody was killed. The crew were left with the rear rotor whirling around. The torque caused the whole fuselage to spin round twice as it hit the ground. The speed of rotating made the aircraft roll on to its side. The blades hit the ground and the impact tore the aft pylon off while the other blade cut the cabin in two as it came round. There was an air-test crew, seven people, on board. They sprinted out. One of them had a broken leg. He was running too.

Less than twenty-four hours later in the Falklands a Chinook was taxiing out to do an air test and exactly the same thing happened. Fortunately, again, nobody was killed. It was eventually traced to one of the thrust bearings being fitted the wrong way round. Further investigation revealed that the alignment arrows on the part had been stamped the wrong way round.

The Chinook has the most complicated control system of any helicopter in the air. Everything inside it is mechanical, not electrical. But because it is a big lumbering beast small mechanical problems can have catastrophic effects. I've lost twelve friends in Chinooks. Some – so the Ministry of Defence insist, though I cannot agree with them – due to pilot error, others due to unexplained mechanical break-downs, a bloody stupid mistake or sheer bad luck. I've come too close to call on many occasions myself. Sometimes I've felt as if I was inside some half-wild beast, one I might con-trol for a while but could never fully tame.

The Chinook does not suffer fools gladly. It takes a crew of four to fly it. That's a team of four. Two pilots. Two crewmen. Who have to work together and trust each other absolutely. All the time. Flying a Chinook is not about showing off at Mach 2 in a fast jet: it's bloody hard work. Sometimes the difference between success and dying is a matter of inches on a moonless night. A Chinook pilot who wants to be top gun is a bad Chinook pilot.

The captain generally sits in the right-hand seat – the opposite of where he would sit in a fixed-wing aircraft. In early helicopters there was only one collective lever, which was in the middle so that either pilot could get to it. The natural reaction was to grab it with the left hand leaving the cyclic for the right. Sitting in the left-hand seat was unnatural for a right hander, so they swapped seats.

The nonhandling pilot is responsible for navigation and radio in conjunction with the crew. Usually they swap leg and leg about: one of the pilots will fly, the other navigate. On the next leg the other pilot will fly and the crewman navigate, and on the next the crewman will fly and the other pilot navigate. It's like musical chairs. I have flown the air-craft with both pilots out the back sitting on the ramp, catching a few rays while admiring the scenery. I suppose it was very trusting of them.

At first sight, because all the controls are duplicated, the cockpit appears incredibly complicated. Directly in front of the pilot are the primary flight instruments, and in the centre of view is the artificial horizon – AI (attitude indicator). When he is unable to see the natural horizon outside – in cloud or darkness – this gives him information about the attitude of the helicopter. This will tell him whether the nose is up or if it's banking to the left.

Moving out from the AI, to the left is the airspeed indicator (ASI), which tells the pilot how fast he is flying through the air, calibrated in knots (10 knots is approximately 11.5 m.p.h.). On the right of the AI is the radar altimeter (radalt) which gives the height of the helicopter above the ground. Directly below the AI is the horizontal-situation indicator (HSI). In its basic form the HSI gives heading information to the pilots, but it also has navigation needles for various radio beacons, and information about the instrument landing system. To the right of the HSI, and below the radalt, is the pressure altimeter – or pressure alt – which gives a reading of pressure altitude (which is not necessarily your actual height above the ground). Directly below the pressure alt is the vertical-speed indicator (VSI), which shows how fast the helicopter is climbing in feet per minute – a normal cruise climb would be around 1,000 feet per minute (f.p.m.). To the left of the HSI and below the ASI is a smaller AI known as the standby horizon (in case the main AI fails).

To the left of the ASI is the torque gauge. One gauge with two needles, numbered 1 and 2, for the respective engines, calibrated in percentages from 0 to 150. Just below the torque gauge is the rotor r.p.m. gauge, calibrated in either percentage increments or r.p.m. (This should always be at 100 per cent – approximately 240 r.p.m.). On the top left of each pilot's instrument panel is a small circular gauge known as the CGI (cruise guide indicator), which measures the stress on the forward and aft gearboxes.

Both pilot seats are adjustable and supposed to be armour-plated. On the floor next to the pilot's feet are rudder pedals (known as yaw pedals in a helicopter). Coming up from the floor between the pilot's legs is the cyclic stick. This is held in the right hand, and controls the altitude of the helicopter. The pistol grip on the cyclic has several buttons, a trigger used for transmitting on the radio, and a trim button next to where the thumb rests.

The 'coolie hat', situated at the centre top of the cyclic stick, is used for fine trimming of the helicopter. Pulling the coolie hat down makes the nose of the helicopter slowly pitch up without the need to move the cyclic. Next to this is a guarded switch with a spring-flap cover, which is used to release loads from hooks or to fire a cable cutter on the rescue hoist.

Coming out of the floor to the left of each seat is a lever with a large handgrip, known as the 'collective lever'. On top of the collective are various 'BEEP' switches used to fine-tune the engine controls. It is used to control the pitch of all the blades. Pulling up the lever during a hover makes the helicopter climb vertically.

All of these controls are duplicated on both sides of the cockpit. The area between the pilots is filled with monitoring and warning gauges. On the top of the panel in the middle are two T handles to be used in case of an engine fire warning. Pulling and twisting one cuts off the fuel supply to the engine and fires an extinguisher into the engine compartment, which, hopefully, puts out the fire. Just below these handles are more gauges, which show how fast the engines are turning, fuel quantity, power turbine inlet temperature of the engines, gearbox oil temperatures, oil pressure, hydraulic pressure, and fuel flow (how much fuel is being used).

To the left of the centre panel is the pilot's favourite, the crew-alerting panel, or CAP. When the CAP lights up there is a problem. A serious problem. The XMSN CHIP DET warning light illuminates when the forward gearbox, the aft gearbox or the combining gearbox has a chip detection. A failure of any of these has catastrophic consequences.

Back in the cabin right in the middle of the aft gearbox, there is a magnetic plug, a metal detector. The oil passes over this and if there are any metal particles in it they are attracted to the magnet, which shorts out the circuit. In the cockpit the pilots see the XMSN CHIP DET caption flash up. If you get one of those captions the drill is to slow down to your minimum speed, putting the lowest possible amount of power through the gearboxes, and land as soon as possible. That means that, if you are over a wood, land on the field on the other side. Don't go to the nearest airfield.

Sometimes pilots would get cocky and decide to thrash around a bit. If, stuck in the back, we got sick of them throwing the aircraft around we stood up with a screwdriver and touched the centre-line chip. As soon as the light came on they shat themselves and eased their approach. Then we'd tell them, 'No, it's OK, I just slipped the screwdriver in – be sensible from now on.' Usually they were.

Below the centre panel at thigh height, and running to the back of the cockpit, are rows of radio and navigation equipment. The roof panel consists of engine starting controls including engine condition levers (ECLs), one for each engine. The top panel also contains controls for arming and disarming the hooks and for the rescue hoist (if one is fitted).

Everything on a Chinook is run by hydraulics. It is simply too big to fly without mechanical assistance. The only way to alter the pitch or angle of attack on the rotor blades is through hydraulic jacks. The jacks operate just like a car jack. Each is an inch and a half in diameter and a foot long with an extending slider. Each contains two chambers in case one fails. When the pilot moves the cyclic stick this raises the hydraulic jacks, which in turn raise the swash plate. As the rotors spin round, the pitch rods will hit the swash plate, which alters the pitch of the blades.

The cyclic stick is linked to aluminium control rods. These control runs are fed into a mixer unit, which works out what you want and puts one input into all the jacks. The mixer unit is situated just behind the pilots above the control closet. Inside it's like a mechanical computer, a Spaghetti Junction full of control runs and hydraulic actuators with wires coming off in every direction. The mixing unit looks like it's made of dozens of little pulley wheels, but, instead of wires, signals are transmitted by aluminium control rods up to the hydraulic actuator valves.

Without hydraulics the Chinook will cease to be a flying machine and become a flying coffin. If the pilot sees both a 'HYD 1' (Hydraulic 1) and a 'HYD 2' (Hydraulic 2) caption come up on the CAP that's it. You might as well unstrap, take your trousers down and stick the cyclic stick up your arse because that will be as much help as anything else you can do. It won't help in the incident but it will certainly confuse the Board of Inquiry.

Even the starter motors for the auxiliary power unit (APU) work on hydraulics. Starting the APU is the only way to start the engines, and the APU is started by pumping up an accumulator to a charge of 3,000 p.s.i. (pounds per square inch). The starting switch is on the pilots' overhead panel. When activated, the circuit is checked by the illumination of two orange lights at the back of the cabin. When the 3,000 p.s.i. is released by pushing this switch, the APU starts to wind up. At the same time a cracking noise can be heard as the igniters (similar to spark plugs) start to ignite the fuel, and then the APU winds up to 100 per cent r.p.m.

With its high-pitched whining noise the APU is far louder than the engines. Once up and running, it powers the auxiliary gearbox. With this on line full hydraulic power and electrical power are available to the Chinook. In flight without the APU running the auxiliary gearbox is driven by a small shaft the thickness of a pencil. If that snaps there are no hydraulics, no electrics, followed very soon afterwards by no life.

Once power is available various control checks are carried out before take-off. Outside the aircraft a crewman watches the response on the blades as the pilots check their controls. There is normally a rotor brake engaged. Similar to a car's disc brake, but much larger and made of carbon fibre, it is mounted on the drive shaft just forward of the aft gearbox, where it can be seen by the crewman. When applied to slow the blades down on close-down, it can glow red-hot. This occasionally ignites any oil that may be hanging around, which demands vigorous use of the fire extinguisher.

The first engine to be started is number 1 (left-hand side), which is monitored by the crewman for leaks and fire. The pilot engages the starter motor, which is controlled by a small switch on his roof panel. Once the engine reaches 20 per cent r.p.m., the ECL is moved from stop to ground idle, which allows fuel into the engine. The start switch is moved to ignition, which starts off the igniters to light up the fuel. This is monitored carefully in the cockpit as the engine winds up, since it is possible to get an over temperature on start-up. If this happens then the ECL is brought back to stop and the engine instantly winds down.

Once the engine has stabilised, the rotor brake is released and the blades start to turn, gradually gathering speed up to approximately 40 per cent rotor r.p.m. (r.r.p.m.). The crewman then goes round to the right-hand side of the helicopter to monitor the number 2 engine start. The ground crew who would normally be standing by the crewman – with a fire extinguisher at the ready – are then dismissed. The pilot puts the ECLs up to flight idle, and as he does this the rotor r.p.m. increases to approximately 98 per cent. This is fine-tuned by the 'BEEP' switches on top of the collective lever to 100 %. (These BEEP switches send small signals to the fuel computers in the engines to increase or decrease the fuel flow to the engine a small amount to keep the rotor r.p.m. at 100 per cent.)

At this point the helicopter is ready to fly, so the chocks are brought inside by the crewman. Although it could lift into the hover it is more normal to ground-taxi clear of the area to prevent the downwash damaging something. To taxi, one pilot holds the controls (the cyclic and the collective) and guards the yaw pedals with his feet; the brakes are released by pressing on top of the yaw pedals and releasing the pressure.

The Chinook has six wheels, two sets of two on the front and one either side at aft, one of which has a hydraulic steering arm. This is controlled by a black circular knob about three inches in diameter, situated to the rear of the centre panel, and is used like a car steering wheel – except that you are steering the back end, not the front!

Prior to lifting into the hover, the aft wheels are locked in the fore/aft position to stop the back end skidding around on the ground. Pre-takeoff checks completed, the automatic flight-control system (AFCS) is engaged by turning the selector on the centre instrument panel to both channels. This makes the helicopter more stable to fly, but it is not an autopilot. It also controls the DASH (differential airspeed hold). The Chinook can be flown without the AFCS, but it is much harder work.

The crewman checks the sky is clear above and the pilot starts to pull up on the collective lever slowly. As he does this the pitch on the blades is increased, the downwash increases and the power demand to the engines increases.

The strain on the gearboxes when the aircraft is heavy can easily be heard. As the lever is pulled up the r.r.p.m. drops a little and the nonhandling pilot 'BEEPS' up the r.r.p.m. to 100 per cent using the switches on his collective lever.

The nose of the Chinook lifts off the ground first, closely followed by the rear wheels. In the hover it will settle in a slightly nose-up attitude. The cyclic and collective are very sensitive controls. If the helicopter is light a few millimetres of movement on the collective can send you rocketing up into the air, or have you plunging rapidly to the ground. Similarly the cyclic stick – held in the right hand – rarely needs any more than a few centimetres of movement to set the helicopter on its back.

For reference points in the hover the pilot looks straight ahead and glances to the side. Any movement either left or right, or fore or aft, is more easily detected by focusing on a distant object. During this 'scan' any changes in the height can be detected and corrected with the collective lever. The average hover height is about fifteen to twenty feet above the ground

A lot of information is picked up from peripheral vision. Problems in maintaining an accurate hover can arise when there are no references to hover on – looking out to sea when there is no horizon, or when it is pitch-black. When the pilot is trying to position the back of the helicopter accurately there are no visual cues at all, and he has to rely on the crewman's instructions. The crewman has to give accurate information down to the inch when he may be hanging out of the front door or off the ramp looking at everything upside down and back to front. Once you start wearing night-vision goggles, which remove peripheral vision and operate in only two dimensions, or the enemy starts shooting at you, that can get very tricky!

Both the cyclic stick and the collective lever are constantly adjusted to maintain the required position. If the helicopter starts to drift to the right, then the pilot applies a small amount of left cyclic to stop the drift, and vice versa. If it starts to drift forward then a small amount of aft cyclic is applied to counter the forward movement, and visa versa. As soon as any cyclic movement is made, it changes the angle of the downwash from the blades, and then the helicopter will start to descend or climb, which requires movement of the collective lever with the left hand to counter this. Any change in the wind strength or direction will change the equilibrium, and to maintain the hover all controls have to be adjusted accordingly.

The helicopter's heading is changed by using the yaw pedals. Light pressure on the left pedal will turn the helicopter to the left just as a boat turns using its rudder. Pressing the left pedal increases the pitch on the right-hand side of the forward head and the left-hand side of the aft head. This changes the thrust and causes the aircraft to rotate.

Once the helicopter is stable in its hover and ready to fly forward, the cyclic is pushed forward very gently. The helicopter's nose lowers. As this happens it will start to descend because the angle of the downwash has changed. To correct this requires a gentle increase of power by raising the collective lever. If more collective is pulled, the helicopter starts to climb. This climb may be stopped by lowering the lever a little or pushing the cyclic forward which lowers the nose. Lowering the nose makes the helicopter accelerate more quickly. It is possible to accelerate very quickly by pulling in lots of collective to maximum power (100 per cent torque), and lowering the nose to stop the climb. When the aircraft is light the nose is pitched down up to twenty degrees to stop it from climbing.

Transitional lift is reached when the helicopter leaves the ground cushion of air behind, and the blades are turning in undisrupted air. A gentle rumble can be felt through the airframe as it goes into smooth air at about forty knots airspeed. The nose is then gently raised with the cyclic to the climbing attitude of about five degrees nose up, at a speed of between eighty and a hundred knots. If a higher rate of climb is needed more collective lever is pulled in. Once at cruise altitude, the nose is lowered, and the speed then increases. A normal cruise speed is 140 to 160 knots depending on the weight of the helicopter and how much spare power is available.

What keeps a helicopter in the air is the blade spinning round. Try sticking your arm out of a car window at 100 m.p.h. with the hand horizontal. If you bend the palm back the arm will be pulled up, bend it forward and it will go down. If you stop or slow the car the arm drops. That is basically what a helicopter blade does. But to make it go up or down you need that 100 knots of forward speed, so the rotor r.p.m. (r.r.p.m.) is very critical.

There is an optimum speed for blades. If there is not enough they will stall which is due not to an engine fault but to the airflow. If the angle is too steep the airflow cannot keep a smooth line and stalls.

In the event of a double engine failure the pilot must go into autorotation. Lowering the collective lever lowers the angle of the blades, which spin like a windmill enabling him to maintain a controlled, albeit very steep, descent. However, very careful judgment and coordination are required during the last fifty feet to ensure a safe landing and stop the blades slowing down and stalling. Each blade on a Chinook weighs 300 kg, so with six of those spinning round at 250 r.p.m. there is a lot more inertia to maintain the rotor r.p.m. This gives the pilot a millisecond more to sort things out than in a smaller helicopter with less inertia. In a fixed-wing craft, if I'm quite high up, and stall, I can light a fag, eat a meal and still have time to sort the problem out. In a helicopter emergency procedures have to be done immediately and they have to be done correctly. There is no second chance.

To descend the pilot lowers the collective lever. The more it is lowered, the higher the rate of descent. Speed is controlled by the cyclic raising or lowering the nose. The transition from forward flight into the hover requires bringing the helicopter from cruising altitude at speeds of up to 160 knots into a fifteen-foot hover at zero speed. It has to descend and reduce speed simultaneously. Lowering the collective lever with the left hand starts the descent, and raising the nose by pulling back on the cyclic with the right hand reduces the speed. Again, careful judgment and good coordination are required to meet the profile.

Once you're in the hover and ready to land, the crewman checks below and talks the helicopter down. The pilot once more controls his rate of descent with the collective, his position with the cyclic, and his heading with the yaw pedals. The rear wheels touch down first, and then the helicopter settles down on to its front wheels. The AFCS is disengaged, and the helicopter is ground-taxied back to the apron.

Shutdown is the reverse of the start-up procedure. Chocks are put in, then the APU is started, the ECLs are then brought back to stop, which effectively stops the engines. Rotors spin freely, until the rotor brake – a lever about eighteen inches long situated on the right-hand side of the cockpit roof – is applied by the right-hand-seat pilot. The crewman monitors the brake for fire, until the blades have stopped turning. The APU is then turned off and silence prevails.

The noise from a Chinook is subdued, because you have

Me aged 18.
I'd occasionally manage to get airborne on a motorcycle – unfortunately usually followed by a police summons for speeding.

Freedom in the sky.
ays like this caused the flying bug to bite me hard.

Another flight over and my cheek muscles once again aching with smiling.

Swinderby June 1984. My second day in the RAF.

September 1984:
day one at Finningley.
Six weeks of torture. Myself,
back left and Bruce Laycook,
back right, were the two out
of the five that make it
through the course first time.

Training in the Yorkshire Dales. Given two pieces of string and a tooth pick I have to get my team over the river.

Another exercise to make sure two nuclear powered ping-pong balls don't touch each other whilst maintaining a six-foot exclusion zone around the barrel.

Me in the middle trying to convince myself that it will all be worth this pain and exhaustion.

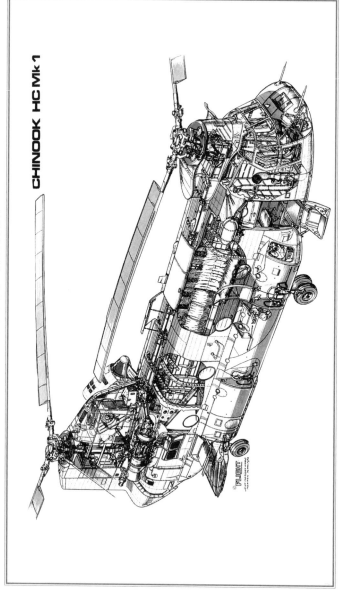

Cross-section of a Chinook HC Mk 1.

CHINOOK HC Mk 1

FADEC — the first Chinook to be delivered to Boeing for upgrade and later the one damaged due to engine over speeds (the RAF sued Boeing for $3million for damage caused).

A Gazelle helicopter looks on as a neverending stream of troops get into the Chinook.

A Chinook carrying a triple load, using all of its three hooks.

The Chinook at work again on an observation tower in Germany.

Lifting other helicopters is no problem for the Chinook. Smaller ones like the Gazelle require extra ballast to stop it swinging around. Here a Puma is lifted.

Formation take-off from RAF Lyneham.

The Chinook displays its agility on the ground

To accommodate the SBS we occasionally had to land on water to recover or drop off troops.

Ramp riding. Good fun unless you are my ex-drill sergeant.

No 13 Chinook course. I am back row, fifth from left; John Sanderson (Captain in the Gulf) front row, fourth from right; Chas Dickenson (Gulf co-pilot) back row, second from right; Jim McMenemy (was killed in a crash in Hanover) front row, fourth left.

After nearly two years training I am awarded my flying brevet. Now to start the SF training.

April 1986. Jill and I get married.

a helmet on, but it's constant and unrelenting – a scraping, screeching sound as if a nail were being dragged across a plate; the regular thud and thwack of the blades coming overhead; a high-pitched whine from the gears; the shuddering from the rotors at 250 r.p.m. Most crew on helicopters go high-tone-deaf. A helicopter crew after a night out at a club is a hysterical sight. For a few minutes after coming out nobody can hear anything at all. Conversation is conducted in a mixture of sign language and bellowing, reminiscent of Basil Fawlty talking to foreigners.

The cabin is the aircrew domain. Crewman number 1 is normally responsible for the running of the cabin. He has the greater responsibility when dropping off troops and the equipment. He sits back left and looks out of a bubble canopy. Just to confuse matters Crewman 2 sits by the front door during operations and talks the pilot down during landing.

When I first discovered that I was going to be aircrew on a Chinook I was really disappointed. Most of the time the Chinook is the aerial equivalent of a horse and cart, or a four-ton truck. Our job was to carry men and equipment wherever it was required. It was easy enough having some grunt back a Land Rover up the ramp and secure that down with ropes and ties. It was a different matter when it came to transporting a smashed-up Wessex or a field gun and two containers of ammunition.

Picking up and transporting loads is the Chinook's bread and butter. It is also when the pilot learns that he has to have absolute faith in his crew. The pilot is sitting there with the first hook fifteen feet behind him, the second at thirty feet and the third is forty feet behind him. As soon as he sees the load go under his feet he can't see anything any more. Crewman 2 leans out of the front right-hand door wearing a harness and gives the pilot directions like 'Go forward twenty units' (one unit is about a metre). Meanwhile Crewman 1 has moved forward and opened the centre hatch – a big square hole in the centre of the cabin. He lies down, looking out for the load, which he can't see as the pilot is going over it. Once he sees it, he calls out, 'My load,' and takes over giving instructions.

It starts to get more interesting when you have to pick up three loads. There are three different lengths of strop, a short one at the front, long on the second and even longer on the third. Many times I've had one load dangling from the front, the second a little lower below it and been desperately trying to position the helicopter over the third with my head hanging out the floor looking behind and desperately calling out instructions.

You expect the pilot to respond immediately. This is a procedure the crew learn to do in all conditions: in the daytime, in high winds, at night and in emergencies. During an engine failure, the crew also have to know how to jettison the load should it be necessary. At very low speeds and high weights, you can't get away with an engine failure, so the pilot has to dive towards the ground to gain some speed, or if there is not enough height to do this, then jettison the load to make the helicopter lighter. The brass were never very keen on our jettisoning loads because it can make a very expensive mess. We did drop a Rapier missile defence unit in the Falklands once. That was the best part of a million quid written off. It was the fault of the grunts on the ground who hadn't tied the chains on properly.

In peacetime every lifting load, both internal and external, has to be trialled by the Joint Air Freight Testing Establishment, who come back and say you can't fly with this particular underslung load at more than sixty knots and you must have these strops and those chains. I soon discovered that when dealing with the Special Forces or in times of war the rule book goes flying out of the door.

Because it is a twin-rotor aircraft, the Chinook has a few other personal idiosyncrasies. When flying a helicopter the pilot always wants to have a 'positive stick gradient' – which means he has the stick pushed away from his body as the speed of the helicopter increases. When testing the Chinooks in the early days they discovered that the faster they went the more lift they got from the rear rotors, causing the helicopter's nose to pitch down. The only way to prevent that was to pull the cyclic stick further and further back. When the stick's wedged in your stomach it's very difficult to fly.

So all the brains got together, cast their bones in the air and came up with the DASH (differential airspeed hold). They put an electric motor on each end of the cyclic stick control. As you go faster the motors wind away and falsely lengthen the control run so you have to push the stick forward to gain speed and create a positive stick gradient. No other helicopter has got this. The DASH control run is very complicated and it's fine when it's working properly but if it doesn't it can be the bane – and possibly the end – of your life.

In April 1987 we were flying out of Odiham and went into cloud to do some instrument training. Suddenly there was a severe vertical vibration, very high-frequency. The aircraft shook so much that the instruments became a blur. The negative G was flashing all the captions on. It was really severe so we put out a mayday call. In clear skies you can see where you are going and try to keep the aircraft level, but to keep level in cloud you need instruments. The vibration was so severe we couldn't see them. You can't fly upside down in a helicopter because the oil goes away from all the oil pumps, which means the gearbox would seize up. More seriously, the blades would slice through the cabin.

Fortunately for us the cloud base wasn't too low and we came out of cloud at fifty degrees of bank and fifteen degrees pitched forward. We saw the ground in time. The pilot managed to recover control and we landed on a racecourse. That incident was traced to a lateral problem on the DASH. It was suddenly getting a signal saying it was going 170 m.p.h., then that it was doing nought. The control run went crazy, which caused a severe vertical vibration that wasn't pleasant and could have been fatal.

There is no difference between flying the Chinook and any other helicopter, unless you take out the AFCS, which steadies the helicopter down a bit. I've had a few goes at flying it without that and it's an absolute bitch and hard to master. Pilots do practise that but there are other priorities. Do you practise making a good approach to an oil rig at night or use the hours to practise flying without a DASH?

That's where the question of cost comes in, and the accountants get twitchy and ask how much money is being spent. It costs £3,500 an hour to fly a Chinook – not including the crew's pay – and the bean counters are becoming increasingly cost-conscious.

CHAPTER 5

COMBAT-READY

On 5 March 1986 I finished the Chinook Operational Conversion Unit (OCU) course. I had put in a request to stay at Odiham. I didn't want to go to Germany because I was getting married the next month. The boss went through everyone on the course, congratulated them all, told them where they were being posted. When he got to me he looked me straight in the eye, turned to the others and announced. 'Apart from McMullon, could everybody leave the room please?'

My first reaction was, Oh fuck, I'm being chopped.

'Do you realise why you're being kept behind?' asked the boss.

'No, sir. What have I done?'

'Was it mentioned to you that you were going straight on to the SF Flight?'

I nodded. He continued: 'You passed the course very well and you're being posted to 7 Squadron Special Forces Flight here at RAF Odiham. Any problems you have won't be with the Flight but the reaction of people on the squadron. You're the first person out of training to go straight in, whereas they have to be on the squadron for a minimum of six months. Expect to receive a lot of flak when you go in there.'

I was so relieved I wasn't even listening. After all, how different could it be? I had survived Spike Edwards! But I still had no idea what squadron life was about, and had even less of a clue about what being on the SF Flight meant. Three days later I breezed into 7 Squadron to introduce myself.

'Dave McMullon,' I said, 'I'm starting on Monday.'

The desk sergeant ran his eyes over a large board before replying, 'I haven't got your name anywhere down here, Sergeant. Look.' Most of the names were printed in red, but at the bottom was a much smaller list, highlighted in green. I could see mine there.

'Look, it's down there.' I grinned. 'Right at the bottom in green.'

'On the SF Flight?' he said. 'First posting – and you've come straight in?' I could immediately see that he was thinking, You jammy bastard. That I shouldn't have been there. I could feel a brick wall come down. It didn't lift for a long time. Even after I'd been there a year there was still a lingering resentment, hovering unspoken in the air.

To begin with I did get a hard time – mostly light-hearted piss-taking from my new colleagues, but there was an edge to it. People told me, 'You will be back here and we'll show you how it's done – those SF blokes are just a bunch of wankers.' There was a hint of jealousy because the SF did more interesting things. It was seen as a career step up and here I was, a wet-behind-the-ears Geordie, fresh out of training, preferred to some old-timer. Worst of all, I didn't have any idea of what I was supposed to be doing. I learned soon enough.

There are usually ten Chinooks in a squadron – give or take. It depends on how many have crashed or are being fixed. To be SF-Flight-qualified you had to be able to do any of the other squadron tasks, so for the first three months I was at Odiham I was under the wing of the squadron, double checking I was up to the job. Once I got all the ticks in the right boxes Sean Calloway, the OC, announced, 'Right we'll have him now.'

On 12 April I married Jill. My honeymoon was confined to a brief weekend. I was right in the middle of squadron training duties and the SF Flight were hungry to get their money's worth. I was scared shitless about getting married, even though we both knew we would do so one day. Jill must have rabbited on about it or we wouldn't be engaged now! Originally I'd promised her, 'When I finish my training at Finningley.' I thought I'd never finish the training so I would never get engaged. After I passed she buttoned on to this and demanded, 'When's it going to be then?'

I said, 'Oh God, all right.' It wasn't the world's most romantic proposal but I can't be bothered with any of the sloppiness – Valentine cards, flowers. I didn't want to get married until I had finished all the training. When I was training at Shawbury, we bought a house in Shrewsbury and agreed a date for the wedding. Then for some reason it had to be brought forward by a month and a half. Jill called me and when she told me I went completely numb. I just stood there while she was shouting, 'David, David, David' down the phone.

'I'm sorry,' I said, 'I'm just in shock.'

The wedding day itself was excellent, the standard church bash packed with people I didn't know. I had some RAF friends dressed in blues and Jill's father gave a speech in which he said, 'When David first met Jill he was working in the bank and we thought he was a man with a secure job and cheap mortgages, and he'd be a bank manager before long. Now we're shocked because he's joined the RAF and soon he'll be dangling out of a helicopter hanging on the end of a rope.' He was joking, but I know he was quite pleased.

For the first year we were married Jill lived in the house

and worked at the Nationwide Building Society nearby. I stayed in the Sergeants' Mess at Odiham and came home back to Shropshire only at weekends. It really wasn't working out so we decided to rent the house out and move into married quarters. I hated that year of commuting but buying the house proved a very shrewd investment. Eventually it was to help secure my future.

The SF Flight had evolved as a consequence of various joint missions between the RAF and SAS during the Falklands War. They discovered they needed to be able to deposit SBS or SAS quickly and accurately after covering long distances, primarily over water, but they didn't have equipment that was up to it. They even practised fast-roping a small group of Paras and high-ranking officers from a Sea King into the water.

On one mission a Navy Sea King helicopter dropped SAS troops off on mainland Argentina. Without enough fuel to make it back, they made for Chile, where the helicopter was torched by the crew to hide the purpose of their mission. It seemed rather an expensive price to pay to blow up a few Argentinian aeroplanes.

However, the basic idea was sound and led to the formation of the SF Flight in 1983–84. The SAS did have two civilian Sikorsky helicopters of their own, flown by a warrant officer (WO) pilot and kept at Hereford. But they can take only a small team. They needed something that could carry two Range Rovers, two tons of equipment and up to seventeen blokes, deploy to a situation ASAP and have enough fuel to get back to base. The Chinook was the only helicopter capable of carrying the extra fuel weight.

This was done by fitting it out with Andover extended-range fuel tanks. Each is 4.5 feet in diameter and 12 feet long with a capacity of 900 gallons (3,000 kg) of fuel. This gave the aircraft a total fuel capacity of just over 9,000 kg, six hours – seven if you pushed it – of endurance and a range of nearly 900 miles. At the same time it could still carry fifteen to twenty troops on the remaining seats.

When I joined the Flight was mainly involved in training with the SBS/SAS in all their roles, and had helped, with 18 Squadron, in the evacuation of the British from Beirut. There were no real secret missions that I was aware of, though we did travel to politically sensitive areas such as Jordan and Morocco, all of which were so hush-hush there were threats of testicle removal if we told anyone where we had been.

I believe the RAF got the SF Flight by default. The SF Hercules flight had been going for a while, so they could claim the expertise, and the bean counters weren't going to re-equip the Army or Navy with Chinooks at £10 million a shot.

It has meant that the RAF have had to change their rather sneering attitude to helicopters and their crew. Historically, the RAF have always been geared to fighters, bombers and transport aircraft. Helicopters are carthorses, without an aeroplane's pedigree. The Army have always been helicopter people, but the way they use them is completely different. Army helicopters hover in the front line, target spotting. They get shot at and they shoot back. But there is no RAF attack helicopter. The Chinook is there for slugging loads around, dropping and collecting people, going in and coming out unseen. It is only recently that the RAF have stuck guns on support helicopters. The Army, and particularly the American forces, are aggressive and love to go in guns blazing. They want to see blood.

Since 1984 the role of the SF Flight has been to take the SAS or SBS exactly where they want to go, unseen, if possible unheard, and with split-second precision – at night, flying so low that enemy radar thinks it's made a mistake. That's fine if you're in a small helicopter, a Huey or a Puma with minimal equipment. They are like sports cars: small, nippy and manoeuvrable. The Chinook is a double-decker bus, so if you're about to drop an SBS team on an oil rig at two in the morning and pilots and aircrew aren't in perfect synch there's going to be a big mess to clear up.

The SF flight crews did twenty per cent more flying time than other Chinooks because we had to fulfil normal squadron commitments as well. On average I'd get sixty hours' flying a month (fast-jet pilots get only a quarter of that, which simply isn't enough). Not that we got paid anything extra for our efforts.

Flying long distances, low-level, over water – depending on the state of the sea, we'd be between twenty and a hundred feet up – is tricky because the sea moves and the computer thinks the moving sea is a vector on the ground. Long-range navigation over water is very tedious: sitting there with heavy night-vision goggles on for eight hours is very uncomfortable and tiring, and boredom and tedium can make it dangerous.

Everything important I'd learned in OCU was magnified three or four times on the SF Flight. Whatever personal differences we might have we had to operate as a team. Both pilots and both crewmen had to be able to navigate to within fifty metres of the target and then drop into it – it was much tougher then, since we didn't have all the high-tech GPS (global positioning system) stuff they do now. All Chinook crews have to be able to do some neat manoeuvring, to drop in and out of small confined spaces carrying men and equipment. The SF Flight have to be able to do it at night, with a pair of oversized binoculars glued to their faces. Using NVGs requires learning your job all over again, learning how to fly in a bizarre world where there are only two dimensions. And the only colour is green.

I checked out my first pair in July. The generation 2 night-vision goggles were kept in a soft green case similar to that of a camera. They cost a mere £20,000 a pair and weighed about three pounds, which does not sound a lot, except that by the end of a long trip it felt like some caring mechanic had welded an anvil on to your helmet. They slid on to a fixed bracket on the front of the bone-dome, and were locked into place at the desired position. They could be tilted up if necessary. A battery pack – about three inches by one inch – was fixed on the back of the helmet to try to balance out some of the goggle weight. This pack was attached by the latest modern design – Velcro.

Once I switched on the battery pack, the two toilet-roll tubes I was looking through turned into green television screens. To get the sharpest image they had to be focused one eye at a time on a distant light – stars were a favourite. When you look up into a clear night sky without the goggles it is covered with stars, but look up with NVGs on and you see a whole new sky with twice as many stars. NVGs need some light to operate, and, if there is a very dark area, the image becomes very grainy as they try to intensify what light there is. Once you'd got the desired focus, the distance between the eye and the goggles was adjusted until the two green TV screens appeared to merge into one. That's all there was to it.

'Easy,' I crowed to the rest of the crew. Malcolm, the pilot, was having problems adjusting his focus. 'Let's go and fly,' I said, adopting an air of absolute confidence. Then I turned towards the aircraft – and walked straight into a wall.

That was when I realised the normal three-dimensional world that we were used to living and flying in had suddenly lost a dimension and turned a funny colour. The NVGs robbed you of depth perception – suddenly a hover wasn't a hover any more. Try driving your car along a country road at night with one eye closed and imagine the only colours you can see are green and black. Now imagine flying in a twenty-three-ton machine at two hundred miles an hour fifty feet off the deck in the dark at night while navigating accurately to within a hundred meters, all with one eye closed!

Once I got used to the discomfort of wearing the goggles, it became obvious that everything I was used to doing was either useless or made the situation much worse. The internal lighting in a Chinook was a very dim red colour but it had the same effect as shining a bright torch directly into the eyes. This was true of any unfiltered light. The smallest amount of 'white light' caused the goggles to 'back off'. In other words blinded us.

Before we were ready to go we placed an infrared filter over all the cabin and flight instrument lights. Once the Chinook lifted into the hover it became obvious that Malcolm was not finding flying quite as easy as he normally did. His usual rock-steady hover began drifting around. Heights were bloody difficult to judge. A new technique was required. To judge height you compared with things around you. So if a tree was about twenty feet tall and we were level with it we were also twenty feet off the deck.

Flying was like starting from scratch, exhausting for both pilots and crewmen alike. Looking out of the back I discovered that I had lost the peripheral vision I relied on for picking up any aircraft movement. I had to scan from side to side moving my entire head to pick up any movement in height and drift. Constant movement of the head and relating to everything else around me partially compensated for the extra senses I had lost. Looking straight down with goggles on, I could see the load underneath but didn't know if I was ten feet above it or just two.

As we climbed the scale of the picture increased. Trees, roads, cars and the fields became smaller and were constantly replaced, like a large green carpet unrolling in front of us. At 500 feet the overall picture was good but there was not a great deal of detail to be seen. Power cables were not visible, just an occasional pylon. Lights from near and distant towns showed up very brightly, and when I looked directly at them the goggles backed off, and became useless for a few seconds. The closer we got to the ground the more detail became apparent: cables three miles ahead were clearly visible. Houses we flew over were perfectly clear – even the TV aerials were visible – and the glow of light behind the curtains became very bright as the people inside the house opened them to see what had disturbed them at this late hour.

'Climbing,' announced Malcolm as the helicopter gained another 100 feet. Although the helicopter was flying level at 150 feet, the small hill looming up as we approached remained undetected by the crew until the radalt warning (a high-pitched note), sounded telling us that the helicopter was now dangerously close to the ground. In daylight we would have picked up the rising ground easily and naturally. It was an important lesson. The whole crew realised we must learn to be more vigilant, both looking out and study-ing the map.

After two hours we sped back towards Odiham at 200 m.p.h., level at 150 feet. 'Tango 62. Fifteen miles west to join. Request all airfield lights off for the approach.' The air-traffic controller dimmed the airfield lights in compliance. We knew from the silence he wasn't happy. Unable to see us on his radar because we were too low, now he could not see us out of his window either.

After two months' training with the NVGs we were getting pretty good. Jill, however, was complaining that she'd agreed to marry a man, not a bat. Summer night flights didn't end until the small hours, so at weekends I was always asleep during the day and wide awake at night.

We moved on to fast-roping training. The roping kit is a large square alloy frame that bolts on to the edge of the ramp. It is hinged so that it can fold down in transit. When erected it stands about six feet high and can take up to four ropes, though normally only two or three are used, so the troops don't bash into each other on the way down. The ropes are thick – an inch in diameter – and green. They come in either sixty- or ninety-foot lengths with a metal eye at the top, which slots into the roping frame and is secured by a large 'T' pin. Directly above the centre hatch is a bracket for fixing another rope to – provided the engineers have removed the centre hook. The final exit is the front door: the step is removed and when the upper door is slid up out of the way it leaves an exit about six feet high and three and a half feet wide. If the helicopter has a winch fitted for search-and-rescue operations, then the end of the rope has a large metal ring on it that simply clips on to the winch hook. Alternatively, the helicopter is fitted with a 'spider', which is simply a metal plate that has a facility for securing the ropes on to, attached by several legs.

Not everybody was able to apply their newly acquired NVG skills to fast roping. During my time on the flight two pilots and one crewman were chopped because, although they had learned to fly again with goggles on, having to apply that in tense situations built up an awful lot of pressure. It took too much out of them, which left little in reserve for safety.

We also learned to operate in NBC (nuclear/biological/

chemical warfare) kit. This was a two-piece green suit which felt as if it was made out of stiff Brillo pads lined with coal dust. Highly unpopular and incredibly uncomfortable and hot. Naturally someone realised that aircrew might find an excuse not to wear the two-piece suit so a special one-piece version was designed – to be twice as uncomfortable. This was worn under the flying suit, which if you were flying over water would be covered by an immersion suit and made you look like the Michelin Man. It was guaranteed to make you lose a gallon of sweat an hour.

Complementing the NBC suit was the dreaded AR5 (aircrew respirator). It resembles a Conservative MP's sex toy comprising a black rubber bag, worn like a balaclava with an airtight neck seal. To breathe through, there was a fighter pilot's oxygen mask, and there was a diver's mask to see through. Two pipes led from the oxygen mask. The inlet pipe was attached to a green circular filter case known as the 'hissing handbag'. The outlet pipe expelled used air. Air was drawn into the handbag, filtered round and passed into the hood. The flying helmet was then put on top. With NVGs on, vision and movement were so restricted that it became a claustrophobic's nightmare. Everything took twice as long to do. We'd have to empty the sweat that collected around the neck seal every fifteen minutes. Pilots could operate in an AR5 because they remained seated, but it severely restricted the crew's ability to perform.

In September I was finally pronounced combat-ready and allowed to make my first unsupervised trip to Pontrailis Army Training Area near Hereford. PATA is the SAS training area.

At the first briefing I attended at Pontrailis I was expecting to hear a detailed brief, carefully laid out, sounding like something out of a James Bond movie. One of the troop warrant officers stood up and gave out the essential information: 'My name is Warrant Officer Pat Stead.' This was his idea of a detailed brief: 'OK, lads, after the crabs have dropped us off and pissed off out the way, we'll reach the enemy location. Remember we are the SAS, so just go in and fuck them.'

After a few moments of stunned silence an arm was raised from the back of the room.

'Yes, sir. You have a question?' asked Stead, looking rather surprised.

'Yes, Mr Stead,' said the officer with his hand up, patiently. 'Would it be possible for you to expand just a little more on the "go in and fuck them" part of the brief?' My vision of these well-prepared professionals was temporarily cracked.

Any walk of life has its wankers and the SAS is no different. Generally they were very good blokes and I was immediately struck by how the normal Army rank structure was ignored. They have a simple attitude: 'Get the job done'. And to do that they have to be well trained, extremely fit and – in most cases – well briefed. But basically they are all trained hooligans who are able to control it – to harness it and put it to a great deal of good. I knew a lot by sight but not their names because they preferred nicknames.

They were always friendly and very happy to let us play with their toys. The RAF give you a 9mm pistol and basic training with the SA80 once a year. When we went up to Hereford they just said, 'There's the range, there is a whole bunch of weapons and as much ammo as you need. Help yourself.'

My first visit they took me on a tour of the Killing House. The Scottish corporal who took me round offered me the chance to sit in the hostage's chair for a demonstration that afternoon. With live rounds.

'You'll be quite safe, laddie,' he said as his right hand started to jerk. 'No one's been killed for years. I'll be leading the team.'

I went white and mumbled some lame excuse about being married. 'Suit yourself, laddie.' His eye twitched as he scowled. Funny thing for such a crack shot: he only ever twitched when he was showing visitors round the Killing House. Drink didn't have the same effect at all.

There is a CT (counter terrorist) unit at Hereford and a Chinook on standby at Odiham twenty-four hours a day. We'd have exercises at least once a month – except we didn't know they were exercises until we got there.

One of the toughest counter-terrorist operations we practised was dropping teams down on to a hijacked car ferry. Going into confined areas at night and roping people down is tricky enough without adding a moving boat, two Lynx helicopters – each carrying an SBS sniper – and three Chinooks. The operation was coordinated by a radar operator sitting 30,000 feet above the water in a Nimrod. Once the AEOP (air electronics operator) had worked out the ship's course, the helicopters' attack heading, the abort heading and the wind velocity, he'd announce, 'Stand by to copy Air Plan Falcon,' and then count us down.

The plan was that the Chinooks would be coming in a stream of three aircraft at ninety-second intervals, but twenty-three tons doesn't stop dead. Also, we couldn't come to a hover, since we had to slow to ten knots, matching the speed of the ship. Come in too low and you can't get any blokes on the rope. Or one is standing on the deck with his mate perched on his head. If you are too high it takes them too long to get down.

According to the plan, we would follow in the two Lynx helicopters, which would provide sniper cover on the port and starboard sides of the ship with the terrorists on, while we dropped our blokes down to ruin their day. The Lynx pilots had no night-vision goggles, no lights at all, so the only way we could formate on them was by the lights on their instrument panels. It didn't bother us at all but one night we took one of the Lynx pilots in the jump seat of our Chinook, whilst following the Lynx helicopters. 'Jesus, I wish I'd never seen that,' he said after we asked him which light we were using as a reference to formate on. It was a parking brake light. He was absolutely gobsmacked because when he was flying the Lynx on previous exercises, he did not realise how close we got to him, or where we were. None of them wanted to come on the flight deck with us again.

The most frightening exercise of all was the oil rigs. It's a major government fear that someone might try to hijack an oil rig. The exercise looked easy enough on paper – except that an oil-rig platform is 200 feet above sea level, so we had to practise in daylight to get it right. The idea was to come in unseen, skimming the waves, flying low and fast and end up thirty feet above the platform with zero speed on. Coming in at 140 knots at a height of fifty feet you have to judge the point at which you pull the nose up. This will make the speed drop but you have to make sure that when the speed comes off you are in a hover. If you pull the nose up too early you will come to the hover in the wrong place, too late. You will either hit the rig or overshoot. The first time I saw this metal monster rising out of the sea I almost shat myself. So did the pilot. We ended up with a section of fish heads preparing to abseil straight into the oggin, with the rig fifty metres straight in front of the nose.

'Try again,' explained a senior pilot. 'When you think you just have to pull up, count to three. Then pull up. The problem is that as the speed drops you need more and more power, which can cause problems.' As the helicopter came into the hover all the lift the blades had with the high approach speed was gone. So this had to be replaced with power – lots of it. But if the power was not applied smoothly or just yanked in, it was possible to overtorque the gearboxes. When so much power is being asked for the rotor r.p.m. can temporarily slow down – this is known as rotor droop. This could cause the electrical generators to go off line, giving horrendous problems at night leaving us with no lights, radios, instruments or AFCS (in itself giving gross handling problems).

Once we mastered the technique in daylight we had to do it at night without lights and it came together quickly. The first time I saw this monstrous thing rushing towards me at night I said five Hail Marys – and I'm not a Catholic. We chopped a few aerials and masts down with the blades but that didn't affect anything: we never even noticed it until we saw the roughnecks waving their fists at us. They couldn't get any of the Continental porn channels on the TV any more.

That November I went out on my first extended exercise with the SF Flight. We went to Jordan for six weeks with a bunch of guys from Hereford. It was essentially a hush–hush public-relations exercise working with the Jordanian special forces. How they could call themselves SF I will never know. I knew more about the business end of a gun than they did, though I admit I didn't have their expertise with camels.

One day the Jordanians were playing with their mortars. Unfortunately they decided to use the helicopter landing area as their target, just as we were landing a cargo of high explosives. We saw this SAS Land Rover zooming across the desert, then bodies tumbling out of it and beating the shit out of the mortar crew.

The following morning they threw a box of live ammo on to the cooking fire while we were eating breakfast. It was very noisy and did not aid digestion. Having to swallow a mouthful of sand instead of pork and beans did not improve relations. The pilots managed to get a little revenge, scaring the hell out of our Jordanian passengers by flying to the edge of a cliff. In the cockpit they'd be hovering six feet off the summit, but then we'd lower the ramp and it was 3,000 feet looking straight down.

After a couple of weeks the helicopters were given a break while the SAS instructors went out into the desert and showed our hosts some advanced desert tactics – what a gun looked like, where to point it, that sort of thing. Scott Hudson, one of the aircrew, begged the boss for permission to go with them. Scott was one of the lads and loved all the jockstrappy stuff even when he was the butt of it. It was his only character flaw if you didn't count his love of a pint. Underneath he had a heart of gold and he was very reliable on ground and in air. He might have had forty-eight pints of ale but he'd still turn up for the job.

Because we weren't sure how the Jordanians reacted to drinking we'd brought an entire NAAFI beer tent over with us. As the flight commander was worried that with nothing to do Scott would drink us dry he gave him permission to go out into the desert for a couple of days with the SAS to do some training with the Jordanians.

When they all came back to camp they had a monumental party and got totally pissed. We were sleeping in this dormitory and my bed was next to the flight commander's. I heard the door open and in the pitch-black I could see a shadowy figure bouncing from wall to wall. Eventually he got into bed. I rolled over until I heard murmurings. It was Scott getting up again, obviously with a desperate urge for a pee. I saw this perfectly stable figure walking around the bed, then I lost sight of him and all I could hear was the sound of pissing.

Then there was a yell: 'Scott, you stupid bastard. You're pissing on us!'

'I know, sir,' came the reply. 'I can't help it!'

The only thing Scott could think of to do was salute his superior officer. So he stood there saluting the flight commander while pissing all over him. The next day he spent a long time cleaning the boss's sleeping bag. He was not the most popular sergeant for a while but he was never disciplined.

Working – and drinking – closely with the SAS and SBS blokes helped establish a good relationship. Some of them became pretty good mates but in the end they still viewed us as 'crabs' – a necessary evil but not to be trusted. It was hard to be on a level with them because the rigorous training and tests they go through bring them together as a unit. Anybody who hasn't done all that is outside because he has not met their standards.

We never failed to produce the goods. But that was in training. We always knew that the only way we would earn their real respect was when it really mattered. When bullets were flying and lives were at risk.

CHAPTER 6

OPERATIONAL ACTION

The ops tent had the usual set-up. At the back a few chairs were gathered around three large boards. Two were covered by drawings of the area and an Ordnance Survey map. The third had a list of names allocated to Blue and Red Teams. Every available bit of space was taken up by SAS guys, already dressed in black boiler suits checking and rechecking their kit, fixing torches on to weapons, adjusting body armour and checking respirators. Some of the respirators had tinted-glass lenses, presumably to stop any flashes blinding them, but it still looked as out of place as someone marching into a nightclub wearing a pair of Ray-Bans.

'Everyone listen in, please!' A loud bellow silenced the place in seconds, commanding instant attention. The bellow belonged to Major Jerry Sinclair, a tall, slim man with ginger hair curling over the back of his collar. 'Bob here will give the immediate-action orders.'

Bob was an SNCO whose dark hair was in contrast to that of his officer, cut shorter than normal for the SAS. He flipped open his standard-issue M.o.D notepad as if it was a *Star Trek* communicator.

'Right, this is the situation.' Bob might have looked as if butter wouldn't melt in his mouth, but his voice was loud enough to shatter windows miles away. 'At oh six hundred this morning a group of terrorists hijacked a train two miles to the northwest of here. We know there are at least six X-rays, but as yet we don't know, for certain, if there are any more. There are at least twenty Yankees on board. Our mission is to secure the safe release of these hostages. I say again: our mission is to ensure the safe release of the hostages. The immediate action plan is as follows...'

Bob went on in detail, going through every piece of information that was available. He pointed at drawings of the layout of the train, where the doors and windows were in each of the three carriages, and allocated each one a code name. While it was important for us to have the big picture about the operation, the exact detail of what the teams would be doing once inside was something we did not really need to know about. However, it was interesting that the way they looked at the task was similar to the way that we'd do it. Every single option was looked at and Bob went into lots of 'what if' scenarios.

'Red Team will go in with the Chinook and get in through the rear and the side of the back carriage. That will coincide with both Range Rovers going in and taking out the front and the sides of the two forward carriages.' On the drawing of the train Bob indicated the entry points for each of the teams. 'As we speak Gary and his blokes are sorting out a distraction. It'll be the usual fuck-off explosion.

'When in position the order will be, "Standby. Standby. Go!" Radios on channel one – for the Chinook that is frequency 33.62.' Every member of an SAS team would have a radio with the preset channel secured on his body with an earpiece clipped on to his ear. We had to dial in the frequency manually.

'If there are no questions so far I will brief the assault for once we're inside. At this moment the Chief Constable has not handed over control to us, but we have got to have our shit in order for when he does.'

That was our cue for a crew brief. Danny Sharp grabbed a map and we all studied the area where we had to drop the guys off. The train had been stopped at the bottom of an embankment, about two hundred yards from a tunnel. The sides were fifty feet high, too steep to approach from either side on foot. Just to compound the immediate problem posed by the embankment there was a copse of trees on the eastern side. To drop off Red Team we would have to fly below the lip, and the lower we had to go, the closer the blades would be to the side of the cutting. Over the next two or three hours there would still be daylight, which would be good for positioning, but bad for concealment.

Next question: what ropes should we use? Sixty-foot ropes should be long enough, and preferable, since they are lighter and easier to pull in after the drop-off. But there was no margin for error there, so better to use the ninety-footers just in case we had to fly higher than planned.

Bob joined us after he had finished the briefing. Danny advised him of the problem with the embankment and the possibility of our having to go in quite high. (The ideal is to be about thirty feet, short enough to get down the rope as quickly as possible, but not so short that the guys land on top of each other.) He could see the problem.

'That's OK. I'll tell the team to wear an extra pair of gloves for the slide down. We wouldn't want to get any blisters.' After discussing a few more options we finally settled on having the rear of the Chinook hovering just over the back of the train. This allowed the teams quick-roping access at the rear of the train, and we could put the front rope down just on the right-hand side of the train, allowing direct access through that side.

Danny then briefed us on the immediate-action option to make sure we all knew exactly what was required. Normally after an assault we were called in to pick up the hostages and take them to a safe area, and then return for what was left of the terrorists. If there were any. We decided there was enough space to land between the engine and the tunnel entrance which should save some time in the extraction of hostages.

'If we lose an engine in the hover over the train,' continued Sharpy, 'we're light enough to be able to maintain the hover, complete the drop-off. Then we fuck off sharpish.'

We discussed every option from engine failure to one of the crew being hit by small-arms fire. The SF Flight prides itself on never having had to call an abort due to a helicopter problem. Although our safety was the main factor, when people's lives depend on getting the job done, it would take a skipper with balls of steel to abort. For any crewman to call an abort basically means that continuing the mission would have completely catastrophic consequences.

Bob – like most of the SAS – did not like the sound of our 'what if' problems. The only time they had no command over their destiny was on the helicopters. They much prefer it when the helicopter is a noise disappearing in the distance and they're firmly on the ground.

'That's good for us,' he hollered after we discussed the drop-off. 'I'll go back and brief the guys on the roping area. I want to go through a dry run on the ground, so I'll bring them up in ten minutes.'

Wes and I went to prepare Echo X-ray for the drills. The Chinook needed the ramp to be just above the horizontal to lift off the ground, otherwise it would tip back on to the ground, which would not be a good start to a rescue mission. The roping frame required the ramp to be just below the horizontal, so the frame was down when we lifted off and needed to be put up bloody fast. It was a fairly simple process, but there was always the possibility of its jamming if it was lifted in the wrong place. Once the frame was up it was just a matter of locking it in position with two pins, and checking the ropes were locked on to the frame.

Bob already had the teams sorted out. Six would be going down the front rope next to me and ten would go down the two ramp ropes. In practice it took each man less than a second to clear the doorway. They just leaned out of the door, grabbed the rope with both hands and launched their bodies out and down the rope, using only the pressure of their grip to control their descent. I never knew why they bothered with the rope: they wouldn't get down any faster if they just jumped out. The most important thing was that they did not go until we gave them the signal, which was either the green jump light flashing on, or the bell sounding. When the guys were all hyped up ready to go, there was the temptation to just go when they spotted the target.

'If any of you jump before we've finished manoeuvring you could end up compromising the whole mission,' I stressed as the guys nodded their heads with that well-worn I've-heard-it-all-before expression. ' And we're not scraping any of you buggers off the track.'

There was nothing to do now except wait. We made our way back to the ops room ready to consume several gallons of coffee. Just as we walked in, I heard Range Rover engines burst into life.

A loud voice shouted out, 'Stand to. Stand to.' We sprinted back to the Chinook, scrambling in just behind Bob. His team was already in position on board, fully covered by their hoods and respirators. I caught the occasional glimpse of the whites of their eyes.

'Two lights,' Wes screamed, and the APU burst back into life once more. There was no time for the usual checks as both engines were started in turn. The rotors stabilised at 100 per cent. Wes gave me a thumbs-up.

'Cabin ready. Clear above and behind to lift.' Danny heaved in the lever. The Chinook beat the air into submission and we leaped skyward.

At 100 knots Danny banked hard right to position us in the holding area. I was squatting down with nothing between me and the ground fifty feet below. We passed directly over the Range Rovers, speeding off to their holding area. From the air they looked like toy cars covered in ants. Blokes wearing assault gear were hanging on to the bonnet, the roof and anywhere else there was a hand hold. As we passed overhead a couple somehow managed to give us the usual two-fingered salute and not fall off.

The airwaves were alive with radio checks.

'Bravo Three.'

'Bravo Four.'

'Tango One.'

'Tango Two.'

Andy checked in. 'Charlie One in position.'

Danny reduced the speed to sixty knots as we orbited the holding area at fifty feet. I checked around the cabin for any oil or fluid leaks, while Wes got the frame in position. He was surrounded by black bodies, each one rehearsing in his mind his exit from the helicopter. From the go, it would be less than thirty seconds to the drop zone.

We had been stood to because the X-rays had threatened to top some Yankees if their demands were not met. Good news for us, going in daylight with the embankment on one side and the trees on the other, but SAS teams always preferred the cover of darkness.

'Cabin ready'. It seemed like hours but we had been airborne for only three minutes. I slid the clear visor down on my bonedome to stop the airflow blowing in my eyes and positioned myself with my arse half into the heater compartment so that I would not block the exit. Bob's eyes were fixed open, staring into the distance, in his mind his boots already hitting the train roof. The adrenaline was in free flow, all ears waiting for the call to go. Every crackle on the radio sent my heart racing in expectation.

'All stations! All stations stand down! I say again: stand down!'

The call came in loud and clear. On board everyone breathed out hard, an exhalation half relief, half disappointment. Presumably the X-rays had thought better of executing any of the Yankees and were talking again. Back to the waiting game.

Less than six hours earlier I'd been standing on the tarmac at Odiham carrying a brown holdall full of minging kit. Chocks in, rotors winding down. Paul Harris and I left the pilots completing the paperwork. We chucked the crew bags on to a trolley and hurried our way across the apron. After four weeks living in a damp tent somewhere in the middle of Germany, ferrying grunts from one muddy field to another, I just wanted to spend a couple of days at home.

Before heading home we dropped into the ops room to see if there were any changes for us. Tim White was the duty ops flight sergeant, a tall skinny Mancunian with wispy mousey hair, and another skimpy rodent draped over his upper lip, which he claimed was a moustache. Aircrews liked Tim. Not only was he good at his job – efficient but not officious – but he possessed a sense of humour so sick that it belonged in hospital.

'Any changes for me, Tim?' I asked.

'Not really, Dave, but Matt Colyer's gone sick. He's got AIDS again or something equally unpleasant. He was on standby this afternoon, so would you be able to cover until twenty-two hundred tonight?'

'Yeah, that's no problem. I can cover that from home.' Standby was not a bad duty, since you could stay at home. You just had to get into the squadron and airborne within one hour of the callout. At least I could see Jill.

With everything sorted out I packed the NVGs away and took my flying helmet into the safety equipment boys. It was shagged. In Germany the strap of a grunt's Bergen had caught the arm of my microphone and ripped it away from the helmet mount. For the rest of the exercise the mike was held in place with thick, black bodge tape.

Paul gave me a lift home to our married quarters in the camp area. I threw both bags into his boot. The two holdalls should have been moving by themselves as they both contained a most unpleasant assortment of socks, underwear and other clothing carefully and economically rationed to last four weeks in the field. Paul declined my offer to come in for coffee or beer, as he was desperate to get home for some intimate personal reasons.

As I opened the front door Amy, my beagle, leaped off the chair, and started running around in circles with excitement. Then she peed on the floor. This was soon followed by her first flying lesson since my return home.

Jill had seen me through the window and ran in from the garden. She flung her arms around me, then glanced at the bag on the floor. 'The usual,' she groaned. 'I suppose it'll need a ten-mile no-fly zone around it until it's been through the washing machine three times.'

Half an hour later, just as I was settling into my armchair, finishing a cup of tea, Jill brought me the normal huge pile of mail. Car insurance, house insurance, bank statements and a hundred other things that needed to be looked at. I groaned and picked up the first brown envelope. The phone rang. Jill picked it up.

'Hello. Tim. Yes, he's just come in. Give me a second.'

I walked over to the phone, cursing, thinking, This can't be. I can't believe it.

'Dave, I'm really sorry,' Tim's voice echoed down the line, piling on the bad news. 'There is a priority-one call-out. It's probably some twat who's left a strange brown bag of shit in a car park, but they still want us up.'

It wasn't Tim's fault, so there was no point in shouting and bawling. 'I'll be there in five minutes.'

That left me with the job I really hated. I stared at my feet for a moment, then slowly looked up at Jill, hoping not to see the look of disappointment that first crept, then flooded, over her face. 'We've had over half an hour,' she sighed, trying to put a joke on it once again. 'That's longer than last time!' Poor lass. At least she could cope under the strains that RAF life puts on any relationship. Many of the wives couldn't – and didn't.

'I'm sorry,' I said, though, as usual words were superfluous. 'It's a call-out. I don't know where I'm going. I don't know if I can call you when I get there and I don't know when I'm coming back.'

Jill packed a few things into another bag, then gave me a lift back into work.

At the squadron it was the usual call-out chaos. The wing commander's car looked as though he had abandoned it at 30 m.p.h. and left it to park itself in his nominated spot. Engineers rushed around trying to find an aircraft that was both serviceable and had enough hours left to last for the call-out. I kissed Jill goodbye and I hurried into the squadron in a foul mood.

The rest of the crew were already waiting. Danny Sharp was the skipper. I had flown with him many times and I had a real trust in his abilities. Fortunately it was mutual.

'What's the crack, Danny?' I asked

'Oh, hi, Dave, glad you could make it.' He waved his hand at a chair before letting it rest once more on his beer storage facility, which had lately been increasing in size. 'Fuck knows. It's like trying to get blood out of a stone to get information out of this lot. All I know for certain is that we're going via PATA to pick up the boys.'

'Right. I'll make sure the CT role kit's put on to whichever aircraft we get.'

'OK, Dave. I'll try to squeeze the stones a bit more. Wes is already out there.'

Wes Hogan had recently finished his training on the SF Flight. While this was his first SF call-out he was a sound man. He'd just split up with his wife, moved back into the Sergeants' Mess, and seemed much happier as a result. It was decided that I should take the number two crewman's position at front right, and Wes would take the number one aft left.

Our first task was to sort out the role equipment. Fortunately Wes had already nicked one of the engineers' Land Rovers with attached trailer. There was masses of kit, anything and everything that might conceivably be needed on a call-out. Baggage nets, strops for tying down vehicles, armour plating for the cockpit which was supposed to deflect any small arms fire (but also restricted the field of view for the pilots), body armour for the crew. We had to load AR5s in case gas was to be used.

Wes carried on loading up the kit while I went off to the safety equippers to get my helmet. They had given it the death sentence so I had to have a new one, which I was not keen on, since new helmets take a while to become comfortable. There wasn't enough time to argue, so I grabbed the new helmet and signed out six pairs of NVGs (a mere 120 grand's worth of taxpayers' money).

'Going anywhere nice, Sarge?' asked the corporal

'Wish the fuck I knew,' I snarled as the door closed behind me.

I walked back into the briefing room to check that the goggles worked. The copilot, Andy Morley, was in the briefing room frantically sorting out the flight planning and the weather information.

'The weather's fucking shite so we'll have to go low level up to PATA, and that means navigating around all the airfield air-traffic zones!' said Andy, a skinny, well-spoken Scot (it always sounded strange when he swore).

'But we're on a priority call-out,' I reminded him, 'so if we use the call sign "snowball", any air-traffic unit must give us our requested routing!'

Andy checked the call-out orders and confirmed this. It would certainly make things easier. Wes came back in, scratched his balls, took one long drag from his weedy roll-up before he announced, 'The kit's on board. We've got Echo X-ray and the engineers are fitting the fast-roping frame now.'

Danny Sharp gave us a briefing: 'Right, guys, we all know it's a call-out but we don't know if it's real or exercise, so we'll treat it as real. There's been an incident that requires SF support. It will probably be the CT team. The weather is a problem; the average cloud base is from two to six hundred feet so we'll be on the deck all the way up to PATA. The call sign will be "snowball". That should cut through the crap with air-traffic and get us direct routing. It's forecast to clear up later so the weather for the job itself may be OK. The aircraft is Echo X-ray. Details, Wes?'

'It's got full fuel, seventeen green lines, mainly cracks which hopefully won't join up in flight, one red line with an aft hook that's u/s, and we've got twelve hours until the next check.'

'Thanks, Wes,' Sharpy continued. 'We will travel as direct as possible. When we get there we will land at the refuel pad and shut down there to do any loading while we refuel. I don't know where we're going after PATA or how long we're going to be away. Accommodation will be sorted out when we get there but it will probably be the usual five-star tent. There's no engineering support so we'll have to look after the machine ourselves. If there are no questions we will get going. See you at the aircraft.'

Only forty minutes after the phone had rung at home I was standing on the tarmac preparing to monitor the blades while the pilots did the control checks. The engines started and after I heard the familiar thump thump I climbed in the front door with the chocks over my shoulder.

The visibility – viz, as it's usually referred to – was down to about 2,500 meters when PATA appeared out of the murk forty-five minutes later. We knew the area well and kept a careful eye out for the various masts and aerials on the western edge. As we flew over the entrance gate I could see the vehicles and trucks driving up to meet us.

I called out, 'Visual with the refuel point, forward sixty descending, forty and right dead ahead thirty descending.'

The helicopter reacted instantly to my directions. 'Twenty descending, ten, eight, six, five, four, three, two, one and right, steady clear below down five, four, three, two, one aft wheels on and the front.' The Chinook settled its weight on to the grass as Danny lowered the collective lever and the engines breathed a sigh of relief. The APU wound into life once more as the engines were closed down.

Danny pulled on the rotor brake handle and the blades came to rest once again.

By the time I had the fuel hose plugged into the side of Echo X-ray, Wes already had the ramp down. It only took a few minutes to fill the tanks back up to 3,000 kg and by the time I had finished the refuel, Danny, Andy and Wes were talking to Mac, the warrant officer on the CT team.

Mac was only about five and a half feet tall but he had a neck the size of most blokes' waists. We had met a few times before on other exercises and he always made a point of coming across to brief the crew on what was happening and what was wanted.

'We have a hostage situation, and all I know is that it involves a train and up to seven terrorists. This is where we need to get to.' He pointed on his map to an area about sixty miles to the southwest of Newcastle. There appeared to be nothing more significant there other than a railway line.

'What are we loading on board, Mac?' I enquired. He nodded towards the oncoming fleet of vehicles, followed by a massive truck which could hold the entire contents of Buckingham Palace. 'The usual quart into a pint pot, then!'

Mac laughed and inclined his head slightly. Nodding was for wimps. 'It's only two Range Rovers, all the kit, and fifteen blokes, perhaps a few more – if we can fit them on.'

While Danny and Andy worked out the routing and tried to get some weather reports for the area, Wes and I folded all the red canvas seats up ready to accept vehicles. 'If we reverse the first one in,' I suggested, 'and drive the second one in forwards it'll give us some storage space on top of the bonnets.' Wes passed the message on to the drivers. Time was the important thing now. We needed to get on site and put some sort of plan into motion.

A ground party had been deployed ahead of us as soon as the call-out was initiated. The small Augusta 109 helicopter used by the SAS had been deployed ahead of us from its base in Hereford Stirling Lines with a recce party on board.

The Chinook was like the TARDIS of *Doctor Who* fame – bigger on the inside than the outside – with a never-ending supply of equipment going into the front door and up the ramp. Soon the walkway into the cockpit was covered up by the loading. I shouted to the pilots, 'If you don't get into the cockpit now there won't be room to get in!'

Danny climbed up the step and saw the amount of kit being loaded on. 'Fucking hell, you're not kidding,' he shouted as his arse disappeared into the tunnel that now led to the cockpit. A large plastic drum was handed to me and I was about to hurl it on top of the pile when a loud voice screamed, 'For fuck's sake, don't throw that or we'll all go up.' I didn't dare ask what was inside it so I just put it down gently, right next to where I was going to sit. Where I could hurl it out of the window if there was a problem.

By this stage I could not see the back of the cabin. The two Range Rovers dominated the space, with bags and equipment lining the sides of the cabin wall. Guns, ammunition and other large unlabelled boxes were stacked high beside me blocking the entrance into the cockpit. On the ramp the fast-rope frame took up most of the remaining space, but still more equipment was stacked up high, so much so that it was impossible to close the ramp completely. The only thing left now was to get the seventeen blokes on board. Arms and legs stuck out of just about every window of the Range Rovers as they scrambled to get into the only comfortable seats on the flight. Others were laid across the roofs of the vehicles while two more wedged on top of the boxes behind me.

Any Civil Aviation Authority inspector would have had instant heart failure. There are RAF regulations to ensure every passenger is secure, but for SF call-outs this was waived.

OPERATIONAL ACTION

After less than forty minutes on the ground the APU came back to life, the engines started and the rotors began to beat the air. It was difficult to accurately assess the weight of the helicopter since we did not know the weight of all the stuff put on, but it was obvious that we were right on, if not over, the limit.

'Our weight is about twenty-three thousand kilos,' I told Danny. Andy replied, 'I thought as much. I'll check the torques in the hover. They should be ninety per cent.' The heavier you were the more torque was required. The problem with being too heavy was that if an engine failed we would not be able to stay in the air and would have to land wherever we could. The Chinook could hover on one engine only up to a weight of between 16,000 to 17,000 kg.

Danny pulled in the power as the engines wound up. All the crew could hear and feel the strain on the gearbox. The grass, trees and shrubbery flattened out as 120 m.p.h. of downwash from the rotors hit them. I looked down the side of the fuselage outside and saw the familiar wrinkles and creases on the skin of the Chinook that appear only when it is really heavy. The amounts of torque produced by the forward and aft gearbox fought against each other, attempting to twist the fuselage as if they were wringing out a wet towel.

As we lifted into the hover Andy called out, 'We're at ninety-six per cent.' Bloody heavy.

To compensate, Danny lowered the nose and we started to accelerate very gently to try to avoid over-torquing, riding on the ground cushion. At about forty knots transitional lift cut in and we left the ground cushion behind. Still ten feet above the ground we continued to accelerate until at about eighty knots Danny pitched the nose up gently and we climbed away.

Ninety creaking minutes later we started our descent into the field site. I could already see that the ops tent had been set up and a number of vehicles and blokes were setting up other tents. We were over two miles away from the railway line but made sure that we approached downwind so as not to be heard. This was no time to be hanging around so we just identified a field on the approach that was just to the south of the ops tent – but not too close in case we blew it away.

Now we were back where we started before that first mad scramble and the aborted mission. Back in the Ops tent, sipping lukewarm brown liquid waiting for the situation on the train to resolve itself one way or another. Continuous updates of information came in from the snipers or other observation posts. With this new info the immediate action plan changed, but not for us: they still wanted us at the back of the train.

Darkness arrived. The teams had the cover they wanted but the crew of Echo X-ray were now condemned to operate inside a flat green world. Wes brought over the NVGs and we all checked and prepared them by looking up into the now clear skies, focusing on some distant star trying to get the sharpest image. The stars would produce ample amounts of light for the job. We walked back into ops just as the OC started his brief for the preferred or 'deliberate' option. This was similar in format to Bob's IA (immediate-action) brief, but by now there was more information. Someone had brought some Hornby railway carriages and laid them out in the same position as our train was in. There were large drawings on the ground, with masking tape marking out every compartment to scale. The team's footprints could be seen all around the sides as they rehearsed their drills once inside the train.

'Look like someone's practising for *Come Dancing*,' smirked Wes.

'Do you want to suggest that?' I hissed back.

The new information was that there were now at least eight X-rays, most of whom appeared to be lurking in the forward carriage. The exact position of the hostages was not known other than that some had been seen in both the forward and middle carriages. The plan was still to use a combined ground-and-helicopter assault, but we were now required to go to the front of the train, which would mean starting our run-in along the length of the train. This would necessitate flying below the level of the embankment, which left no margin for error.

Negotiations had collapsed so the Chief Constable had handed over control to Sinclair. We were going in twenty minutes. Bob once again joined us in our brief to decide which way we were going to drop them. The only real option was for us to stick the tail of the Chinook slightly over to the right of the front carriage, with the front-door rope going down just at the front of it. This meant kicking the tail right about thirty degrees as we came into the hover, and required careful coordination between all of the crew.

With our briefings done we made our way back out to Echo X-ray to adjust the lighting levels in the cockpit and cabin. There was only a very faint blue light illuminating the instrument panel. I went outside to make sure no light could be seen from the outside that might give any sharp-shooting terrorist a target. The SAS did not have NVGs so could see nothing in the blacked-out Chinook. The cabin lights were three cylumes, each taped up around the middle, leaving a circle of light the size of a penny coin. Two were positioned on the ramp hinge so that the teams knew where the start of the ramp was and one was just at the rear edge of the forward door. They were totally invisible from the outside.

This was the real thing but compared with the mad scramble of the immediate-action plan it was more relaxed. Once more the rotor r.p.m. settled at 100 per cent. Bob and his team were on board. We used the extra few minutes we had rechecking our goggles, the ropes' security and the engine and gearbox oil temperatures and pressures. We lifted into the hover, accelerated to 100 knots and turned right again for the holding area. This time Sharpy only made a gentle thirty-degree banked turn. At night without the natural horizon, and wearing NVGs, there was a greater risk of disorientation. The toy cars passed beneath us again, but this time they couldn't see us. With the noise of the Range Rovers' engines and the airflow as they accelerated towards their holding area they would not hear us either. No V signs this trip.

'Bravo Two.'

'Bravo Three.'

'Tango One.'

'Tango Two.'

'Charlie one in position,' Andy checked in as we came to a forty-foot hover in the holding area pointing directly towards the target. The railway line was closing from our left-hand side and we were ready to fly up the line to the train.

'Ramp's ready,' Wes called.

'Cabin ready,' from me.

The radios were dead silent. Strangely so. I could feel my heart pounding as we waited for the call. Something wasn't right.

'It sounds bloody quiet, Danny,' I said finally. No reply.

'Fuck, they're moving,' Danny yelled. He could see the glow from the exhausts of the vehicles as they accelerated away. We were all supposed to move together on the command 'Go'. Somewhere along the line the comms had fucked up. Bob looked as confused as we did as Danny lowered the nose and accelerated towards the train at 100 knots. The Range Rovers were going to get there before us. This was not good news for any of the hostages in the forward carriage. A lot of people can die in five seconds.

We levelled at about sixty feet. 'Clear on the left,' Andy called. I was pressed into the heater compartment with just my head peering out of the door. Bob was hanging on to the rope over my shoulder looking out into total darkness.

I could see the carriages now, with faint glows coming from the windows.

'OK, visual with the target, forward sixty. Height is good.'

'Roger.'

We were just over the rear carriage. Danny gently raised the nose to start the deceleration, lowering the lever to maintain our height. With no advance warning a blinding white flash flared. Directly in our line of sight. The effect of the distraction explosion was immediate. The goggles went haywire, totally backed off. Both pilots were now blind. I couldn't see anything straight ahead.

'I can't see a fucking thing,' Danny screamed, but he held the helicopter steady.

'Up twenty,' I called. Danny kept the collective lever in place, which allowed us to climb twenty feet. Now we had clearance above the embankment, which was still lost in the white light.

'I can get us into position,' I called. As soon as the flash went off I had looked away so my goggles were working fine – as long as I looked straight down.

'Carry on.'

'Height is good. Forward thirty.' I could see straight down, so I knew that I could position Echo X-ray where I needed it. Blinded to the outside world, Danny was flying totally on instruments. That is quite a skill at 20,000 feet, but at night, at eighty feet, surrounded by obstacles that can kill, it was a mammoth task. Danny had to trust my judgment as much as I trusted his flying ability. If either of us made an error the consequences would be fatal.

'Forward twenty. Tail right twenty degrees.' The tail slewed round the twenty degrees, and the blast of air from the side-slip pushed against my face. We were now flying sideways, blind and on instruments, with sixteen blokes hanging out the side of the helicopter. I was glad my life-insurance broker couldn't see this.

'Tail right a further ten degrees,' Wes called. He could see the area below the tail clearly and could fine-tune my directions.

'Forward fifteen, ten, eight, six, five, four, three.' The front of the train passed directly below me, and I could hear – if not see – the flash-bangs going off.

'Forward two, one. Steady.'

'Tail good,' Wes called. He threw both his ropes out the back and I followed suit.

'Height and position good.' Danny knew the ropes were in the correct position.

'Go!' Danny gave the exit command. Andy hit the buttons, the faint green light illuminated and the bell rang. Unable to see the ground Bob did not try to go early, as was the tendency. I shouted in his ear, 'Eighty feet high. Go! Go!'

He nodded and disappeared down the rope, followed seconds later by the rest of the team. Within five seconds all fifteen were down and their tiny dark figures vanished as they crashed into the train. Through the NVGs I could see the reflected torch beams bouncing off the carriage glass. Then the muzzle flashes which meant some of the X-rays had been slotted. For an instant I almost felt sorry for the poor bastards. It passed.

'Front rope clear,' I called, shortly followed by Wes.

'Aft ropes clear.'

'Clear above up. Gently!' The initial departure was straight up gently in case the ropes snagged on the train. With the ninety-foot ropes I could see the front and rear ones by lying on the floor with my head outside looking underneath the Chinook.

'All ropes clear, clear above.' This was the call we all loved because it meant that we could now piss off quickly. Until comms were restored there was no way we were going to try to take any liberated hostages on board. Danny heaved in the lever, and the gearboxes whined away as we climbed at a phenomenal rate. The train got smaller until it resembled the Hornby model in the ops tent. The speed was kept at sixty knots while Wes and I did our muscle-men acts pulling the ropes in.

'Excellent,' shouted Danny. 'Well done, guys. That was fucking hard work. Good call to continue, Dave. I couldn't see a bloody thing.' He called out the pre-landing checks: 'OK, holds are out, CAP's clear, Ts and Ps are in the green, LCTs are programming. Fuel's sufficient. Brakes are off. Swivels are locked. Check harnesses and ramp.'

'Ramps up secure for landing,' I said as Wes lowered the frame, raised the ramp and gave me the thumbs-up. 'Hang on, boss. I need to do this. Forward twenty. Height is good to clear the trees. Forward fifteen. Clear of the tree. Forward ten descending, five, four, three, two, one, steady, down three, two, one. Height is good. Forward one and right, steady, down three, two, one. Wheels on.'

We were landing in a field and normally we'd put the thing on the ground without buggering around in the hover. I knew I was going to get some abuse for holding Danny in the hover. I waited until the APU stopped and the rotors were stationary.

'What the fuck's all this height-good-left-one-right-one shit?'

'Well it's because I'm a lazy bastard,' I replied.

'What do you mean?'

'When we took off I forgot to bring the chocks in, so instead of having to walk across the field I just talked us over and got you to land back in the chocks again!' Danny thought about a bollocking but then just laughed. It was probably what we needed to break the tension of the pretty hectic day. Anyway, he was secretly pleased with himself, since it takes accurate and stable flying to position a wheel six feet behind him back in a set of chocks only twelve inches apart.

Leaning against a fuel tank Wes lit another one of his sculptures and took a long drag. It was still holding over 2,000 kg of fuel. He obviously didn't think flying around at two hundred m.p.h. fifty feet above the deck, roping people out of the helicopter, with gas and bullets zapping our way, was risky enough. Danny, Andy and I looked at each other but there was nothing anyone could say or do. We laughed. It echoed around the field breaking the sounds of silence

The whole excitement from lift-off to touching down again had taken less than eight minutes. It felt like eight hours. Twelve hours earlier I'd been sitting comfortably in my living room. Perhaps tomorrow I might get to finish my cup of tea.

But then tomorrow the call-out might be the real thing.

CHAPTER 7

SQUADRON DUTIES

I had been on the run for six days and six nights. It was bloody freezing. I hadn't thawed out since fording a river which turned out to be deeper than it looked. Our daytime hideout was far from weatherproof. The skies were alternating snow and hail. Both of us were starving. We'd failed to catch any rabbits. Our attempts to kill a sheep had ended in dismal failure. We weren't supposed to kill them and anyway they'd gallop off every time we got within twenty yards. After a few half-hearted attempts we gave up. Maybe sheep aren't so dumb after all.

Studying our small hand-scribbled sketch map we saw we had to cover ten miles that night. We knew there was a Para unit hunting stray crabs and that they thoroughly enjoyed catching their prey. The outlook was, quite frankly, bleak. But I didn't care. I should have been dead.

Thank God for the SF Flight. Being on it does not normally excuse the crew from normal squadron duties and four weeks earlier I'd been due go on a detachment to the Falkland Islands. Instead the Flight demanded I go on the Combat Survival Rescue Officers' Course on Dartmoor.

99

CHINOOK!

They asked this other chap if he'd mind stepping up in my place so we swapped slots. Andy Johns got to the Falklands on Tuesday lunchtime, took his kit up to the squadron and said 'hello', and they asked him if he'd mind doing an air test. They took off at 1300. Ten minutes later he, the crew and the engineers on board were all dead. The aircraft was flying along at 500 feet and it fell out of the sky, hit the ground at 190 knots, nose down at sixty degrees. To this day it has never been officially announced what the problem was.

Because they couldn't find the problem everyone thought Chinooks were going to be grounded. In the briefing room the wing commander stood up and gave the usual stuff about how sorry he was about loss of life, but then he said, 'Many of you may be wondering whether we will still be flying them. We are.' There were mumbles, groans and moans. 'I've been told to give you the reasons,' he continued without enthusiasm. It was as if he was reading parrot-fashion from some M.o.D memo. 'We cannot not continue flying the Chinook because of what happened in the Falklands, because if we ground the aircraft and can't find the fault we'll never be able to justify the aircraft flying again.'

Talk about a Catch 22.

So he led by example and took the first flight accompanied by the senior crewman. For weeks after that, every time there was a slight vibration in the aircraft, maydays were being put out and helicopters were landing in fields all over southern England.

I believe they do know what happened. I think it was a problem with the internal workings of one of the hydraulic jacks which move the blades. On the Chinook if you lose control of the hydraulics or have a problem with one of the jacks the aircraft will adopt the aerodynamic qualities of a rock. There were some very sensitive tests when I finally made it to the Falklands seven months later, ground runs where only the wing commander and the senior engineering officer were allowed near the aircraft.

The wreckage from the crash was put in a skip on Mount Pleasant. During my Falklands posting I was driving past when I saw our ground crew rummaging around in the skip.

'What's wrong?' I asked.

'The hydraulic control run on your aircraft's broken and we haven't got a spare,' Sam Forbes, one of the engineers, called back. 'I came to see if there's one in here. I've found it and now we've got to go back, clean it in paraffin and see if it'll fit.'

I wasn't very happy. The reason for the crash of that first helicopter was more than likely a hydraulic problem. Now the ground crew were having to use a part from a crashed aircraft in the flying-control system of an operational Chinook. In my Chinook.

After my good fortune the combat survival course was a doddle. We were shown how to use a parachute to make a tent, to protect ourselves from both cold and desert heat. In peacetime your job was to protect yourself from the heat and cold, try to make yourself known by location, then find water and food. In wartime you were looking at protection and concealment. After the theory sessions, they dumped us in the middle of the Dartmoor winter.

We did pretty well that last night. We covered seven miles over bog, rock and scrub. We'd just scurried across a road and hopped over a gate when six Paras jumped us. We were chucked into the back of a four-tonner and taken away for interrogation. It wouldn't have mattered if we'd made it or not, since everyone was hauled off to a twenty-four- or thirty-six-hour interrogation. At least we could get warm again. It wasn't going to be particularly pleasant but I did know that my balls weren't going to be put in a vice. An hour and a half later I was standing in a stress position up against a refrigerated wall. I could feel the cold creeping down and my body going numb. If they'd stuck needles in my arm I'd never have felt a thing.

After that the interrogation was a relief. There was Mr Nice, who kept asking if I wanted a cup of tea while slipping in the odd question, and Mr Nasty, who had chewed fifteen cloves of garlic before he came in and kept making helpful suggestions like, 'I'm going to find out where your wife is and then I'm going to shag her,' just to rile me.

Then they brought a woman in to do a strip search, made me bend over while she shoved her finger up my arse and made rude remarks about the size of my cock. That was supposed to make me feel bad, but, as I'd been living rough in the field for a week, if somebody wanted to stick a finger up my arse that was their lookout. I was kept blindfolded for hours and every so often somebody would come in and kick my feet away. The idea was to make the subject disorientated and unaware of time passing. The interrogators kept saying, 'Any time you've had enough stick your hand up and it's Endex.'

There were times when I felt I couldn't take much more. Even though I knew it was an exercise it felt real enough. But I had to pass the interrogation – it was a pre-requisite of staying on the SF Flight – so I kept my hand down. Two blokes did crack and put their hands up. They were both Army Air Corps and they'd been the macho people on the course, boasting, 'We're Army and you crabs are poofs.'

Aircrew wear flying suits most of the time. This means you generally get mistaken for an officer. Because of the SF Flight's small size the divide between officers and NCOs is much narrower than in other branches of the RAF. Like most sergeants I carried a collection of flight lieutenant and squadron leader rank tabs so that on our travels we could use the Officers' Mess if necessary. Our pilots used to encourage this, though most of them admitted the Sergeants' Mess was more fun. In the air nobody pulled rank: it was all first names. But once on the ground I would never embarrass an officer by calling him anything other than sir in public. In private we could go back to being good mates.

I suppose I was different from a lot of the other aircrew in that I loved flying myself and so naturally gravitated to talking about it with the pilots. In May 1987 I did a conversion course as a crewman on the Gazelle. This was a nifty little five-seater that we used for reconnaissance missions. In peacetime if you are flying low levels and using NVGs you are required to recce that route up to a week in advance. It's a lot cheaper to use a Gazelle than a Chinook.

I did a lot of recce flights with Rick Cook. Flying was in his genes. He was completely relaxed and never made a mistake that I saw. Even when he let me fly the Gazelle and we were chatting away he'd always be keeping a wary eye on both the controls and the ground. His dad was one of the chief training captains on Concorde and somehow our recce missions always ended up at Filton, just outside Bristol. We'd land there, jump into the Concorde flight simulator, have a thrash around in that for an hour and then fly back to Odiham.

Seven months after Andy Johns died in my place I went down to the Falklands for the first time. I was really excited at the idea of being there because, in my anorak phase, I had followed every engagement during the war. I lost that feeling within a day of being there. Mount Pleasant Airfield is a huge place. At the time there were Phantoms down there, search-and-rescue helicopters to pick them out of water and Chinooks to transport the troops to the radar sites on Mounts Kent, Byron and Alice, all combined in 78 Squadron.

CHINOOK!

Down there you worked very hard. Played hard, too.

We all lived in the respective messes, which were linked up with what seemed to be miles of corridors. The resident Army unit was billeted about half a mile's walk down these corridors, which seemed to have endless numbers of exits towards some barrack block. When we arrived we were warned not to walk the corridors at night by ourselves since there had been quite a number of muggings. A few months before I arrived a man died after falling head first through a reinforced glass window. Whether this was an act of violence or just an accident we never discovered. However, most people were sensible and did not roam the corridors at night solo.

Our basic task was supplying the mountain sites. Ten-hour flying days, picking containers of supplies off cargo ships moored off the coast, hauling them up to the radar sites, logging stuff in and out. The downwash from the Chinook was so strong it caused the whole ship to rotate around its anchor chain, so the hover had to be constantly adjusted. On one occasion when were winching a diver down to the ship, Matt Lomax, the crewman, put him out before the helicopter was stable. The wire started swinging and ended up wrapped round the front wheel of the helicopter, with the diver dangling thirty feet below and not in the best of tempers. Matt was about to winch him back in when I stopped him. This would have either snapped the cable or torn through the hydraulic pipes around the wheel. Instead we kept him dangling there while we gently descended to drop him on the deck of the ship.

We'd have to do a refuse trip twice a week. We'd carry empty rubbish containers up to the radar sites, just using the red strop attached to the middle, then bring the full container back down to Mount Pleasant, drop off the strop and come back and pick it up later after the vehicles had come along to clear the crap out. In the high winds down there we could fly at only forty knots. The container still swung round and round like some demented fairground attraction. The general consensus was that if you saw the container swing up to window level, you pressed the button and jettisoned the load.

One day we needed to pick the strop up so we landed. I was walking back to the container when suddenly the door was opened from inside and out jumped a dozen Royal Green Jacket squaddies, en route to a piss up in the pubs of Stanley. They told me they'd come down twice a week, then either hitch a lift back up or hop into an empty container for a return flight. I reminded them that the week before I'd had to jettison a load. They seemed more interested in going to the pub.

For relaxation we would try aerial sheep herding, thrash around at low level and try to herd them over the divide between East and West Falkland. The sheep could hear the aircraft but didn't know where it was coming from. Being very dim animals they would thunder over the rise and gallop over the edge. We'd usually get a dozen before we had to pull up.

A few weeks later we had a Notices To Airmen, which usually details important things to be aware of – live firing here or a radar that doesn't work here. They came up with a new thing called a Sheep Tam which was a notice to aircrew about not over-flying sheep. It said, 'It appears that sheep are disappearing in numbers and farmers request that all aircraft do not fly lower than 100 feet above sheep'. Nobody took any notice.

The worst part was having to spend Christmas there. Some general came down to say hello to the chaps, to visit all the mountain sites. On Christmas Day the general went off to the radar site leaving four pissed-off aircrew and his camera. When he got back on board another twenty frames had been shot. I'd love to have seen Mrs General's face when he had the pictures developed. Everyone had their arses or their knobs out, and there was one picture of somebody holding his bag open pretending to have a dump in it.

We were quite unlucky to get the general because top brass didn't usually fly in a Chinook. Whenever political nobs arrived signals would arrive ahead saying that they were not allowed to fly in the Chinook. It was obviously not safe enough for Maggie Thatcher to travel in. She got a Sea King.

In the Sergeants' Mess that we shared with the Royal Green Jackets (or RGJs), the bar was about fifty yards long. The most popular post-scran game was the Grunts v. Crabs Deck Landing Contest. First everyone got pissed, then all the tables were lined up in a row and beer was thrown over the surface. The idea was to run like hell, hurl your body down the tables and see how far down you got.

On New Year's Eve Andy Fairfield and Chris Scullen, aka the Dangerous Brothers, were bored rigid in the Officers' Mess. They staggered down to see us in the middle of a vital match. 'Hey, Dave,' yelled Andy, 'what's the score?'

'The grunts are well in the lead,' I said, just as this RGJ launched himself at fifty knots down the deck.

'Can't have that,' Andy said. 'I'd better even the score a bit.' He pulled a table out from the middle of the deck and this bloke went straight into the gap, flew into the side of the table, broke his collarbone and was carted off in an ambulance.

I always thought that the blokes I knew dragged the depths for being disgusting. Until I met the submariners. They are the worst, no question. When men who have been underwater for months come ashore all they want to do is shag lots of women and drink lots of alcohol. Once they had got through the first set of penguins down in the Falklands – all that was available down there – they concentrated on drinking. At breakfast they were all completely pissed. They were drinking crates of champagne and orange juice – by the pint. We came back in the evening and they were still there.

'Hey, Charlie,' I said to one petty officer who could hardly sit up, 'there's only an hour's drinking time left and I don't think you're going to make it.' It was like calling his mother a whore. 'Fucking crab bastard,' he grunted and staggered off. Five minutes later the door burst open, smashing the windows – which happened a lot for some reason – and Charlie comes back in with a cardboard box under his arm.

He demanded the barman fill an ice bucket with beer. 'In the event,' he slurred, 'that I pass out and am unable to drink never let it be said that I can't continue until closing time. Right, you crab bastards.'

With that he took his trousers down, opened up the box, pulled out a stirrup pump, put the inlet end in the bucket and shoved the other one right up his arse. He was swaying like a tree so a mate came up and helped steady him. 'This is the way the Navy deal with it,' he said and pushed the handle down. He got about halfway and suddenly said, 'Oh shit.' He froze, let go and wandered off with his trousers flapping round his ankles. The tube tugged and tugged and eventually fell out. He walked away round the bar shaking his head saying, 'No, no.' He pulled his trousers up and slowly this dark patch appeared around his arse, a wet fart of beer all the way down his trouser legs.

I was in fits. I turned round to his mate, who was just shaking his head. 'That Charlie never could take his beer,' he sighed. Then he picked up the pipe – the end that had been up his mate's arse – and started drinking from it.

I had never been in such close contact with all the other services before and everybody was always trying to get one up on the others. The biggest rivalry of all was between the Phantoms and the helicopters. The jets would scream across the pan at thirty feet and 500 knots showing off, so in retaliation we'd take off, hover over their crewroom and shatter all the windows. They'd go lower, we'd hover closer. Eventually we won by dropping 800 gallons of water from a large bucket, used to help fight peat fires, on the crewroom.

Our boss decided this was most unsafe so he invited OC Phantoms and OC Ops over to bollock them. He was banging on the desk saying, 'My young chaps are trying to do their jobs and these Phantoms are screaming over their heads,' ignoring the OC Phantoms, who was protesting, 'But they keep shattering all our windows.'

While this was going on I was out flying with Andy Fairfield. We were bored, so he decided to go back and buzz the squadron – which meant they would have to retile the roof of the squadron hut afterwards. We came screaming across the squadron at 170 knots. Andy stuck the Chinook on its wingtip to go round the corner. This changed the angle on the airflow and caused 'blade slap'. The shock wave made all the paintings in the crewroom fall off the wall.

Thirty seconds later the voice of the ops corporal came over the radio: 'Could the captain of the aircraft please report to the flight commander's office immediately on landing.' There was a pause, then a different voice, as the OC grabbed the microphone and yelled, 'And tell him to put his fucking hat on.'

After the Falklands it was a relief to get back to sanity, female company and SF duties in Britain. In April 1988 I was taking part in an exercise up at Hereford doing fast-roping practice on to a wrecked aeroplane fuselage when we heard that a jet had been hijacked at Larnaca in Cyprus.

Realistically in a hostage situation it is not a smart thing to rope people down on to an aircraft because the element of surprise goes when the terrorists hear the helicopter overhead. However, the authorities decided to have the SF out there and the favoured option was to fast-rope down, kick the windows in, kill the terrorists, bring the hostages out and wave to the cameras. The problem was getting some Chinooks over to Cyprus in time.

There was a Wessex helicopter squadron stationed on Cyprus so some bright spark thought of giving us a refresher course and flying us out there. It was a ludicrous idea to give us a few hours' practice on an unfamiliar aircraft and then expect us to operate beyond the edge of its flying envelope at night. The Wessex crews were very bewildered about having to hand over the aircraft to people who had forgotten where the master switch was and how to start it. As an option it should have been a nonstarter. In the end we got as far as the disembarkation rooms at Brize Norton. We were held there for eight hours until the operation was called off. The situation had fortunately ended diplomatically and our services were not needed, and we could be stood down.

CHAPTER 8

LOCKERBIE

You can see terror on somebody's face. When they are dead it is etched there for ever.

The Pan Am stewardess was curled up in a ball with her arms, her legs and her fingers crossed tight. Lying in the field, she could have been asleep. But from the position she'd adopted she had obviously been aware that something terrible was happening. There was an expression on her face that I was to see a great many more times.

You can always remember the look on the first dead face you see. And the second.

The woman next to the stewardess had very small hands. She was in her early thirties with a very pretty face framed by dark-brown hair cut in a bob. What I can never excise from my memory is how her hands were pressed hard together, her fingers locked, knotted together in a futile prayer. Very small hands, beautifully manicured. We couldn't get her right arm into the body bag because it was locked from rigor mortis and sticking straight out.

'That one has to go on top,' I said.

'No it doesn't,' said the policeman. He grabbed her arm hard. As he shoved it inside the bag I heard this great crack of bones.

My first sight of the dead in the fields above Lockerbie

wasn't what I had expected. They had all fallen 30,000 feet reaching a top speed of 120 m.p.h. After hitting the ground at that speed the bodies should have looked like sausage meat. Or so I thought. There were a few piles of flesh and bone that weren't recognisable as human, but the majority were intact. Some were sitting there still strapped into their seats, upright in rows of three. Some had Walkman headsets on, books in their hands, waiting to be served their drinks. There didn't appear to be anything drastically wrong — except, of course, they were all dead.

It was just after daybreak on the morning of 22 December 1988.

Less than twelve hours earlier I had been at 7 Squadron's Christmas party in Odiham. I'd been up since 0600 ferrying the Army around and I was slow getting into party mood. The NAAFI Club was buzzing, all the wives were dressed in their posh frocks, the disco was pumping out sixties classics, the bar was open and beer was ten pence a pint. After two years of marriage I was really looking forward to my first RAF Christmas alone with Jill.

I'd had maybe a couple of pints and was chatting away to Jill and friends when I noticed the OC Operations come into the bar. Somebody walking into a party in uniform always catches your eye. He started talking to the wing commander, who made a beeline for the stage, killed the music and grabbed the microphone. I knew something was up.

'Any aircrew who haven't been drinking come and see me now.'

The wing commander's initial announcement fell on dozens of deaf ears. Everybody had had a couple of drinks so nobody turned up. Two minutes later the wing commander interrupted the party again. 'Any aircrew who haven't been drinking too much come and see me now.' I got the hint, stopped laughing, went up to him, asked, 'What's up boss?'

'There's been an incident in Scotland,' he said. 'All we know is that it's bad and they need our support now. We're sending two aircraft up there now. Engineers have already been deployed to get them ready.'

Immediately the adrenaline started to rush. I guess I said goodbye to Jill but I don't remember what I said. Probably a casual 'Gotta go – see you later'. While I pulled my flying kit over my civvies the crew discussed our requirements and the routing. All we knew was that there had been an aircraft crash just north of Carlisle.

Bob Stevens was the skipper, a by-the-book, good, solid pilot, an older man in his early forties who'd flown Vulcans before transferring to helicopters. The copilot was John Sanderson from the SF Flight, a crazy Cornishman on the ground but cool and dependable in the air. The other crewman was Bill Thomas, a scrawny Cockney who was never quite as crafty or as cool as he believed. As two of us were NVG-qualified and the weather forecast up north was unbelievably shitty, I signed out two pairs of goggles.

Waiting for us on the Chinook were two bemused corporal medics with boxloads of medical kit. I chucked them each a set of headphones but they never said a word on the flight up to RAF Leeming. They probably thought they'd be bollocked for chatting or were just intimidated by being on board.

To start with there was all this fairly jovial chat about how we were deemed fit to fly but not to drive. 'I've had three pints,' from me, immediately topped by Bill's 'Well I've had five.' Petty stuff. We knew a plane had gone down so everyone speculated on the damage. Up in the cockpit John and Bob thought it might be a thirty-seater that had crash-landed in a field. But once we logged on to the London radio frequencies that control the airways across the country we knew that something more serious had happened.

'Speedbird 3724 passing two five zero requesting direct to Glasgow.'

'Continue flying three one zero. Negative Glasgow, incident in progress around Deans Cross.'

'Roger. Rerouting now.'

That never happens. Usually aircraft fly straight up the side of the UK – now they were rerouting everything in the air to avoid Glasgow. It was chaos. I was used to things on the SF Flight being covert, getting everybody on board, nobody knowing anything about it, doing the job at hand and coming back. Now suddenly there was this job the whole world was talking about. Yet nobody knew what was going on.

It was a simple eighty-minute flight to Leeming, near Catterick in Yorkshire, but the rest of it was conducted in silence. We didn't want to miss any info coming through on the radio. When Leeming told us, 'The ops officer will meet you on landing,' that was another clue. It was teeming with rain and Ops officers never get wet if they can help it.

He came in, sat in the jump seat and used the headset. I was on the intercom outside supervising the rotors-running refuel. Now we knew enough to know there weren't going to be any survivors. We weren't going to need any medics. A four-tonner came up to the back of the Chinook. It was packed to the top, stacked high, boxes of black plastic bags with heavy-duty zips running up the middle. Thirty boxes, each containing ten bags. Three hundred body bags.

As the ground crew started to load them on board the aircraft I felt a really strange sensation, a haze of reality peeking through the pouring rain. I was used to carrying the living, not the dead. The adrenaline was rushing round my body, my heart pounding away, the hairs on the back of my neck tingling.

LOCKERBIE

The medics were offloaded and we took off again within ten minutes of touching down, just us four crew, alone in an aircraft full of body bags. John tried to crack some sick joke but it fell unacknowledged into the ether. Such company didn't make for much conversation so we flew on towards Lockerbie in silence, not knowing what we'd find but expecting the very worst.

It was worse than that.

We arrived in Lockerbie just after midnight. It was a scene of absolute pandemonium. There was no coordination, no central control. It took until the early hours for the police and civilian authorities to establish a plan – not that anybody could have done anything before then. Not in midwinter in such atrocious weather.

I didn't blame anybody then and I certainly won't now. You are getting ready for Christmas and a 747 crashes on your town killing God knows how many people. Suddenly you don't live in a sleepy little place in Scotland. You're in hell. And you don't know why.

In a civilian case, controlled by the police, all the M.o.D can do is offer their equipment. That first night very little happened except endless discussions. Looking out of the window of the school hall I could see the engine embedded in the main road, the flames, the incessant rain, the burning silhouette of the fuselage endlessly, repeatedly, reflected off the water drops. By the early hours of the morning the military had more input and had suggested we implement sweeping searches, grid square by grid square, to cordon off various areas and tick the boxes as we went.

At four in the morning with the weather unrelenting the authorities sent us back to Leeming to get something to eat and the aircraft sorted. Having been up since six the previous morning, I was knackered and soaked through.

Suddenly the adrenaline that had kept me going leeched away. All that was left was tiredness. I sat down on my seat by the door. Closed my eyes for a second. I woke up after I hit the floor. I was going to pretend it was an accident until I saw that Bill had fallen asleep too.

Thank Christ for that, I thought, then I glanced out of the window and saw that the aircraft was descending fast. 'Are we turning back?' I asked. There was no answer. Shit. I rushed inside the cockpit. Both pilots were asleep. I shook them both roughly, screaming at them, and opened every window, though it was peeing with rain and freezing cold. We did the rest of that short flight determined to keep awake.

At Leeming everyone was desperate to know what we'd seen. We were there for about four hours, grabbed a couple of hours' sleep and landed back at Lockerbie just prior to daylight. As I walked back to the control centre I looked up towards the golf course. The green had maybe twenty body-shaped things scattered around it – as if some evil god had taken human-shaped confetti and shaken it all over the grass.

When daylight broke we were the first helicopter air-borne, carrying a team of four policemen. Their job was to log where the bodies were, tag them, bag them and put a pole in to mark the spot. We went over the rise flying at 500 feet for half a mile. It looked normal enough. Scottish border countryside, just a succession of fields, fences and woods. But suddenly one field took on a different complexion. From my door it looked as if a wastepaper basket had been scattered over this green carpet. Except this wasn't waste-paper but bodies, suitcases and rucksacks all strewn in different directions. Within a two-acre field I saw at least forty bodies interspersed with bags split open, clothes and mail scattered everywhere. A truckload of waxwork dummies, lying there forgotten.

We landed and I saw the stewardess. Saw the woman with the perfect hands. Heard the first crack of bone. Over the next four days I was to see and hear a whole lot more.

The wreckage was scattered for miles. All we could do was get on with the job, help by logging where the bodies had fallen. It didn't help to think about what we were doing. Bill Thomas and I took it in turns to help the police. To begin with we were very careful about putting the bodies in the cabin. We were very gentle about where we placed them, neatly in three ranks of three until they completely covered the floor. Then we'd fly back to the school playing fields where the bags would be offloaded into the meat wagons that would reverse up to the aircraft. But there were so many bodies that we couldn't continue to do that. By the middle of that first afternoon we were just throwing them in and stacking them as high as we could. If you had to get through you just walked over and across them. It sounds callous showing no respect for the dead, but we had to get the job done.

Part of my brain must have decided that if they looked like waxwork dummies they must be waxwork dummies. Think of it that way and you just got the job done. Most of the time I would pick up a body and put it in a bag, and that didn't have any effect on me. Most of the bodies weren't disfigured facially, which funnily enough made it easier. Others were naked with tatters of underwear hanging round their ankles, their clothes stripped off by the wind while they fell. That was undignified.

Occasionally some little thing would happen that would force me to relate to them as a person.

I picked up this young lad, in his late teens, reasonably fit and good looking. I zipped up the bag and didn't think anything more of it. But twenty paces further on was some hand luggage that had burst open. Lying on top of the bag was a photograph of this same guy with a glazed half-pissed look in his eyes, standing at a Spanish bar with another bloke, his arms round his girl. Suddenly this dummy was someone who had been alive twelve hours before. A boy who had been going home for Christmas.

There was one field completely covered in mail and one bloke had been dispatched to pick it up and put it back into mailbags. We went over him a dozen or more times. Each time we saw him picking it up piece by piece with his stick until eventually he had cleared it all and there were piles of fully filled mail bags waiting for collection. The last time we flew over he was waving at us like mad.

'He's found something down there,' I said. 'Shall we go and have a look?' We circled and as we landed the down-wash hit, exploded the mailbags, scattering the letters everywhere. I ran over to him through a snowstorm of letters shouting, 'What's wrong?'

'I was just waving,' he said, looking rather hurt. I'm still surprised he didn't hit me. But in the aftermath of Lockerbie people didn't. They kept their emotions tightly buttoned down. One person's anger is so petty in the face of much greater tragedy.

On the first day, as we did the runs back and forth to the school, we began to work out exactly where all the fuselage sections had landed. There were distinct areas where bodies had fallen out. You would see nothing for miles, then bodies, then nothing, then piles of luggage. After about five hours we worked out where the galley area – which was where the booze was kept – should be.

Bugger me, and there it was, completely shattered – bits of metal, galley drawers and fractured trolleys scattered everywhere. There were also hundreds of miniature plastic bottles sticking in the ground. It was like a field of bizarre crops. Most of them were embedded in the soft wet grass and appeared intact. We had a full load on board so we couldn't do anything then and there. John pressed the navigation equipment to fix the position, so we could get back to it. We thundered across to the school playing fields, slammed on the deck, chucked our cargo out and were back on the site within twenty-five minutes. We came screaming across the hill and came into the hover above the area.

There was nothing there. Not a bottle.

We knew it was the right area: there was the house we'd fixed on for a cross-reference, the GPS was spot on – but all the booze had gone. We shot straight up into a 200-foot hover. Going over a rise in the hill, travelling like a bat out of hell, I saw a police transit van. The back doors were still swinging open with half the galley drawers and all the booze clearly visible inside. Somehow they'd got to it first and pissed off. Mind you, I'm sure they were going off to declare it to the customs.

As we had to keep popping to RAF Carlisle to refuel that night we stayed in a bed-and-breakfast joint nearby. The attention was harrowing: you couldn't go for a bloody crap without somebody sitting down in the bog next door asking you what was going on. The truth was we didn't know, we just had a job to do.

The second day was more of the same but now there was more help available. On the first run we were asked to take a couple of young Army lads out to help. Being – or looking – about sixteen they strutted on to the aircraft acting macho. Until we made our first pick-up.

It was a bad one. Almost surreal, like we'd just been dropped into the middle of a ghastly Tom and Jerry cartoon. There was one man who had hit the ground feet first and his body had just compressed. He must have been six foot tall; now he was maybe four foot six standing upright, stuck in the field. The ground was very soft and there were perfect imprints, impressions of bodies, but the corpses had bounced, landing about five yards away. Another man's head had hit a stone and shattered, leaving a perfectly formed brain quivering on the ground fifteen feet further on.

The two lads spent every minute we were on the ground throwing up over a dry-stone wall. I didn't blame them, just thought perhaps I should be doing that too. They didn't come out with us again.

One of the problems we had was with the media vultures. They were hanging out of trees with telephoto lenses trying to photograph the bodies coming off the Chinook. By now most had rigor mortis and a bone sticking through could split the body bag wide open. That delayed the operation of clearing up dramatically because we had to wait for blankets to be brought out to cover them up.

Another problem we had with the aircraft was that body fluids are one of the most corrosive things you can have. They can rot through the structure very quickly. With the bags splitting open, it got very smelly and then some twat up front got cold and put a heater on, which didn't help very much. When we went to RAF Carlisle to refuel we had to get the firemen to hose the aircraft out.

Christ knows why, but somebody agreed that one of the radio reporters could come on board the aircraft with us. I was looking out when we were landing and this stupid bastard was hanging out of the door with me asking, 'What are you looking for now? Have you seen some new bodies?' I shoved him back in his seat, told him to strap in and not move again until I told him to. As soon as we got back to town I kicked him off. He claimed I was overreacting.

Maybe I was. Lockerbie affected different people in different ways. It was the little things that could flip you over the edge. While we were tagging the bodies the local farmers were driving around on quad bikes telling us there was another one over there. We saw this light flashing about 400 metres away so we hover-taxied over and landed right next to the bodies. It was Bill's turn to go out.

He went out attached to a long intercom lead. There was silence for five minutes. This wasn't like Bill so I hurried out to see what the problem was. He was just standing there, staring blankly into the distance, drifting off away into another world. At his feet were these three beautiful little kids, maybe six, three and just ten months old. Even after they had hit the ground together, the oldest two were still holding on to the baby's hands.

I grabbed Bill by the shoulders, shook him hard. 'Come on Bill. Snap out of it, man.' For a moment nothing happened, then there was a light of recognition in his eyes. 'Hi, Dave,' he said. Then the lights went out again. He went into shock, wandered to the front of the aircraft and sat up there for all the rest of the flying we did that day. After that he was never the same. I hadn't had any children back then. Now I try not to think about those three little corpses.

Throughout it all, the people of Lockerbie were amazing. They had just had a 747 drop out of the sky on to their town and yet they would do anything for us. The one thing I do have incredibly good memories of is how it created a very pleasant atmosphere in terms of togetherness. A tragedy like that either breaks people or it bonds them. The people of Lockerbie put themselves out beyond belief. I wouldn't expect members of my own family to help strangers the way they did.

After we'd been there two days all I had to wear was my flying kit over my civvy party clothes. Doing what I was doing, I couldn't help getting bits of body over my clothes, so I was really smelly. Finally I thought, This is ridiculous, and asked the police if anybody had some spare kit. Fifteen minutes later they came back with piles of clothes that had been donated to us.

Jill and the wives down in Odiham had no real idea what we were doing or whether we'd make it back for Christmas Day. We never knew where we would sleep and there was no way of getting messages to us, but if we wanted to phone home we could just knock on a door and ask anybody. We'd always be given a cup of tea and sympathy. It helped.

By Christmas Eve the clearing-up operation seemed to swing perpetually between tragedy and farce. Sometimes we just had to laugh. On top of a ridge line we found a body that had hit a sheep smack on. The sheep had exploded from the force of the impact and its head had been driven backwards straight into a dry-stone wall. It was stuck there, as if it had been professionally mounted on the wall. A big game-hunter's trophy in some baronial hall. Except it had a surprised look in its eyes and a tuft of chewed grass still in its mouth.

'I wonder what she was thinking,' asked one of the policemen.

'Baa,' I said. We all just erupted into fits of laughter. The farmer who was on the quad bike thought we were nuts.

We always tagged the bodies the best we could but this same farmer found a leg cut off above the knee, a perfect slice so the only place to put the tag was on the toe. We'd landed on top of this grassy mound. It was wet, muddy, steep and slippery and surrounded by a large ditch. I grabbed hold of the first policeman and pulled him into the aircraft, but I couldn't see the other bloke. He'd fallen down into the ditch. Suddenly, in a scene like Excalibur coming out of the water, all I could see was this arm holding a leg with its toe tag flapping in the wind. I was in absolute hysterics, I had tears rolling down my face. So did his mate. Then I told him to take it into the cockpit.

John nearly put the Chinook into a tree. 'You're a sick minded bastard, McMullon,' he screamed over the intercom. He was probably right – but then he wasn't the one out there putting on the tags.

Two hours later one of the policemen grabbed me by the arm. 'Come over here, Dave. There's something you ought to see.' Half expecting another sick joke, I went with him. 'What do you think of this?' He gestured at a row of aircraft seats.

There was nothing strange about that. A good half of the bodies we recovered were still strapped into their seats. He pointed to a girl in her early twenties, sitting in the aisle seat next to her boyfriend. She had chestnut-brown hair, black jeans and a mohair jumper with a big thick collar. (It's funny, but I can picture the jumper and its texture as clear as day but its colour no longer has a place in my memory.) Round where her seat had hit the ground the grass was all torn up. Not by the impact but by her fingers. I could see where she had clawed it, scrabbling, digging in the dirt. I could see the indentations of her fingers in the grass all around her. When we got to her she still had tufts of grass in her right hand. But her right hand was not on the ground. It was clenched round her seat-belt buckle. On her cheek was a smear of dirt.

'Jesus Christ,' I said. 'She was alive after she hit the ground. She grabbed on to the grass.'

Nobody survives that sort of impact but I still sometimes wonder how long she lived after hitting the ground. And she wasn't the only one. When we found the cockpit section all the metals had crushed up compressing the pilots together like Siamese twins. Protected by the glass, they had certainly been aware of what was happening to them. So were a lot of other people we found.

The bomb caused the plane to decompress at 30,000 feet. Air is not breathable at that height so any passengers blown into the sky would have passed out. Bodies fall at 120 m.p.h. and from that height it is going to take two and a half minutes to get to the ground. They would have fallen to within breathable air within a minute, maximum ninety seconds. A minute of oxygen starvation is not sufficient to kill you. Many of them regained consciousness before they hit the ground. What does go through a man or a woman's mind while they are falling to certain death? Not a nice thought.

After dusk fell we were tasked to take some police to Glasgow Airport to catch a flight home. The weather had turned horrendous so after we landed we couldn't take off again. We were booked into the airport hotel. It was full of Americans, relatives of the Pan Am passengers, who had come across to find out what was happening. As soon as we turned up in reception wearing flying kit they quickly put two and two together.

Suddenly we were surrounded by dozens of men and women, holding up photographs, screaming and shouting. 'Have you seen my daughter? Here's her picture.' 'My husband always travelled at the back.' 'My son …' 'My mother was coming home for Christmas.' 'My family …' We had picked up eighty bodies that day and we didn't exactly take snapshots of each one. Nor, if the truth be told, did we want to.

'Look,' snapped John, who was exhausted and right on the edge. He spoke for all of us. 'We've been here three days. We've picked up dozens of bodies. We're not very happy about it ourselves. For Christ's sake give us a break.' For a moment there was this empty, hollow silence. Then one of the Americans, realising the effect they were having, piped up.

'Hey, listen, can I buy you guys a drink?' Suddenly they all started offering to buy us meals, drinks. Anything we wanted.

I was too knackered to stay downstairs for long but I had a couple of drinks, told the relatives what we'd been doing, reassured them (though that's not exactly the right word) that the passengers had never known what happened. That there was no chance that anybody had survived. Until then, because nobody knew what had happened, they hadn't been told much and there's nothing worse than the pain of not knowing. In return they told us stories about their loved ones, reminding me, once again, that I hadn't been handling dead meat for the past three days, that it, too, had once laughed and loved and played.

I'm not a maudlin or emotional man – just ask Jill – but I think that encounter helped me come to terms with everything that happened at Lockerbie. Jill had a phone call from the RAF shrink before I came back warning her, 'He may wake up in feverish sweats in the middle of the night.' I can honestly say that since then I've felt no horror, no sickness, nothing. I can put my hand on my heart and say it hasn't traumatised me. I've had no sleepless nights and Jill can confirm that. Instead I got pangs of guilt about why I didn't get affected in that way. Maybe I just don't have enough imagination.

On Christmas Day we transited back down to Lockerbie to complete the clear-up of the bodies. Despite the holiday the school dinner staff came in. For three days they had been continuously on hand to cook meals for people, desperate to play some part to support the operation. They were truly excellent, and remained strong throughout. The people of Lockerbie set us an example and I'm proud to have known them.

The police, too, couldn't do enough to help. The weather was getting worse and worse, heavy rain and low cloud closing in. Bob decided we'd better get back to RAF Carlisle to the refuelling base, otherwise we'd be stuck on the playing fields. Unfortunately, one of our ops lads, Corporal James, was still in the control centre in Lockerbie. We couldn't wait for him any longer so we buggered off. He was coming round the corner when he saw us lifting off.

'Shit,' he announced, rain dripping off his uniform, kit-bag lying in a puddle. 'I'm in the crap now.'

'Have you got a problem?' asked this local policeman sitting inside in his patrol car. 'Where is it heading?'

'Carlisle.'

'Jump in.' Jamesie and the policeman took off, sirens blaring. He radioed ahead and another patrol car met them halfway and took him to RAF Carlisle. He was sitting down in the base drinking a cup of tea fifteen minutes before we got there.

That night we all sat down to Christmas dinner in the Officers' Mess at Carlisle. It was the only time in my service career I was ever served turkey by a wing commander. On Boxing Day both Chinooks flew back down to Odiham. The control tower told us to do a formation fly-past over the married quarters. By the time we turned back ready to land we could see dozens of cars streaming from the married quarters to greet the incoming aircraft. They greeted us like returning heroes.

We weren't heroes. Far from it. I know it sounds like a cliché but we'd just been doing our job, like all the police and everyone else in Lockerbie. The difference was I could get back to a normal life. They had to live with the memory of Pan Am flight 103 every time they walked down the street.

CHAPTER 9

SNOW AND SAND

When I had first joined the RAF my intention had always been to become a pilot. I'd gone in determined to transfer to pilot training after a year, as the careers officer had suggested. It took rather longer than that. Without blowing my own trumpet I knew I was very good at my job because I had a great deal of knowledge about and interest in what the pilots were doing at the front. However, fewer than five per cent of aircrew go on to be pilots. In November 1988 – after four years in the job – I plucked up the courage to go and see the wing commander.

His reaction was really positive. After I mumbled something about advancing my career prospects he said, 'Why don't you apply for pilot training? You'll have no problems because you'll have my full backing. Here's the bit of paper. Now wait while it goes through the system and I'll see you in the Officers' Mess in a couple of years with wings on your chest.'

I knew I'd end up on helicopters. At twenty-six I was old to be starting as a pilot: your reaction time goes down at that age. Anyway, I didn't want to fly a fast jet any longer.

Coming in low level at 500 knots, you have to be in constant practice to do it well. But due to cost the number of hours a jet pilot flies in a month can be as low as five, which is nowhere near enough to keep his skills up to scratch.

The paperwork was put in. I had all the right ticks in the right boxes. In January I qualified as a training crewman on the SF Flight. Now I was the one teaching techniques to new aircrew. The problem was Lockerbie. Horrible though it was at the time, it was a high peak in my life, incredibly hyper and draining. After I came back it was just business as usual, a slump back into normal squadron life, routine, the usual standard inspections.

At least when we deployed out on Exercise Hardfall in January that was a few days out of the trough. It was the annual SF snow exercise, a standard deployment over the North Sea with a prebooked refuel on an oil rig, and an excuse for a piss-up on expensive Norwegian beer.

Landing on an oil rig was a straight admin move, no low-level approaches for a change. We arrived, jumped off, plugged in, did the refuel with rotors turning, did the checks and buggered off, heading for the next turning point. We were fuel critical by the time we reached the rig (maybe a hundred kilos, ten minutes of fuel in hand), which meant we hadn't a lot of time to hang around over the North Sea, so if it's not going right you have to put up hand and say, 'I'm not happy.' You might get a bit embarrassed, get a kick in the bollocks if you were wrong, but it's better than ditching in the oggin. To an oil rig a helicopter is just a menace. If anything goes wrong they will think nothing of taking a crane and throwing it off the side. A huge amount of money can be lost through not being able to transport things off the platform.

The refuel went fine and we were plugging away. Something in my water didn't feel quite right I couldn't say

what or why. The pilot checked the heading: 020 was correct but the rig was going away in a strange direction. So he
rechecked using a normal magnetic compass and discovered
we were ninety degrees out and heading straight for the
North Pole.

The Chinook electronic compass systems detect the magnetic field in the earth. Landing on a rig you are surrounded
by lots of metal, which influences that magnetic field. The
normal practice for helicopters and oil-rig operators is to
realign their compasses, once they get away from the influ-
ence of all magnetic deviations, using a little switch that
reads 'fast slew'. We didn't know that because the only time
we saw rigs normally was from fifty feet up, chucking blokes
down a rope. We warned the aircraft behind us so they
didn't follow us off to visit Santa.

Flying helicopters in Norway is generally dangerous.
Snow landings can cause as many problems as sand, but the
biggest dangers are the logging wires. They are wrist-thick
with no pylons and no markings, and stretch from high
ground all the way down the valleys. The shocking thing is
flying underneath them, then looking back and realising that
another fifty feet higher and you'd have been salami or spinning around the wire like a top.

White-out conditions are potentially lethal, too, not just
through the downwash throwing up the snow but misjudg-
ing where the crest of the hill is. Flying towards one piece
of ground covered in snow you think you will just miss that
but what you are actually seeing is the line below the crest.
It happened to Neville Greenacre in the Falklands.
Someone had committed the cardinal sin of switching the
radalt bug off so there was no warning of rising ground. In
that crash the copilot, one crewman and number of Gurkha
passengers were killed, and Greenacre lost his leg. He was
off duty for a long time, then he came back doing ops work

and eventually talked his way back into flying. Every squadron has its own Douglas Bader.

What finished me off out in Norway was Squadron Leader Nathanson. He wasn't SF Flight but somehow he was out there. One day he gave us the standard brief and finished off with, 'Anyone got any questions?'

My main intention on any exercise had always been to stay alive. Particularly if I didn't trust the bastard in the front seat. 'What radalt bugs will you set?' I asked. The radalt bounces signals off ground and gets the exact height above ground. It's usually bugged to fifty to a hundred feet and when it gets to that point it sets off first a warning light in the cockpit and then a warning bell. It is normal SF Flight procedure to bring this up at the brief.

'It doesn't matter, Sergeant.'

'What about white-out conditions,' I said. 'Radalts have saved my life.'

He begrudgingly set a policy and on the way out to the aircraft I heard him whingeing to the copilot, saying, 'I'm sure McMullon doesn't trust me.'

'Yeah, he probably doesn't,' came the reply from my loyal friend.

'Right, we'll start up now,' Nathanson announced when we reached the Chinook. There was four inches of snow on top of the rotor blades. Blades have to be evenly weighted. If one is heavier than another it will start the aircraft rocking and can turn it over

'Excuse me, boss,' I said. 'We can't start off with snow on the blades. Let's get the engineers to sweep it off.'

'No, McMullon, we'll start up and it'll throw off.'

I could see rank pulling through, so I quickly got inside – if a helicopter is going to turn over on the ground the last place you want to be is outside – and strapped myself in just underneath the gearbox where the blades can't get you. I sat there and counted: 'One thousand and one, one thousand and two.' The aircraft started bouncing around on its four wheels, lifting off the ground. There were shrieks from the front – 'Shut it down' – and much heaving on the rotor brake.

'It must be the snow on the blades,' Nathanson says. 'I'd better get the ground crew out to sweep it off.'

'I hate to say I told you so, sir.' I couldn't resist having the final word. Nathanson didn't take kindly to me after that. It started to worry me that if I became a pilot I'd have to drink with and support the likes of him. There was no guarantee I would get back on the SF Flight so I'd end up being confined to normal squadron duties.

Soon after Norway we went on an exercise on Salisbury Plain. Three days of pissing rain, living in tents. I came back one afternoon, shook the water off like a dog, sat in the crewroom, looked around, saw all the pilots were as fucked off as I was and thought, What the hell am I going to do with my life? On pilot training, I thought, I'll have the usual year and a half of bullshit, of being called 'You horrible little man'. If I get through the system I'll be back on Chinooks sitting in the same crewroom, wearing different rank tabs and getting paid slightly less. (Being commissioned means you have more expenses in the Officers' Mess.)

The haze cleared. It was time I thought about coming out and doing something else. There are a lot of good people in the RAF as well as a lot of tossers, but the longer you stay in the deeper the rut is. I've seen a lot of mates come croppers once they step outside – suddenly this protected environment is no longer there to protect them. There is no job outside the RAF unless you are a pilot – navigator, flight engineer are all things of the past. Loadmaster didn't enter the market.

I knew Jill would back me. She's always had a lot of confidence in me – more than I do – and has supported me in everything I wanted to do. I went to see the wing commander and told him I'd like to withdraw my application for pilot training. Shock. Horror. He wanted to know why.

'I'd like to become a civilian pilot, sir.' There was a moment of silence.

'I should be talking you out of it,' he said, 'bollocking you for wasting our time but, honestly, I can't put my hand on my heart and say you're doing the wrong thing.'

'Thank you, sir.'

'Oh, and Dave?'

'Yes, sir?'

'When you get your instructor's licence will you do my conversion for me?'

I bought a share in a Piper Vagabond two-seater at Popham Airfield to start getting the hours for a commercial licence. As I needed 700 hours and the hire rate was £60 to £70 an hour, it was expensive. Fortunately we had sold our house at Shawbury for a handsome profit – enough to pay for all my licences. Once I got sufficient hours to get my instructor's ticket I could fly loads and loads of hours and get paid to do it. That was the recognised way of doing it, but the Civil Aviation Authority (CAA) have stopped that now. A year later I had to do twenty commercial pilot's exams, real balls-aching flying tests, then I got my instructor's rating after a course in Coventry. I was very popular with the pilots at Odiham, who all wanted me to do their conversion from helicopters. I did the wing commander first.

For some reason the RAF seemed very keen to keep me. Out of the blue I was called up at home and told to go and see the boss right away. There was another sergeant with me. 'Stand to attention,' he snapped. 'You are both improperly dressed. The dress codes are very strict on this squadron. You are not wearing the right rank. You have been promoted.'

He gave me this letter telling me I was being promoted to flight sergeant. It was a serious pat on the back to be promoted after only six years – usually it took fourteen. And I got more money. I read the letter and said, 'Excuse me, sir, but it says you've got to be signed on for twelve years.'

'Yes, you have to make a big decision. I know you want to go out and be a pilot.'

'If this means I have to stay on for another four years,' I said, 'there's no decision to make. I can't take it.' He was gobsmacked. I must be one of the few people in the RAF ever to turn down a promotion. The system couldn't believe it.

I had to sign the bottom of this blue letter, signed by the chief nob, accepting it. I signed saying, 'I do not accept it'. I took it into SHQ – the old blunty's paradise – and handed it to the desk corporal. I was walking out and he rushed after me saying, 'Sarge, Sarge, you've signed the wrong bit, you've turned it down!' I said, 'Yes, I know'.

Finally I got a snotty phone call from the bloke in charge who told me pompously, 'Do you realise how many people have written good things about you and what an honour this is?'

'I will gladly accept it,' I replied, 'if I can still come out in two years' time.' He put the phone down.

Even Jill, the most patient of souls, was getting fed up with SF call–outs, frustrated because we could never arrange to go out. Once, after she'd just fallen pregnant with Andrew, we were going home for a family wedding. The car was packed. Then the phone rang. It was the station, who wanted me to come to work on standby. She lost her temper and told them, 'No, he's coming home with me.'

They called back ten minutes later and said they'd managed to find a replacement.

Soon afterwards I was standing in the next room when I heard the flight commander talking to a new pilot, giving him a briefing on what to do and what not to do.

'Is there anything else I shouldn't do?'

'Oh yes, for fuck's sake, whatever you do, don't piss McMullon off!'

'Who's that,' asked the terrified voice.

'One of the sergeant crewmen.'

'Why's he a problem?' At that point I decided to knock on the door and introduce myself. The pilot shook my hand nervously and then retreated against the wall, where he studied me as if I was some kind of tyrannosaurus throwback. The flight commander just grinned and said, 'Oh, Dave, tomorrow you'll be flying with our new recruit. Show him the ropes, will you?'

Otherwise it was RAF business as usual. I was sent up to Spadeadam near the Otterburn ranges on an EW (electronic warfare) course. It was all left over from the Cold War, learning how Russian radar and SAMs (surface-to-air missiles) showed themselves and how we could evade them. I thought it was going to be a waste of time and, since the East–West option was never going to happen, I didn't take it too seriously. But you never know what is round the corner. I didn't know that out in the Persian Gulf the Iraqis had been buying up Russian arms and missile systems for years.

We were told what sort of missile was being used – a SAM 7, SAM 8, whatever – and then we'd listen on the RWR (radar warning receiver) to the noise it makes. On the second run we'd have a look to see what to do to stop the radar looking at you. Flying evasion, turning away, turning towards it. The best defence was always terrain screening. Hide behind a big hill and the radar on the other side cannot see you.

SNOW AND SAND

On the third run-through we'd try defensive measures. Firing chaff (a cloud of metal foil) was effective but you had to have the skill to know when to release. If the aircraft moved first, then fired, it didn't do any good. The missile would come straight through the foil and take you out. The idea was to fire the chaff so there was a huge screen of metal foil and move away sharpish while the radar got confused looking at that. The aircraft would have between two and three seconds before the radar started to look for you again – by which time you would have buggered off and they would have lost you. Hopefully.

Learning how to cope with attacks from jet fighters was much more fun. Near Leeming was a corridor about fifteen miles wide and fifty miles long and we would tootle up and down there, wait to be attacked by Tornadoes and evade them the best we could. The Tornado pilots thought it was going to be a turkey shoot. Fast jet against lumbering Chinooks. No contest. You could see their moustaches twitching as they thought, Goody, helicopters! We'll go and bag ourselves thirty and come back in plenty of time for tea and medals.

On the first day their gun-camera films showed there was not a single incident where a Tornado even got a shot off at us. Actually that's not true. After several sorties when they couldn't find us at all we were asked to switch our radar transponders on. It clipped the macho image somewhat when they had to ask us to squawk. That was like putting up a big smoke signal and saying, 'Here we are boys.' When we squawked and the pilot got a radar lock he was able to fire one of his missiles, but in a real scenario they wouldn't waste one on a helicopter. Missiles are saved for either a bomber or another fighter attacking them.

Flying in a helicopter, if you see the fighter first, with the exception of the Harrier, they'll not get you. For a start you have four blokes looking out. Flying in battle formation with another helicopter a mile apart doubles those odds. If I'm looking back I can see over the back of the other helicopter and see anything coming in on him and vice versa. So if you are looking out for each other and wiggling about all the time, flying at fifty feet and 150 m.p.h. you become very elusive.

The biggest defence you have against a fast jet is its own speed. Their biggest problem is acquisition of the target. If you spot a jet coming from behind, you must turn and fly straight towards it. The fighter's environment is 2,000 feet at 600 knots, and if we are flying towards him that gives a closing speed of 750 m.p.h. To use his guns he has to stick the nose down. That leaves him very little time to do anything about it. If he tilts his nose down two or three degrees the time to impact with the ground is ten to fifteen seconds. When you factor in manoeuvring – because the helicopter will not be going in a straight line – that gives him less than five seconds. The pilot has to be bloody good to get a lock on. These days most of them don't get enough practice.

When we did the same exercise with Harriers I caught the fighter coming in time but all the boss did – another case of a boss who shouldn't fly – was move the stick from side to side very fast. Unfortunately, when you throw twenty-three tons of Chinook around like that, it ends up going in a straight line. They got us that day. The Harrier was more difficult to escape because it can turn tightly, and it flies more slowly. While a normal fighter is limited by the amount of G it can pull, the Harrier not only uses its wing to get round but also vectors its nozzles like a rocket, pushing it into the centre of the turn.

In May 1989 I went out on Exercise Transit – an eight-week SF exercise. It was the usual cloak-and-dagger stuff where you never knew where you were going until the last moment. We launched out in a four-ship formation from Portsmouth and rendezvoused with the *Ark Royal*. It was flat calm – we could see the reflections in the water, not a ripple.

That was better than my last flight to an aircraft carrier. We'd landed on the *Illustrious* a month before. The matelots had run on and locked four 10,000-pound chains on to us so that in the bouncing sea the aircraft didn't roll off the side. We had 40,000 pounds of restraint on, then a sudden gust of wind whipped in from the side, created lift under the blades, pushed us straight back up into the hover and snapped the chains. Caught unprepared, the pilot turned the wrong way, and the blades whirred over the bridge, nearly decapitated the captain and scared the hell out of everybody. He heaved in a whole load of power, dived away to the side, sorted the problem out and came back in again.

Whatever the conditions, I am terrible on water. I am always bloody seasick. As soon as I stepped on the deck of the *Ark Royal* I was absolutely gone. Then they put us in bunks right at the pointy end. I didn't get a wink of sleep, throwing my ring up all the time. That amused my fellow crewman, Kev Hardie.

Kev never got seasick. He had started off in the Navy and had been in their display team – the guys who race the field guns at the Royal Tournament – before transferring to the RAF and fetching up on the SF Flight. He was Mr Muscle Man, Mr Trainer. To Kev you weren't a man unless you drank twenty pints and shagged thirty women a night. I usually have suspicions about somebody that much over the top but I couldn't help but like him and he was great to have on an exercise like that.

The next evening we launched off the coast of Portugal, heading for Morocco. It was a very fuel-critical operation.

There on deck in choppy seas (I had nothing left to throw up by that point), were four aircraft, rotors turning, packed with long-range fuel tanks. The inertial navigation system has to have a stable platform so we had problems aligning them. After fifteen minutes we had to refuel, then they ran out of fuel, which had the boss running round in circles, getting hysterical.

It was a day-into-night transit. We went into cloud at 1,000 feet, 100 yards apart. The first Chinook skimmed the top of the clouds and the vortices from the blades created a little bit of turbulence. After three more aircraft scudded the cloud, we found ourselves flying through a circular white tunnel. I'd never seen the effect before – it was like flying through the flexitube from a tumble dryer, but more dramatic.

Observing radio silence, we crossed the coast of Morocco flying at 100 feet. The moon was fingernail thin, and there was low cloud obscuring the stars, so it was as black as hell, even with goggles on. We were third in the four-ship formation and suddenly I saw Number One pull up, then Two as well. The copilot said, 'Hey, there's a mast at ten o'clock, one mile.'

I called, 'Mast at one o'clock, one mile.' Fuck. Masts tend to be joined together. By wires.

'Pull up fast,' I screamed. The masts were 300 feet up and we were heading straight for them. It went from bad to worse. There were wires everywhere and we were supposed to be flying low.

What was ridiculous was that we'd sent out a non-SF pilot in a Gazelle to recce the routes. The information we had got back from him was very detailed. Words to the effect of, 'The whole of Morocco is an excellent low-flying area. There are no significant wires or masts. Enjoy yourselves.' I don't know what he had been doing – shagging all the local tarts or something. You really can't miss a 300-foot pylon. He could have wiped out every one of us.

We split into two pairs each carrying a six-man team plus an LDV. The next big problem was sand: 120 m.p.h. of downwash creates a lot of sand.

Our first drop point was a clearing 200 feet wide surrounded by big trees. We went in side by side in the pitch-black. The visibility was almost nonexistent and what had looked like a small rock suddenly turned out to be much bigger. I was at the door watching the other helicopter land while talking my pilot, Chris Scullen, down.

Suddenly the downwash hit the sand. It came up in torrents. I couldn't see anything. We were in the shit. We couldn't move forward because we'd hit the trees, couldn't pull out left because there were more trees, or right because of the other helicopter. Hitting that would be calamitous. The only safe way was down and we could see bugger all. Fully aware of the problems, Chris Scullen announced, 'We're going for a landing guys. Let's get the thing down.' Chris's was the correct decision. It also focused the crew's attention on helping in any way they could within the formation.

What saved us was the sparks. As the spinning blades hit particles of sand the friction warmed them up sufficiently so that with the goggles on I could see sparks coming off the blades and judge where the other aircraft was. If the blades hit the trees I reckoned it might knacker them but we'd live through it. If I hadn't seen those sparks I'd have gone home in a black bag. Sand sparks have saved my life twice.

I kept on giving instructions until we hit the ground. Hard but firm with all four wheels digging in, a bit of forward momentum so the aircraft nose tipped forward before it settled down. Like pedalling a bike on the beach. We made it down more through luck than judgment. I was shitting myself.

That night we didn't shut the rotors off for eleven and a half hours. We'd land on a desert strip behind an SF Flight Hercules, which would refuel us, and then we'd take off again. After about ten hours we heard that one of the SAS guys had rolled his buggy off the side of a cliff and we had to rescue it. Kev had a few choice words to say about that.

We put a strop on this LDV but as it was a very dark night with very little starlight, we had to stare even to see the edge of the cliff. We had to hover down to pick up the LDV with the blades five foot off the edge of the cliff. Because it was so dark you got very little perception of whether you were drifting left or right and very little height perception. The pilot was next to the side of the cliff. I was at the forward door making sure we didn't drift into the SAS bloke beneath us or rip the LDV off the side. Kev was literally hanging off the back of the ramp making sure that the blades didn't hit the cliff wall on the other side.

The chatter that went on was constant, nonstop for thirty-five seconds, three voices all interacting, not blabbing at the same time. It was very high-pressure. We were all tired and attempting something we'd never done before. If anything had gone wrong we'd have been pointed out as a bunch of wankers who shouldn't even have tried it. Yet each one of us knew where the priority was and if we called it the others would shut up. Chris became a voice-activated autopilot who reacted precisely to instructions, which made our job easier. If the flying was accurate, fewer corrections had to be given.

No sleep, eleven hours in the air, almost zero visibility, and in a situation where the slightest mistake could kill you – at times like that you know what real teamwork is. We were lucky in having Chris Scullen at the controls. He was one of the few pilots who could have maintained that kind of performance despite being totally shagged.

Then we went off and spent two nights in a hotel getting completely pissed. The Gazelle pilot was there too, but we were still so angry with him that he spent the whole time talking to his engineers.

CHAPTER 10

EXERCISE COCK-UP

Aircrew always believe a Chinook is at its most vulnerable when it's come out of the shop after a major refit. We believe that if the aircraft looks like a heap of shit anything that was going to happen to it already has. If it has oil spewing out everywhere we know it's got oil in it. When a pristine, immaculate, gleaming machine rolls out of the hangar we are very suspicious. The first thing that happens is that we go for an air test.

It's not that we don't trust the engineers – far from it – but these days with all the cutbacks they are under pressure to save money all the time. When that's the prevailing attitude from the big brass, corners are bound to be cut.

Mistakes happen and the Chinook does not forgive mistakes easily. Sometimes it got personal, and it felt as if one particular machine really was out to get you.

Once one of our Chinooks, Echo ZA712, had a gearbox problem. It went into engineering at Odiham and came out all gleaming, ready for an air test. Engineers have loads of aircraft to fix and not much time to do it in and so they are always overstretched. But as with everything in the RAF there are procedures, so when everything has been done a supervisor has to come along and say, 'Yes I'm happy the wheel nut has been tightened OK'. Then he puts a tick in the right box. Somebody had signed to say Echo ZA712's gearbox was now A-OK.

My ground job was to do the walk round on the outside of the aircraft. I checked everything was OK and secure, that the engine oil levels were full. I tapped the engine cowling because if that was cracked it would not make a ringing sound. I climbed up the aft pylon and did all my checks, but when I got down I wasn't happy. I went up again, rattled everything and as it still seemed all right I walked back along the walkway on top of the cabin. I knew something was wrong. Suddenly the mist in my head cleared. The Jesus nut hadn't been tightened up. The Jesus nut held the rotor disc in place. The nut was about eight inches in diameter. I put my fingers on it and spun it like a top. As soon as we'd started up the gearbox the rear blades would have spun off – causing God knows how much chaos – and we'd have been left inside the fuselage whipping around on the torque reaction.

Four months later I was sitting in Echo ZA712 once again, preparing to transit out to Gütersloh in Germany for a squadron exercise. The Iron Curtain was still up so the plan was for 24 Airmobile Brigade to deploy to Germany. There we would link up with Pumas and the Chinooks of 18 Squadron to transport the ground forces, heavy guns and all the paraphernalia of a major military exercise. It involved mass movement of helicopters transiting back and forth across the FEBA (forward edge of battle area). The idea was that we would spread ourselves across the German country-side and take over barns and base ourselves in them. In return the government would pay the farmers huge sums of money.

We were the last three aircraft to fly out of Odiham, laden with all the supplies and spares. We thrashed out in a loose formation about a mile apart and crossed the coast at about 1,000 feet. The first thing that caught me was the smell of transmission oil. You get used to the sounds and smells of an aircraft and quickly pick up something that isn't normal. I could smell and taste something was wrong. I looked up and saw this mist coming from the aft gear box. I went to have a look and as I got there the whole pipe split. It was a big bastard – two inches in diameter – but not, thank God, a high-pressure one. There was still masses of oil erupting out of it. If you lose the oil out of your aft gear box the bearings will seize up within a minute or two. Soon after that the Chinook will have forgotten it is supposed to be an aircraft.

'Gearbox oil problem. Head for land,' I called to the skipper, Barry Tinslow. We were ten miles out to sea. He turned back and put out a mayday call while I clambered down the back and saw what was happening. It was serious.

'Keep an eye on the oil pressure on aft gear box. We're losing everything. It's split from arse to elbow.' I wrapped my glove around it to try to seal it up. It was piping hot so I was burning my hands, hanging on for grim death, trying to keep every last drop of oil in. We pulled up, just on to land, and there was a farmhouse with some nice gardens. Barry said, 'Bollocks, I'm not looking for a landing place.' So we landed on this perfect lawn and shut down, scaring the hell out of an old lady who was busy pruning her roses.

She was furious to begin with but, as soon as we explained, she got out the silver teapot and started plying us with biscuits and cake. Especially after we told her she could claim for any damage caused by twenty-three tons of aircraft landing on her perfectly manicured lawn. The engineers on board worked out what part we needed. Naturally it was on another helicopter, so they peeled off, dropped it and the engineers off at Manston where they got transport over to us. It took about six hours to fix, then we had to do ground runs and seal checks before we buggered off again.

If that had happened fifteen minutes later we would have had to ditch. The decision was difficult. Do you fly until the thing ditches? Or do you do a controlled ditching and be certain to get everyone out? Once the oil pressure starts flicking in the cockpit you have thirty to sixty seconds, which isn't enough. Theoretically the Chinook should float but I wouldn't bet a day's salary on that. All the weight is on the top and most helicopters that land in water promptly turn turtle. In training we all went through dunker drill, which was not a pleasant experience and certainly not one we wanted to repeat for real. The idea is to stay strapped in your seat until all movement stops. Most people feel one impact and think, Right, let's get out of here, but then they get thrown across the cabin by the second impact. Once the aircraft has rolled upside down and movement has stopped you know where you are. In my case right by the front door!

Exercise Long Stride should have been rechristened Exercise Cock-up. Everything that could possibly fuck up did. When we eventually reached Gütersloh we had our briefing and headed out to the field sites. Tim Lockhart took over as pilot and his copilot was Phil Simms. It was dark and we were trying to find this field site, flying without NVGs, and he called out, 'Turn right after this wood.'

I objected. 'If you do that you'll hit the wires coming down from the top.'

'No they're not there.'

Tim interrupted: 'Are they there, Dave?'

'Well, I can see them.'

'OK, Phil, shut the fuck up. Dave, tell us where to go.'

On the SF Flight it was a basic necessity to be able to

navigate. There are always two primary navigators: the non-handling pilot and the forward loadmaster. But the aft load master will also be checking the position. If they can't navigate to within fifteen seconds and 100 metres at night, low level, they won't be on the SF Flight. It wasn't the same on regular duties.

That night we were putting Echo ZA712 to bed, by putting covers on the engines and tying the blades down with ropes to stop them sailing up in the wind. In order to put the ropes on the blades, we had to turn the rotors by hand to be able to reach the individual blades. Mick Bell, the other crewman, was at the back and suddenly announced, 'What the fuck's that noise?'

As we turned the blades there was a loud grinding sound that could not be heard with the engines running. We traced the noise to the right-hand cross-shaft at the front of the engine. I climbed up, undid the six fasteners holding the fibreglass cover on, and removed it. I peered inside and immediately invented a few new swear words. Then I jumped down to show the rest of the crew my latest discovery. Laid along the bottom of the cross-shaft was a large open-ended spanner about one foot long. Part of it had just been touching the cross-shaft, which made the grinding noise. Another millimetre and the spanner would have dug into the cross-shaft like a lathe tool into a piece of wood, torn into it and eventually broken it. The engine would then have been unable to deliver its power to the combining gearbox, and then the rotors.

To add insult to our potential injury not only had the spanner been left there, but it had been painted over with green undercoat. This became a source of much argument among the crew. Who was the biggest arsehole? The bloke who left the spanner there? Or the one who painted over it?

The exercise itself went fine, though the farmer's barn left a lot to be desired in the way of five-star accommodation. We were giving him a load of money for upsetting his cattle but it was important to maintain good public relations. At the end of the exercise we took him up and had a bash round so he could see his farm from the air. As we were flying I could smell hydraulic fluid.

I could smell a hydraulic leak at a thousand paces. Still can. It's one of my gifts, thank God.

After we landed and shut down I said, 'Boss, I'm not happy with this.' I climbed up on to the fuselage to look at ZA712's forward gearbox pylon and it was peeing out hydraulic fluid. I opened up the casing and it looked like somebody had just killed a chicken. Red liquid everywhere.

'That's it,' I said, to the engineer who came running over. They were all packed up and ready to leave. 'Endex. There's something wrong with that jack. The seal's knackered. I'm not flying anywhere in that machine. It's grounded.'

'No it's not,' he said, having wiped all the fluid off. 'It's bloody all right. We can't see any break in the seal.' Then he said to the pilot – not to me, of course, since I was interfering – 'It's OK, sir, ready to go.'

The officer looked at me. He was a brand-new squadron leader whom I didn't know. I wasn't sure if he'd back me so I just said, 'You can go, sir, but I'm staying on the ground. I'm not happy to fly in that.'

'If Sergeant McMullon's not happy, I'm not happy.' It was like I'd farted in church. All the engineers came round with their senior NCO shouting, 'How dare the aircrew override a ground-crew decision.' They were mega pissed off, claiming that the reason it had fluid there was the weight of the blades pressing the jacks down. 'Bollocks,' I said. 'After five years on these things I've never seen that.'

'We'll leave it ten minutes, then power it up and see how it goes,' said the corporal technician.

Inside the Chinook in the Falklands: taking a break from the job – packed in like sardines for a day trip out.

It's not just astronauts that can practise zero gravity!

Monitoring an underslung load from the centre hatch. The red seats were removed in Saudi.

United Arab Emirates, prior to deployment to Saudi. The sand camouflage proved too bright/reflective at night.

On a visit to the other half of 7 Sqn, based 300 miles south of us.

Kuwait International Airport with US Apache helicopters parked. This was the day after we arrived at the airport.

Kuwait. Crew 4 relax while deciding which souvenirs to take back with us. Wes sitting on the box, John Sanderson, the captain, sitting next to him, Chas Dickson holding the sign with me and Nick Kirk, the regiment gunner, bending over.

Midday but the smoke from the fires made it seem more like midnight.

The rib cage and engines of the 747 brought back memories of Lockerbie.

Roping the SBS down on to the British Embassy in Kuwait.

Flying the Kuwait flag over the city.

HMS *Ark Royal*. Refuelling prior to our flight to Morocco.

The other part of 7 Sqn and 18 Sqn got involved in transporting Iraqi POWs.

The road leading north out of Kuwait, with destroyed vehicles and Iraqi bodies scattered everywhere.

We saw lots of evidence of the accuracy of the Allied bombings. This bunker and its contents has seen better days.

A Chinook beds down for the night in Wadi Rum Jordan.

SAS Pinkie Land Rover and motorcycle in Jordan.

View from the front door of the Chinook looking down into a wadi 1000 feet below.

Some bedtime reading during a Scud warning in NBC (nuclear, biological and chemical warfare) gear.

Leaving the Kuwait oil well fires behind us, going back to Saudi.

Kev Hardie (right) with some of the other crewmen model the latest aircrew kit. (Most of us used this due to the cold when flying and we supplied most of the SAS teams with them when they requested extra clothing due to the cold.)

'You can power it up as many times as you like, I am not going up in that.' So we waited, then powered it up. I was standing behind the corporal technician, who had a smug smile on his face. Nothing happened. He turned to me and said, 'See.' At that moment there was an almighty crack and the whole jack exploded, showering him and me with hydraulic fluid. If that had happened even in a hover, it would have been an irrecoverable situation. In flight you were dead.

Back at Gütersloh we indulged in our favourite activity. Drinking. The Officers' Mess was quite boring so one night the pilots came back to the Sergeants' Mess to get pissed. We started drinking all sorts of weird concoctions and eventually Chris Scullen told me, 'It's time you came back to our mess.' I know he dragged me back there because the next day I could see the heel marks in the snow but the only thing I actually remember is being shaken awake in the toilet. I was in the middle trap and had thrown up everywhere. Unfortunately, the door opened directly on to the reception hall. I next woke up in my normal accommodation – in a room that looked like a chicken slaughterhouse – with John Sanderson screaming at me.

'What the fuck have you done to our mess?'

'Yeah, but I was in the toilet.'

'Oh no,' he said. 'You were on the toilet when you threw up, but it wasn't in the toilet. You'd better sort it out.'

So I slapped some squadron leader rank tabs on, went to the Officers' Mess and opened the toilet door on to a river of vomit flowing out on to the reception floor. A cleaning lady came up and said, 'I wouldn't go in there, sir. Some dreadful person's made a terrible mess.'

'I know,' I said. 'I'm that dreadful person. I've come to clean it up.'

CHINOOK!

'Very good of you, sir,' she said and thrust a bucket in my hand. Chris and John managed to cover up the tracks in the snow so no more was heard of the incident.

At the end of the exercise, the formation leader, one of those illustrious leaders with scrambled egg under his cap, had a brilliant idea. The boss's job is not to fly, but to manage the squadron. However, he decided to climb into the cockpit and lead the squadron back to Gütersloh airport – twenty-four Chinooks flying between one and two rotors' width apart (sixty to a hundred feet) in a step-down pattern. The idea was to fly round the airfield in a circuit with the wind behind, then peel off and land into wind.

Leading a formation, you have to think about all the other blokes' problems. It's like a motorway traffic jam. If you have 400 cars on a motorway and the car in front slows down by five m.p.h., the car behind him brakes and slows down by seven m.p.h. and by number 100 you are locking your wheels, going sideways and trying not to crash. It is the same in an aircraft formation: the slightest movement at the front sends ripples that get bigger all the way back.

Suddenly the boss decided to make a split-arse turn at the front. The aircraft behind him had to slow down and pitch up. As each bloke pitched up the guy behind had to pitch more but couldn't peel out because anyone doing that would take out the aircraft behind with his rotor.

Echo ZA712 was twentieth back, 1,000 feet above the leaders at 800 feet. To avoid a collision we had to pitch twenty degrees nose up – which doesn't sound a lot but it makes a change of speed of sixty knots. Minus sixty knots. I looked down and saw the aft rotor disc of the aircraft in front going beneath us. At this time the pilot was completely blind and I was saying, 'OK, keep the same rate going, don't sink.' Actually it was more of a prayer.

I'd survived everything the helicopter could throw at me for the past four weeks only to run into the macho factor. Human error. We could have lost fifteen helicopters and sixty lives because the boss decided he wanted to lead the formation.

Aircrew have their own rule to cover such situations: 'When a man with more than three bars announces he is going to lead the flight, take cover!'

CHAPTER 11

WELCOME TO SAUDI

I was hugging Jill and Andrew, kissing them goodbye with an urgency I'd never felt before. Andrew was barely eight months old. He was born on 3 April by emergency caesarean section, so I hadn't been allowed to see his birth. I'd already been away from him over half his short life. Now I wondered if I would ever see him walk or talk, let alone grow up to drive me crazy. Neither of us would cry, though there was no point in pretending, in keeping up the macho posture. All around me blokes were doing the same thing, trying to hold back their emotions, saying goodbye to their loved ones.

It was just after dawn on 15 December 1990. Freezing fog covered the runways at Odiham. In just a few hours I would be in the Arabian Gulf, facing the burning heat of the Arabian desert and God knows what Saddam Hussein had in his arsenal.

I had been down in the Falklands when I heard that Saddam had invaded Kuwait. When you're stuck on a windswept rock with nothing between you and the South Pole, what's going on in some sandy hole halfway across the world doesn't really affect you. Information slowly filtered down about the build-up of troops, but the Chinese whispers that reached Port Stanley told us 7 Squadron (SF) would not be needed. You always prefer to believe in the Good News.

As I turned to get on to the bus, Jill squeezed my hand. 'Be careful. See you when you get back.'

'We're only going out as cover,' I said, trying to reassure her. 'They haven't got a role for us.' That was true enough. Word had it that there was no defined role for either the SAS or the SBS but General Peter de la Billière had insisted they be out there. What I didn't add was that every nutcase in the Special Forces would be racking his brains to find a way of getting into the action. That would inevitably involve flying Chinooks behind enemy lines.

'I'll be fine,' I lied. 'I'll probably spend my days ferrying grunts around behind our lines and living it up in a luxury hotel.'

Usually a busful of blokes will start farting and shouting obscenities before the driver's passed the main gates. Not this time. I waved goodbye until the little group of wives and kids were just a blur, then sat in silence, and wondered whether this would be the last time I ever saw my little boy. Jill told me later that for all her trying to keep calm she had burst into tears as soon as she got into the car.

I'd been back from the Falklands for only a couple of weeks. So much for Good News.

We flew from Brize Norton to Riyadh on a Tristar freighter, with thirty seats crammed in at the back. Harry Secombe was on board flying out to boost Christmas morale for the troops. He improved our morale tremendously as we nicked all the meat out of his sandwiches. We had these crusty pieces of shite to eat and he had a huge butty box. While he was busy, shaking hands, chatting to people, we whipped all the innards leaving him with the dry bread. He was pretty cool about it, chewed his crusts and never said a word.

Riyadh was complete bloody chaos. Every man and his dog were flying in troops and equipment. All I wanted to do was have a dump. I ran into this hangar full of communal crappers pursued by a movements officer screaming, 'McMullon your aircraft is leaving.' I wasn't going on a Hercules in that condition. There's only a little chemical toilet covered by a shower curtain and, the moment you head down there, there will always be a chat on the intercom. Then just as you are sitting comfortably the aircraft encounters severe turbulence. It happens every time.

Personal business complete, I leaped on board, engines running. In the United Arab Emirates a Chinook came to take us out to Bateen airbase. Things started to look up. Helicopter crews were put in the local Intercontinental Hotel and to drive to the base we were given a brand-new Toyota Land Cruiser. We blew one up within twenty-five minutes.

Kev Hardie was in the driver's seat. I was in the passenger seat, and Wes Hogan and Jim Tench were in the back. We each had a control to operate. Kev had the clutch, I had the accelerator, Wes had the gearstick and Jim the steering wheel. Whatever one person did the others had to accept. We came to some stop lights and I kept the accelerator on the floor. They had the choice of dumping the clutch or blowing the engine up. So we blew the engine up, pushed the vehicle into the side and called up the car-hire firm. They came out with another. That lasted nearly two days.

We weren't drunk, just in manic high spirits – convinced we were all going to die so it didn't matter any more. If you think you are going to croak, it's a natural defence mechanism to flake out, go doolally, drink too much and do all sorts of stupid things.

We soon discovered that if we wanted to stay alive there were a lot of things that needed doing. Our aircraft had standard desert camouflage, a sandy-coloured paint job. When we started flying we discovered light was reflected off this paint, which for anyone wearing night-vision aids made it the best target in the sky. The boss told us to sort it out. We went and bought fifty tins of black paint from the local market, then everybody on the base – all the ground workers, crew, everybody – slapped bits of black paint on. Not one of the aircraft had the same colour scheme: some had zebra stripes all over, others had explosions of black spots like some modern art painting. It was perfect, gave us sufficient colour, but we were toned down so it didn't affect the goggles and completely camouflaged us flying at night. To formate on each other we needed only the heat of the engines. The tails looked like white dots.

In the SF Flight we were used to swapping around but in the Gulf the squadron commander decided that we would split into specific crews for the duration. We had four aircraft and six full crews. Allocations were made by Steve French, the flight commander, and Julian Mason, the crewman leader, who tried to spread the experience level out over the crews. Initially I wasn't sure about the idea but the way things turned out Crew 4 was an excellent unit. Until Rupert Campbell-Smith turned up.

John Sanderson was the captain. I'd done a lot of flying with John since we went through the Chinook OCU together. John was thirty-seven, five foot ten, slim with a growing hint of beer belly, very dark hair and piercing green eyes that could charm the ladies from the trees. John hadn't been to university and was loafing around when he saw an RAF recruiting picture in a mag and decided to have a go at this pilot lark. He didn't know anything about it. He'd turned out to be a natural pilot with a wicked sense of humour and a Cornish accent that went as thick as clotted cream after a few beers.

At the time John wasn't my favourite chap. I didn't dislike him and he was a good drinking companion who'd helped save my bacon when I threw up in the Officers' Mess in Germany the year before. But under severe pressure John had a tendency to become slightly headstrong. A few months earlier in the Falklands we were carrying an underslung BV from one side of Mount Kent to the other. As we lifted in the hover, two of the eight legs of the strops came undone, which meant we were overstressing the remaining six. He wasn't interested in stopping to restrop. The big problem was that our flight track was over the troops' living area.

Chas Dickson was nominated as copilot. On the outside, Chas (or Chicks, though we sometimes called him Elmer Fudd because he couldn't pronounce his r's properly) appeared to be a real nob, a standard-issue RAF officer who does what he thinks an officer should do. He looked the part, well spoken, well built, six feet tall, in his early thirties with a small weedy tash and a deep baritone voice that could make your headphones vibrate. Educated at public school and university, he also liked to put on a show about 'us' (pilots and officers) and 'them' (aircrew and ground staff). It was deliberate self-mockery but many an outsider would think he was being serious. It certainly fooled Right Rupert.

Chas stayed calm under pressure. Initially he did have a small chip on his shoulder because he wanted to be commander of the aircraft and he wasn't, though, to be fair, he never said as much. He was excellent in the non-handling role, what little radio work there was, navigation, monitoring the RWR visually and aurally. No one ever got lost if Chicks was navigating.

I was delighted that Wes Hogan was my fellow crewman. In the three years since I'd trained him he'd grown even calmer. Nothing fazed Wes so long as he could have a cigarette. He still managed to smoke like a chimney though he was banned from sneaking one on the Chinook because we had seven tons of fuel on board.

People liked Wes. He was a smashing bloke but he didn't do himself many favours. He'd come through the ranks as a fitter – where he'd lost the top half of the index finger of his right hand in a machining accident – and remustered as loadmaster. He was from Anglesey, but no trace of his Welsh accent remained. Perhaps that was a survival mechanism, since he'd married some local bird there and it didn't turn out too well. After a lively spell in the Sergeants' Mess he'd settled down with a new girl. We'd been in the Gulf three weeks when she 'Dear Johned' him. Such a thoughtful girl. If it hurt him – and I know it did – he didn't show it. Fortunately, he had someone else, much closer to our tent, he really, really hated. And he came with a double-barrelled name.

In the helicopter world you tend to live the life you are working. After all, we're just grunts who wear blue uniforms. Living in the Intercontinental was too good to last. After two weeks we were deployed to Victa, a field site in the UAE. It was a compound with a couple of hangars, a small landing strip and four blokes to a tent, sleeping on camp beds. This was the excuse we needed to start complaining about the serviceman's favourite gripe. Money.

In the Gulf the Americans earned about eighty per cent extra, what with warzone pay tax-free golden bollocks and all the Coca-Cola they could drink. The Tornado pilots were in Riyadh living in five-star hotels on £100 per day allowances. We were living under canvas and, because the M.o.D were supplying our accommodation, being charged £1.20 per day for the privilege. The blokes who were living in Germany were even worse off. Although their families were still overseas their extra cost-of-living allowance was taken away. For the privilege of being allowed to die for Kuwaiti oil we were £1.50 per day worse off.

On New Year's Eve we celebrated by drinking bottles of water, sitting on the sand wondering what 1991 would bring and whether we'd ever see another New Year's Eve – preferably one with booze in it.

The carefree insanity of the first few days in the Gulf had now been replaced by more measured discussions about what might happen. This was certainly helped by a very near miss we'd had with another Chinook during a night deployment exercise. After that Crew 4 decided sanity was the best route to survival.

In the build-up there was never a predefined role for the SF. They were desperate to find something to do, so all sorts of weird and wonderful options were proposed, no matter how crazy. Then they made us try them out. Sometimes the SAS didn't appreciate the dangers they could be put into by the aircraft. Among the things tried for rapid extractions was flying around with six SAS carabinered on the end of a sixty-foot rope. They thought it was a great idea but the crew were terrified that they could crash into each other or get tangled up. Not to be outdone, the SBS made a careful study of Iraq. Once they realised there was a large area of water on the map up by Baghdad we had to practise landing on water and letting them crawl up the ramp using a net.

On the first Special Forces mission inside Iraq the SBS destroyed the fibre-optic cables linking Saddam Hussein's headquarters with his Scud missile launch sites. Two aircraft were dispatched and had to shut down the rotors on site – not a good idea in enemy territory a mere forty miles north of Baghdad – while the SBS went out, dug up the enemy cables and destroyed them. If the crews couldn't get the engines started again the fallback plan was for everyone to put on their dry suits, mask and snorkels, jump into these bloody rivers, waddle their way down to the bottom and be picked up by another helicopter. It is a strange mission when you are deep inside enemy territory, parked up in the middle of a desert and your getaway kit consists of two flippers and a dry suit!

The strange thing was that after all the daft stuff we'd been trying out that seemed almost normal. Because it was a wartime situation all the usual rules were off and as the ferry boys we were getting increasingly concerned. Originally the SF Hercules Flight was going to be involved in resupplying any missions behind Iraqi lines but it quickly became apparent that the potential loss of a Herc and crew was deemed to be too expensive politically. It was different for the Chinooks. We were expendable.

One option that was seriously considered was a mission on the night of the outbreak of the war which involved all four aircraft going out to deposit the troops and sufficient supplies. As long as we got the troops on target and left them there, the acceptable loss rate for that mission was half the SF Flight – three crews and three aircraft. We weren't terribly amused.

We were whingeing about this when Ben the Dog announced, 'If there is a one-way mission I would happily volunteer for it.' We called him Ben the Dog because he looked and behaved like an old dog, barrel-chested with a Pancho Villa moustache and a bunch of old scars on his cheek. He was a droll sort of bloke, with a what-I-don't-know-about-it-you-can-write-on-a-flea's-testicles attitude, but actually he was a bit slow. He'd struggled to get on the Flight and only made it because he had so much helicopter experience.

'Be my guest, mate,' I said, glad he wasn't in my crew. I reckon that if there is no fear in a man there is something seriously wrong with him.

Another favourite topic of conversation was what would happen if we had to crash-land with SAS on board. Did they want a bunch of relatively unfit blokes doing an escape-and-evasion run with them? One of our worries was that the first thing they might do after surviving the impact was put a bullet through each of our heads. Face it, we were a liability.

When we were just doing exercises, they were a tightly knit group, who trusted in their mates. Suddenly all these outsiders were there every day. Now for the first time we started to mix socially. In the air we were part of the team but on the ground we would be a big weakness. They did offer that we could stay with them if we went down and they were happy to take us along. Kev Hardie, Ben the Dog and Jim Tench – who all fancied themselves as lean, mean fighting machines – thought that was a great plan.

I reckoned the safest option was to say, 'You go your way and we'll go ours.' Once on the desert floor we would drag them down and if we got captured with a bunch of SAS it would be our balls the Iraqis cut off first to get information.

Because of the perceived threat from biological and chemical weapons we had to practise operations wearing full NBC kit. It was worse than training: we now lost two gallons of sweat an hour and it drastically reduced our ability to operate efficiently. In the end we decided to lose the suits and risk the gas.

One day everybody at Victa – aircrew, engineers, SF – was ordered to report to the sergeant medic for a course of injections. We were told all sorts of things, including that the Iraqis might be poisoning food and water supplies with anthrax, and we needed protection. Everyone groaned and complained that we'd had the standard holiday-type jabs – polio, typhoid – before we were sent out. But nobody questioned it or refused to have them. There was no doctor so we went to the medical tent in groups and were given a series of jabs. I lost count how many injections I had. Five, maybe six. We were also taking the NAPS (nerve-agent poisoning) tablets every day. If we came in contact with nerve gas we were supposed to give ourselves an injection, which would work in conjunction with NAPS tablets. We did it for the first couple of weeks, then we threw the bloody things away.

After this devil's concoction of anthrax, hepatitis and God knows what else all within a day or two of each other we were told we might feel mild discomfort. I – like everybody else – was laid up in my camp bed for a couple of days feeling absolutely ghastly. One of the engineers took it really badly: he came out in red blotches and was in such a bad way he had to be medevac'd out in a Hercules. After I recovered I never gave it another thought. Instead I developed a terrible toothache.

Little did I know it at the time, but Jill's family had plans to save me from Saddam. Her sister Jane is the secretary to a hospital doctor in Saudi and she had written to Jill saying, 'Don't worry, I've got it all sorted out. If David crashes – and he lives – I've made sure he'll get the best possible care in the best hospitals!'

Crew 4 settled into our luxurious – and expensive – tent. The view was exquisite. Sand, sand and – occasionally – rocks. Of course there was the odd personality clash but we rubbed along well. And we were a great team. Naturally at that point the powers that shouldn't be decided to foist a couple of extra crew members on us. They wanted another pilot to sit on the jump seat and monitor the RWR.

'But boss,' John implored the flight commander, 'if the RWR goes the shit has hit the rotors anyway. It's just another person to get in the way.'

'Sorry, guys. That's the directive. They arrive tomorrow from 18 Squadron.'

'Who've we got?' asked Chicks.

'Rupert Campbell-Smith.'

Saddam must have heard the groans. Spy satellites shuddered in their orbit. Campbell-Smith was a legend in his own lunch box. He'd been at Odiham and then disappeared off to do an OCU as an instructor, gone to Germany, and now here he was in the Gulf. He wasn't SF but he modelled himself on a Spitfire pilot: blond floppy fringe and a handlebar moustache. Not naturally posh, he put on all the public school airs and at home must have had a standard RAF-issue black Labrador, four legs, walkies, for the use of. He arrived in our tent and it was chalk and cheese. It had nothing to do with rank or class. He pissed everybody off equally.

Every morning the first one to get up in the tent put the brew on and made everyone a mug. Rupert would get up in the morning and make one for himself. The only contact we had with the outside world was short-wave radio. John had a tiny one and we would all huddle together to hear the BBC World Service. Rupert arrived with this huge machine, and a hang-up aerial that could pick up radio signals from Mars. He used to put it on and plug his headphones in and listen to it on his tod. Selfish prick.

When we reached Al Jouf there were very few washing facilities bar a bucket of lukewarm water so we weren't the sweetest-smelling bunch of people. He'd spend six hours spraying himself full of bloody crap, washing himself with soap, pruning his moustache like a dog licking its balls. The second he walked into the tent it was just like the Tarzan films – Wes used to sniff the air and declare, 'I can smell white man.' They could recognise his soap in Iraq.

Right Rupert – no guesses how he got that nickname – could quote you the RAF law manual from Page One. Now anyone who wants to do that has something wrong with them and that attitude and behaviour was normally kicked out in a multicrew squadron. He was a real 'them-and-us' type, unlike Chicks, who just pretended. He didn't like the idea that sergeant crewmen were lying around. He'd bull his shoes every day and expected other ranks to do the same.

One day he said to me, 'You're a disgrace to the RAF, Dave. Look at the state of those boots. They need polishing.'

'I'll do that straight away then, sir.'

I hadn't anything better to do so I went away and bulled my right boot until it was gleaming. I showed it to Campbell-Smith. 'That's much better,' he said, 'nice to see.'

'But I prefer this one sir.' The other boot I had sanded down completely and drawn a little 'What, no polish?' face on it. Chicks and John fell about. Rupert didn't laugh at all. He gave up on me after that.

His refusal to interact with the team pissed all of us off so what we did was sabotage his camp bed. He had an army-issue cot with springs underneath; we had the American cots, which were quite sturdy. Wes had nicked loads of them. Right Rupert went out and so we cut every second stitch with a razor blade. As soon as he lay on it, it collapsed, so he spent the whole time lying on the sand asking if anybody had a spare. Of course it was childish behaviour and wrong for us to let something like that happen to him but it was a welcome release. Once we started flying missions we would have eased up. If he had.

Wes got particularly pissed off with Right Rupert. One day in the tent he was cleaning his weapons. 'Why bother?'

I said. 'You won't kill anybody at the range we're flying.'

'The range I need is three feet.' He joked about filing the end of one bullet down and engraving the letters RCS on the casing. I still don't know how serious he was.

We all carried Gulf Kit – water, compass, some food, a first-aid kit – so if we went down and survived the crash we could run away and escape. Normally we'd hang them up on the rails above the seats in the Chinook. One day I was doing stuff in the cabin and Right Rupert came in picked up Wes's bag put it on the floor and hung his own up. Wes's face went dangerous so I said, 'No, not now, wait until the Land Rovers are on.' We got his bag, put it under the back wheel of the Land Rover and told the SAS boys, 'Lads, when we put you off you might feel a bit of a lump but just keep driving – it's the arsehole's bag.' His bag was completely shagged.

After that Wes never took Gulf Kit with him. He said, 'If we go down then I will be taking his.' I feel sure he would have done too. One thing is for certain: if we had gone down Right Rupert would have gone his own way. We couldn't have survived with him.

Our other new addition was nicknamed Guy – short for Guy the Gorilla – who'd started with us in the UAE. This was Corporal Nick Kirk, from the RAF Regiment, six foot three and big with it. He manned the second minigun where the forward left window used to be. The other was mounted on the forward right door and could be unlocked and swivelled inside the helicopter. Initially we wasted time trying to give the Regiment blokes basic training as additional crewmen but it was asking too much to expect them to have any effect. We kept them on purely as gunners. Guy never let us down.

The Gatling miniguns were a fairly old design that had been used during the Vietnam War by DC3 Dakotas in their role as gunships. They have six barrels that spin at high speed and two trigger buttons capable of firing 4,000 rounds a minute. Having the miniguns was a big psychological boost. Especially once we learned what they could do. For target practice an old tractor tyre was thrown out. After a two-second burst from the minigun we saw two halves of tyre flying through the air. There was another occasion when there was some live target practice on a camel. It disinte-grated, was unrecognisable as a living creature.

Not very nice for the camel but very reassuring for us. We needed it. On the night of 16 January the coalition air-forces started bombing military targets inside Iraq. The war had started and we were going to be a part of it. Twenty-four hours later we deployed from Victa to King Fahed International Airbase (KFIA) and then onward to Al Jouf. To celebrate, Will and I nicked a roller conveyor from a Hercules. We reckoned it would speed up unloading sup-plies. Every second saved increased our odds of survival.

The war might have started but my tooth was such agony that my mind was more on that. All our medic had was stuff to paint on if a filling dropped out, which was as helpful as a bucket of water in a sand storm. During the flight to KFIA I couldn't concentrate on anything so I told the flight com-mander I had to get it fixed or I might be a liability when the missiles started flying.

KFIA was a huge airbase with every single aircraft imaginable and loads of aprons. In typical American style they had everything laid on, including messing halls and good food compared with the crap and sand we'd got used to. We got there late at night and my tooth was so painful I was banging my face against the wall. I found the dental surgery – a tent – but there was nobody there except the receptionist, an American Army girl. She told me to come back tomorrow. I told her I was flying a mission tomorrow and I needed to get sorted now. Begrudgingly she called out the duty dentist. Eventually an American captain appeared in a foul mood and told me it had better be serious. At that point I couldn't have flown anywhere. If he hadn't done anything I'd have taken some pliers and pulled it out myself. That wouldn't have been any worse.

The dentist took one look at my tooth and said, 'Christ, we'll have to get into this.' The only light in the tent came from a generator and the power was so low it was flickering on and off like a strobe. First he demanded another generator be put on but the lights just flickered faster. Then he put me in the chair. I was in it for four hours. He had to give me five injections before the pain went away. Because there wasn't enough electricity the drill kept getting stuck in my tooth. Next he brought out some files that were about a foot long and when he was right at the bottom of the root I felt it was coming out the bottom of my jaw.

Then the Scud alert went off. 'Don't worry, this is much more important,' said the dentist, adding helpfully, 'They usually miss.' I couldn't say a thing because my mouth was clamped wide open. He did a bloody great job. That tooth hasn't given me any problem since.

The next morning we flew up to Al Jouf. On 18 January 1991 Saddam started firing Scud missiles at Israel. None of the high-tech satellites or AWACS spotter planes could find the Iraqi mobile launch platforms. We learned later that the Israelis promised to stay out of the action only when they heard that the SAS were going to be sent into Iraq to take the Scuds out. At last the boys had a really important job to do.

But first someone had to take them behind enemy lines.

CHAPTER 12

BRAVO FOUR ZERO

'We are now in enemy territory.'

John made the announcement quietly. It was the night of 24 January 1991. Call sign Whooper 41 was out on Mission 4553. We were 100 feet above the ground. Below, all I could see was sand, more sand and then some more sand. Iraqi sand. The voice in my headphones repeated, 'Everybody alert. We are now in enemy territory.'

You see it in the films, but the first time it really happens is different. I didn't really believe it. I was living inside the green world created by the NVGs. A two-dimensional world, like a map unfolding in front of me, but this map was not paper but the sand of the Iraq desert. A desert that was very unforgiving of mistakes.

My grip tightened on the handles of my minigun; my right thumb flickered across the two red trigger buttons. Reassured, I glanced across the cabin at Guy. He was looking out of his window, his huge frame perched uncomfortably on a three-and-a-half-foot-square, black metal box. Housed in this box were the extra avionics fitted on the helicopter for the Gulf War – the Loran C navigation system and the Mode 4 IFF (Ident Friend or Foe), which was supposed to identify us as friendly to any Coalition fighters.

Protruding down from the cabin roof area just above Guy's head – so he could bash it every time he jerked upright – was the bottom half of another box. This box was supposed to save our lives. Inside were the controls for the SAM distracter, officially known as the ALQ157. There were two mounted externally, just below the engines. Each looked like a giant green bible with mirrors housed in the centre. Their job was to confuse any missile fired at you and prevent it getting a lock on – but only if that particular missile was programmed into the system. It was my job to check the programme prior to departure. I'd done it twice before takeoff and a dozen times in my head since.

Between Guy and me was the walkway into the cockpit. By leaning slightly left and looking forward I could see into it. Usually the engine and gearbox gauges were clearly visible together with the crew alerting panel. However, as the jump seat was occupied by Rupert Campbell-Smith my only view was a flight-suited back and a pair of dangling legs.

Normally the sides of the Chinook cabin were lined with red canvas seats but they had all been stripped out to allow us more space. We were encased in an oppressive grey world, grey soundproofing fabric covering the walls, a grey alloy floor interrupted only by two black nonslip strips for vehicle wheels to run up and down.

Lying on the floor between me and Guy were two long thin coffins, each three feet long, eighteen inches high and six inches wide. Each held 6,000 rounds of 7.62 bullets for the miniguns. At maximum rate of fire these would last less than ninety seconds. At the end of those ninety seconds my target would cease to exist, not recognisable as once living tissue. I'd seen what had happened to that camel.

Everyone was hyped up. The crew were all keyed up although we pretended calm over the intercom. The seven SAS boys were far tenser than I had expected – after all they'd been ready for action for months. But in the back of everybody's mind was Bravo Two Zero. There had been no contact since they were dropped off last night. Were they on the run? Had they been captured and tortured? Or was it the worst-case scenario – the one nobody dared put into words?

Just behind me, next to the ammo boxes, Jim, Bravo Four Zero's comms man, hunched over a satellite receiver, constantly monitoring the messages from the AWACS spotter planes circling high above us. Our dropoff point was an area about fifty miles southwest of Baghdad, right in the heart of Iraq. Behind Jim and Guy was a large, square, black plastic tank, containing a further 2,400 kg of fuel. We needed every gram of that fuel but aided by the overhead heater – a truly useless piece of kit that overheated the cockpit and scarcely took the chill out of the cabin – it was guaranteed to stink the cabin out for the whole flight. The ever-present stench of aviation fuel could cause even the toughest SAS operatives to go a little green. A few had been known to start blowing chunks.

Lurking behind the fuel tank was the silhouette of a Pinkie – an SAS desert vehicle with a powerful engine and modified to carry enough weapons to start a small war. Although it was tied down with every quick-release strop available, whenever we rode through any turbulence it bounced up and down. Protruding from behind the shadow of the front wheel were disembodied legs belonging to a brace of troopers trying to lie down. The hunched shapes of two more men were down the aft end next to Wes. Sitting with their backs against the cabin wall and their feet up on the fuel tank, were the final two SAS. Both were plugged into the intercom. Every time the conversation was about anything more than map references their team leader, Captain Paul Stains, a tall slim chap with mousy hair and just a hint of a Scottish accent, started upright.

It was bitterly cold in the cabin. The wind howled in through Guy's open window and my door. Every few minutes one or the other rose to his feet, staggered alongside me, trying to keep out of the slipstream from the open door. Then he would strain to catch a look at country they would soon be walking over. Since neither was wearing NVGs there was nothing to see, so they sat back down again.

Out of the desert blackness I saw the lights of vehicles travelling on the Iraqi main supply route. Crossing the MSR was always a potential problem since vehicles travelled along it twenty-four hours a day. If you saw anything you called it. Just in case.

'MSR closing from the left,' called Chicks.

'Visual with that,' I confirmed. 'I can see vehicles stopping on the side of the road. They've probably heard us. I'm marking them.'

Marking them was a euphemism. What it meant was that I was zeroing in on them with the minigun. I watched the vehicles closely in case they started firing on us. Our policy was not to fire unless we had no choice. I called their positions in case we had to manoeuvre away. 'Two o'clock now. Enemy getting out of vehicles. No threat at the moment. Three o'clock now.'

The conversation soon attracted the attention of the two SAS plugged into the intercom. The atmosphere in the cabin was suddenly charged with tension. The cold forgotten. Without ever seeing them I felt the presence of people all around me, looking left and right. Then I saw gun barrels poking out of the window right alongside me, following the directions of my clock code, paralleling the position of my minigun. None of them could see a thing without the NVGs.

'Tell us where they are, Dave,' hissed a voice in my ears.

'Five o'clock,' I called. 'No hostile ground movement.'

'Six o'clock,' from Wes aft. Then a few moments later. 'Lost visual.'

The SAS settled back down on the floor, grumbling, seriously pissed off at not being able to shoot at anyone. Funnily enough it lightened the mood in the cabin. I wasn't sure who to feel more sorry for, the blokes on the ground if we had opened fire on them – or my eardrums. We settled back into routine.

I was looking out of the door when I saw the missile take off. It was fifteen miles away. A flash of white fire a hundred times the length of the rocket. It was the biggest thing I'd ever seen on NVG goggles, but far enough away not to cause them to back off. It looked as if Saturn 5 had taken off. And it was heading straight for us.

'Incoming. Two o'clock,' I shouted. John must have already seen it because the Chinook lurched right and dropped twenty feet as the words left my mouth.

'Shit, that's big,' murmured Chicks half to himself. John threw the aircraft around the sky taking every evasive manoeuvre he'd ever learned and adding in a few extras. There were yells of surprise – and anger – from a couple of SAS troopers as they were bounced off the Pinkies into a pile of Bergens.

After five frantic seconds both pilots realised that the missile had no interest in us at all. It continued to move straight up, heading southwest towards Riyadh, with some other poor buggers' futures tattooed on its warhead.

'It's a fucking Scud.'

I had already seen a few Scuds from the ground at King Khalid Military City. Initially when Scud warnings came out everyone dived for cover under sandbags, but after a while we'd stand outside and watch the Patriot missiles try to take them out. It was like Bonfire Night. We would see these flashes in the sky, see the Patriot rocket fly up and lots of bits coming down. One that hit above us blew a big piece of Scud off, which crashed into a compound killing seventeen of the US National Guard.

'Dave,' said Chas Dixon, cool as a trout stream, 'I have the Scud launch position marked as north thirty-three degrees, twenty-four point six, east forty-one degrees, fifty point two. Can you confirm?'

'Roger. Confirmed at north thirty-three, twenty-four point six and east forty-one, fifty point two.'

'Alert AWACS. Maybe they can nail the bastards.'

I relayed the information to Jim. Within half a minute he'd squirted it to the AWACS and left them to sort it out. We never heard if we had a confirmed kill. By the time they sent in the F-15 and F-16 Scudbusters we were long gone.

'Ten minutes to drop.' Chas's languid call came through breaking any reverie as the sands hurtled past below us. Everyone acknowledged. I advised the troop commander, who had already heard the call over his intercom. Wes helped the troops sort out all their kit. He untied the Pinkie in preparation for landing, leaving just one strop holding it from bouncing off the fuel tank if there was a heavy landing. Any time on the ground must be cut to minimum. Paul Stains moved down towards the ramp so he could be first off to view the area. In his hands were a set of PNGs (passive night goggles), which were similar to our NVGs. Nowhere near as efficient, but still better than the naked eye.

As we approached the drop-off the aircraft speed slowed down. The whine of the engines and gearboxes changed note as the Chinook decelerated to 100 knots for the approach. I began talking us down on to the ground, paying particular attention to the sand cloud created as the aircraft got slower and lower. The idea was to get the wheels on the ground at the exact moment the sand cloud engulfed the helicopter. Otherwise we would be completely blind.

'Down eighty.' We had eighty feet to go. I leaned right out of the door looking forward, right and aft trying to pick up references to judge height and speed. Looking behind I could see how far the sand cloud had formed.

'Continue down sixty. Cloud starting to form. Down forty. Cloud twenty feet behind us. Down thirty. Down twenty. Cloud ten feet behind us. Down ten, nine, eight, seven, six, five – cloud at the tail now, two, one.'

The helicopter touched down firmly just as the cabin filled with flying sand particles. I caught a mouthful of grit. Outside, the only things visible were two large rings of sparks. John reduced power. The sand began to settle.

'Wheels on,' I called.

'Ramp down,' from Wes.

'Now let's get these blokes out and fuck off sharpish,' said John's voice in my headphones, but I saw little of what was happening until the sand in the cabin settled, mixing with the petrol fumes of the Pinkie as the engines roared into life. The view was similar to looking out to sea on a perfect day with excellent visibility. Dead calm without a ripple in sight. John and Chas checked the position with the GPS (global positioning system) and prepared for takeoff. We had intended to be off the deck in forty seconds. After a minute the Pinkie had not moved.

'Clear at the back, Wes?'

'Stand by,' came the reply. 'The troop commander's not happy about the terrain.'

'Shit.' We stood out like someone dressed as Tarzan at a dinner party when everyone else was in a tuxedo. This thing we were in was a hundred foot long and sixty feet wide, and could be heard for miles. This was not going according to plan. I could feel my heart pumping faster.

I saw Paul Stains gesticulating furiously at the other team members. John and Chas double-checked the fuel to see how long we could hold.

'They've got three minutes then we've got to piss off,' said John in a voice that brooked no argument, 'or else we'll all be walking back.'

Stains grabbed a headset from the side of the cabin. 'Listen, it's like a baby's fucking arse out there. There's no cover at all. We'll be in the shit come daybreak. Any chance of trying twenty miles north of here?'

'Not a chance. We've only got two minutes' fuel left to hang around here before we must go,' snapped John. 'That's as long as some raghead doesn't blast the shit out of us while we're making such a nice target for them.'

'OK, bollocks to it. Let's go home.'

'Ramps up,' called Wes, before the words were out of Stains's mouth.

With that I called 'Clear to go.' The engines wound up, and as the gearbox whine increased the cabin filled up with the sand cloud. John heaved in the collective, the downwash hit the desert floor, and we lurched forward. Airborne again, leaving only the cloud of sand drifting in our wake. Level at 100 feet, 170 knots, homeward bound again

Paul Stains resumed his position behind me. For most of the trip back he did not put on the intercom, just sat there with his head in his hands. I left him to it. He felt he'd let everybody down but in fact he was the bravest man in the aircraft. It really does take balls of steel to make an abort decision and return to face your mates.

Fear gets to people in different ways. Some guys would be fine until they got back to Al Jouf, when their legs would just turn to jelly and their stomachs would rebel. Some, like

Right Rupert, were too determined to be a hero to think about it. He was really pissed off that the mission had been aborted because he'd asked me to get him a piece of Iraqi soil for a souvenir. (I picked him up a piece of rock at Al Jouf and he was thrilled.) Others would let it nag and worry at them like some internal cancer. Me, I just didn't have the imagination to worry about what shit might happen. It either did, and you coped if you could or it didn't, in which case you'd soon stop worrying about the what-ifs.

A couple of my fellow crewmen did not exactly cover themselves with glory. Funnily enough it was the guys who always fancied themselves as hard tough men who cracked worse. Perhaps their personal expectations were greater.

Ben the Dog, the man who wanted to volunteer for a suicide mission, didn't exactly flip but the pressure got to him. He went completely moody. We couldn't speak to him without his snapping back. Then he went very incommunicative when on the aircraft. On the ground, he was completely withdrawn socially and wouldn't speak to anybody.

Jim Tench was really tight with Kev Hardie, a lean, fit and wiry man. One of those odd blokes in the RAF who'd rather run than lie in the sun. A couple of missions into the Gulf War, his Chinook was locked on and fired at by a SAM 7. Jim just lost it, didn't do his job at all, just screamed and shouted, 'There's a missile, there's a missile. It's going to take us out, it's going to take us out.' Training is all very well but when this shit started coming in the pilot needed every bit of information he could get and it wasn't happening. In the cockpit they knew he was shouting from the rear left-hand side so they turned to the left and managed to evade the SAM.

Tench had lost the big picture from fear. He had panicked. Back at base the skipper had a serious crew chat about what they would like to hear rather than what they did hear.

Jim apologised, swore it would never happen again. Others weren't so sure. A character will either do that or he won't and they knew if it happened again he might react in a similar way. It was a serious problem because if they downgraded him, said he was unfit to fly, the Flight would be a crew short. So they had to carry him and pray the Iraqis continued to have a lousy aim.

Every man wonders how he will acquit himself when the bullets start flying. We all want to be, believe we can be, heroes. But deep inside there's a little doubting demon. He makes us wonder whether when the time comes we will do our job – or if we will cut and run.

I found out how I would react soon enough.

CHAPTER 13

LOCK-ON

'Beeeeeeeeep.'

All I could hear was a high-pitched single note. High-pitched means high danger.

I'd heard it before up at the electrical-warfare centre in Spadeadam and it had scared the hell out of me then. But if you hear that high-pitched beep and you're deep over enemy territory the chances are it will be the last thing you ever hear. It is serious shit if this happens – it really is. An irrecoverable situation. You aren't going to live.

What it means is that somebody on the other end of a radar beam is looking straight at you. They press a button and a rocket is going to fly down this beam. And to you.

It had been a perfect night for flying. There was a half-moon overhead and it shone down on the aircraft, casting a shadow on the ground. Using the night-vision goggles we could see brilliantly – it was almost like daylight.

Doesn't that look nice? I thought, looking out of the door. If the aircraft rises, the shadow will recede; if it drops, the shadow will come into us. It's just perfect for judging our height.

We were flying low and fast over the desert, maybe eighty feet above the sand. Time had, as usual, come to a standstill. Suddenly as we came over this shallow rise I heard this sickly sound. No prior warning. Just a never-ending beep.

Depending on the type of radar the Iraqis were using we had between four and eight seconds before the rocket impacted.

The source of the screech was the RWR (Radar Warning Receiver), a tiny screen the size of an ashtray surrounded by a square box, with four little eyes, *one* in each corner. This little gadget picked up any radar aimed at the aircraft, told us who was looking at us and why.

Radar theory is pretty simple. If I am in an airliner coming into Heathrow but still out over the ocean and the air-traffic controller wants to look towards me and check there are no problems he uses a very slow long-range radar, which fires the signal very slowly. On the RWR what I would hear (in the aircraft) from a low-threat, long-range radar like this one, is a low-pitched 'doo' and I'd see a dotted line coming out from the centre of the RWR screen (rather like the spoke of a bicycle wheel) pointing towards the radar's position. As the aircraft comes closer into Heathrow the controller is no longer so bothered about planes further away but he is interested in checking I am on the correct approach path to land. So he uses a different radar, which sweeps a smaller area and the signal will register as a higher-pitched and faster 'zzt zzt'. Once again, the dotted tracer/spoke on the aircraft's RWR shows the direction that the radar signal is coming from.

If an enemy radar is interested in me and nothing else, it can direct a stationary radar signal straight at me, which bounces off the aircraft and straight back to the radar or missile. The radar beam is locked on to the aircraft all the time. The RWR shows a solid line pointing in the direction that the missile will be coming from, complemented by a high-pitched 'Beeeeep'.

This one meant death.

'Lock on.' I screamed it out.

'Ah, yeah, lock on,' confirmed Campbell–Smith from the jump seat. The only piece of information we required from him was the direction of the lock-on so the pilot could start evasion procedures but he burbled on, 'It could be a SAM 8 or a—'

'Which fucking direction?'

'Uh – four o'clock.' I didn't need to see his face to know he was sitting there staring at the screen, white as death, transfixed by the unwavering thick line that had locked on to us. I knew he was going to be as useful as a sack of shit.

'Break right!' I called out desperately. John was ahead of me. He had already reacted and broken right. The sound of the gearboxes decreased as he reduced the power to dampen the heat signature from the engines. We were banked sharply to the right, travelling at 160 knots, descending steeply towards the ground, dropping below sixty feet, turning straight into what is known as a Zero Doppler Notch.

I'll try to explain this strange-sounding phenomenon. Because a radar measures velocities it bounces off you and will sense whether you are coming towards it or going away. However, if you fly across the beam it gets no sense of your speed. The first thing to do is confuse the radar as to which way you are going, to turn until the aircraft is on the beam at a ninety-degree angle and then go backwards and forwards so it has no idea of your speed. That evasive manoeuvre is called the 'Break Lock'. John had already instinctively lowered the collective lever, reducing the power so the aircraft descended. A heat-seeking missile may be lethal but fortunately it's not that smart. It picks up and homes in on the heat from the engines. One way to baffle it is to reduce their power.

'Chaff gone,' from Chicks.

'Flare gone.' That was Wes. I counted. One thousand and one. One thousand and two. My finger twitched above the flare-release button, ready to hit it the moment he forgot the routine. No need.

'Flare gone.' I counted. One thousand and one. One thousand and two.

Wes fired five flares at three-second intervals. Each one emitted such an intense heat for two to three seconds it might be enough to confuse the missile – if it was a heat signature SAM 7. Chicks fired the chaff off to confuse the missile's radar in case it was radar-controlled not hand-launched. The RAF have been using chaff since World War Two – thousands of strips of silver foil are fired to create a giant cloudburst that can blind the radar beam for a few seconds. After confusing everything you piss off out of the way. Well that was the theory, anyway.

This was the practice.

Campbell-Smith offered another piece of the world's most useless advice: 'Go for terrain screening.' A hill or large sand dune would indeed have been perfect to hide behind except that the ground below us was so flat that if it had been covered with green felt it would have made a perfect billiard table. There was nothing to hide behind. Stop clogging up the intercom with useless crap, I wanted to say.

It had all happened in a space of milliseconds. We'd broken right, the chaff was gone, the flare was gone, we were descending to get to cover and banking sharply. Then, I heard the rattle of small-arms fire out the back. It was Gonz lying on the ramp firing his GPMG (general-purpose machine gun) at the bloody flares because he thought they were a threat to the aircraft. Perhaps I should have left him behind at the resupply point.

This had just been a routine mission, aimed at getting water, fuel and ammo to the SAS units who were Scudbusting deep inside Iraq. We didn't resupply just one unit – that was too dangerous. We always did three or four at once. They would rendezvous at a prearranged location in the desert, cordon off the whole area and wait until the middle of the night. When they heard our engines the squad commander flashed a one-letter code on an infrared, covered torch. It was clear as day in the NVGs.

The way the SAS had cordoned off the area defensively was really impressive. We came in at about five feet right over the top of the lookout. The downdraft set off a sand storm that must have blasted the shit out of the poor bugger but he didn't twitch a muscle, his head didn't move. For the few minutes they were being resupplied the SAS were at their most vulnerable. His job was to watch that area and that was what he did. All he was hoping was that we wouldn't land on top of him.

That night we were resupplying three units. There were three palletloads of equipment. Each one included three fifty-gallon drums filled with water, which were bloody heavy. Each load weighed a ton and a half, which is difficult to move in a hurry. We'd learned fast how to improvise. The roller conveyor Wes and I had nicked from the Hercules didn't fit properly. We'd had to bodge the job, wrap string round it and pray it didn't break during the landing. It wasn't pretty but it meant that when we landed we could just slide stuff out on to the ground.

The aircraft was so heavy that we almost got stuck in the sand, but we shoved the pallet out really fast. With one load out the aircraft hopped forward ten feet, like a frog in sludge. It was a bit like having a dump on the run, surrounded by sparks flying up everywhere as the sand hit the blades. By the time we had the last load out, the first pallet, water drums and all, was already loaded on the Pinkies. We were all ready to get the hell out of the rendezvous point (or RV).

CHINOOK!

One of the major problems the blokes had out there was the cold. I'd never been so cold in an aircraft before, horizontal snow would fly in through the doors so I flew with seven layers of clothes on. The troops on the ground who thought they were prepared for desert conditions were almost freezing to death. The previous day Gonz had gone out to the local market where he'd bought a load of goat-haired furry coats to give to the blokes. They were ugly, they stank, but they were warm.

We'd unloaded everything. I was ready to lift when I saw that Gonz had disappeared. We needed a certain amount of fuel to get back to our base and we only ever had reserves for ten minutes over that. That meant we could not stay at our target rendezvous for longer than ten minutes. We'd been here six already. Our safety margin was being shaved every second. And now I couldn't find Gonz anywhere.

'Where the fuck's the QM?' I snapped at an SAS corporal. 'I'll give him another minute. If he's not here we leave without him.'

Someone went and got him in a real hurry – I'm sure the SAS blokes didn't want Gonz left behind to help on their next Scudbusting exploit. He ran back and explained he'd been busy getting his blokes to sign for the coats. I suppose he thought that a bit of red tape would be a morale boost for the chaps. Remind them they hadn't been forgotten.

I never did get to know Gonz's real name. He was a human pit bull terrier, as wide as he was tall, and the regiment's SQMS out in the Gulf – the man in charge of getting them the kit they needed. So long as they signed for it first. But Gonz was no desk jockey, he'd seen it all.

Now he was lying in the back of a Chinook blasting away at our own flares thinking he was shooting down Iraqi SAM 7s, probably wondering why he didn't stay on the ground. It's much easier to down missiles if they aren't in the air coming straight at you.

My job was simple. To look out at the area of the lock-on and watch for the incoming missile. Stay cool, keep calm, wait for visual contact and keep the skipper informed. Otherwise keep my mouth shut.

Sometimes, thank God, a sixth sense saves you. Something didn't seem right to me, once again time started to slow right down. I looked down at the ground. I couldn't see the crisp moon shadow of the helicopter I had been admiring a few minutes before.

Where the fuck was that shadow? Alarm bells sounded in my mind. I couldn't see the shadow because we were already in it. Dropping down into it at 150 knots.

We'd been somewhere between fifty and eighty feet off the floor when the enemy radar locked on. The blades are sixty feet in diameter, so if you tip the helicopter at a sharp angle the tips of the blades get closer to the ground. I looked up and because the aircraft was banked over and descending the blades were creating vortices which were throwing up sand as they got close to the desert floor. The blade behind was hitting the particles, which were being thrown up, causing the sparking effect. The last time I'd seen similar sparks we'd been on the ground – but we were not on the ground. We shouldn't be anywhere near the fucking ground.

'Up! Up! Up!'

I didn't think, just shouted.

The helicopter responded immediately to my call. John knew from my voice we were in a deadly position. He applied maximum power, rolled level and climbed.

'Five feet, ten, thirty.' That was Chicks calling the heights from the radio altimeter without any emotion – until we were clear. 'Forty, fifty – fuck, that was close.' Just as I called the climb Chicks had seen that we were five feet above the ground in a banked turn dropping fast. If I had just been looking out for the missile we would have been wiped out for sure. If I'd paused a fraction of a second longer before screaming, the tip of the blade would have caught the ground and the impact would have sent the twenty-three-ton helicopter flipping into the sand.

But we weren't out of the shit. Power on, John took us above forty feet. 'Beeeeep.'

Locked on again.

'Chaff gone.'

'Flare gone.' One thousand and one. One thousand and two. If you could count you were still alive.

'Flare gone.'

We had to transit for forty miles, never more than thirty feet above the ground, travelling flat out at 160 knots. We hugged that terrain like a frightened mouse knowing there was a hungry cat out there waiting to pounce. Every time we popped our head above forty feet we got locked on again. On the third lock-on Chicks fired only half a load of chaff. No more left. Nothing we could do except to keep firing the flares. Keep counting. Keep praying.

The routine and the physical responses that followed never got any easier. First that high-pitched 'beeeeep' screaming in my ears. Then the black hole opening in my stomach, muscles tensing like steel across my shoulders. Bracing myself for an impact that never came while the aircraft dropped like a rock back into silence. My robot head scanning from side to side, willing myself to see my death before it had a chance to see me. At the end of each rotation my chin dropping down as my eyes scanned for moon shadows. It took us twenty minutes to get out of range of the radar but it seemed to last ten hours. It felt as if we were crawling, not flying, home.

We should have been taken out. It must have been down to the people operating the radar. It was simply due to bad training that they didn't get us.

From the moment I heard that first lock-on I didn't feel frightened, not even during the cat-and-mouse, wadi-skimming, camel-hump-high skirmish that followed. But when we got back to Al Jouf the reality seeped in, my stomach felt like jelly, the blood drained away from every extremity. We all realised how close we had come to getting it. Even Gonz seemed pretty pleased.

We were bloody lucky we didn't lose it out there. Of course some of it was good judgment. The intensive training we'd been through had meshed us together so we were like four heads on one body. But the main reason was luck. There were no big wires or overhead cables out there in the Iraqi desert. If there had been we'd have been taken out loads of times.

CHAPTER 14

KUWAIT AT LAST

Three nights after we'd survived the lock-on, Whooper Four One was back in Iraq. I was scanning the horizon, an hour into the flight 100 miles over the border heading for another resupply drop when the SAS comms bloke tapped me on the shoulder.

'Farmhouse,' he mouthed. I stared back at him blankly.

'Codeword Farmhouse,' he yelled. The penny dropped, or rather hit the floor, with a tremendous crash. The AWACS had sent us a coded message down through the satellite comms system. They would never risk compromising our position unless it was serious.

'Farmhouse, codeword Farmhouse,' I repeated over the intercom. No reply. I tried again. Nothing. Except a succession of howling feedback and squeals. Shit. Water, snow or something had got into the system. We had to abort this mission right now and the intercom didn't work.

I disconnected and grabbed Campbell-Smith by the shoulder. He had his eyes glued on the RWR. These days he watched it like a hawk.

'Codeword Farmhouse. Tell John we've got to turn back immediately.'

'I can't tell him that,' he said. 'We're in Iraqi territory.' What did he want? A medal for landing in Iraqi territory? I ripped his intercom out and just as I plugged in, I heard John say, 'I don't give a fuck, I want Dave McMullon on intercom now.'

'I'm on, I'm on. Message is Farmhouse. Repeat, Farmhouse. Return to base immediately.'

When we got back we discovered that by accident the American Ops commander had wandered in to see our chaps. On our map Ops had all the various SAM sites that could be potential threats marked out. 'Oh,' he said casually. 'You haven't got the SAM 8 site our satellites picked up yesterday.' It was less than a mile beyond our drop point. A blind Bedouin with a hearing aid could have picked us up at that range. A SAM 8 would have spread tiny bits of us over several square miles of desert and taken out a dozen SAS for good measure. The balls went into motion double quick and the message was relayed down to us to turn back.

Returning southbound we passed over the Iraqi border trenches. The policy was never to fire at anyone if you were going into enemy territory because it gave your position away. That way they knew which direction you were travelling. They could hear you but it is difficult to judge where a Chinook is going just by the sound.

On the way back it didn't really matter so much. Particularly if you were extremely pissed off.

Normal calls were coming in. 'We've got movement at seven o'clock,' called Wes.

About five miles north of the border there were all these long slit trenches. I could see movement, shapes scurrying in the darkness about 400 metres from us. Through the goggles

I saw three ragheads pointing something at us. Then I saw muzzle flashes. What it was I had no idea. They weren't loaded with tracer so there was nothing coming towards us I could fix on. But they were shooting at us. I reasoned that one of them might have a SAM 7. After the last time I wasn't going to wait to find out, or rely on the ALQ157 doing its job.

'We're being fired at. Two o'clock. Returning fire.' I just opened up with the minigun. Let rip.

The principle was to acquire your target with the lower (2,000 rounds per minute) rate of fire and once on target engage the higher rate of fire (4,000 r.p.m.). The ammunition belt was loaded with 1 in 17 tracer (in every seventeen bullets there was one tracer round). In the black desert night it looked like a solid beam of light. One that destroyed anything it touched. After pressing the high-rate button the first impression I felt was this complete, awesome, destructive power. The sound frequency was similar to a bee or a wasp but no insect swarm can ever be as loud as 100 rifles being fired simultaneously.

Through the handles I felt not the chattering and bucking you get from a machine gun but a vibration, a tingling. All the pilots heard was a faint crackling, as if a seatbelt clip had been left outside and was rattling along the fuselage. Two of the Iraqis were hurled against the back of the trench as if they'd been punched by a giant invisible fist. It didn't look as if they were diving for cover. The other crumpled, dropped down into the dirt, and I didn't see what happened to him. I knew I'd hit all three of them. I don't know if I killed them or not. I hope I did.

When I stopped firing the barrels kept rotating for a few seconds, whining and clattering in their frustration. Wisps of cigar smoke drifted gently away from their tips. As if for good luck I touched the sides of the turning barrels. The leather fingertips on my flying gloves smouldered from the heat. The smell of cordite filled the cabin. As if someone had set off a firework. It smelled better than aviation fuel.

I had to fill in a contact report after I came back in. The flight commander had no problems with that. The ground crew did. A formal complaint was put in by one of the chief engineers who said the crew of Whooper Four One had left the aircraft with empty shell cases in and hadn't cleaned them out. We had been behind enemy lines for three hours, dodging under radar, being fired at and firing back. We had arrived back just before dawn. We were knackered and here was this prat complaining about a few shell cases!

The boss had a very one-sided conversation with him.

Stan, the chief engineer, was a tall chap, maybe six foot two, skinny with thick glasses and an attitude to match. He was about forty-five and had been in the RAF since the year dot – one of those career sergeants who didn't like seeing aircrew come in and get their rank within fourteen weeks. He came from somewhere in the Midlands and spoke in a flat Brummie accent that made it difficult to tell if he was telling a joke or just being a miserable bastard.

By this stage there was a lot of resentment building up between the ground and air crews. It had been simmering away for weeks. Years probably.

Basically most ground crew see aircrew as going off, getting pissed, shagging lots of girls, flying around, waving out of the window, coming back home in time for tea and medals. Usually they put up with it but, now that they were stewing in the heat of Al Jouf with nowhere to go, and nothing to do when they got there, it got worse. By the end all the ground crew could see was them working hard all day while we were lying around like lazy bastards, soaking up the sun, and then pissing off at night before coming back and complaining that everything was broken and needed to be fixed.

There is an element of senior ground crew that will always think the aircrew are a bunch of wankers. They don't usually see the skills and training required. And they will pass it down to their crew. You will never see a chief technician calling a pilot by his first name, though generally in the RAF you get more out of a person by calling him by his first name. (The exception is the regular army blokes: once you do that they start to relax too much so you have to exert your authority.) I couldn't blame the other lads who worked for Stan: you can't be too much of a rebel against your boss.

I thought Stan asked for it anyway. First he used to draw cartoons of all the aircrew sunning themselves while the ground crew worked all day. We all laughed. Then he started pushing it too far, kept saying things like 'You boys, well your chances are reducing every time you go out. Soon there'll be one helicopter less to service.' OK it started as a joke, but we were the ones risking our necks every night. The ones who'd been out looking for Bravo Two Zero, the ones who knew what it would be like to crash in Iraq. When you have been fired at for real those jokes aren't quite so funny any more.

Especially when we were ordered to do a border patrol. In daylight. In a huge slow Chinook that was very risky. Chas asked drily if we should paint a large target on either side of the aircraft. I decided to even the odds a bit. I mentioned to some of the SAS blokes that we were doing a border run and would some of them like to give us some support? When I pulled up at the aircraft there was a four-ton truck parked at the back. All the windows had been taken out, sandbags were in and there was a GPMG hanging out of every single window. The Chinook looked like HMS Victory with rotors. The whole floor was covered with ammo cases and if one single round had come in there they'd have blown us to pieces.

We did the patrol, never saw a bloody thing and the natives at the back started to get very restless. Eventually there came the requests over the intercom: 'Permission to test our guns captain.'

'Go on, then.' Christ, the noise. One person firing a gun on an aircraft can rattle the fillings in your teeth. Ten machine guns blasting off at once is like someone setting off a string of firecrackers inside your skull.

On another mission, just after the Falklands War, we had to take a mass of gear on a resupply. The helicopter was carrying nearly twelve tons of cargo, three and a half tons above its maximum weight. 'We can't get airborne with this,' I told the skipper. 'We're not on Mount Kent.' Because of the winds down in the Falklands, which helped to create extra lift, one of the Chinooks there was regularly lifting sixteen to seventeen tons (eight or nine tons over maximum weight). As a result the actual aircraft fuselage was bent and the gap between the front and rear rotor mountings was eight inches less than on others. To travel straight and level you would have to fly it slightly wing down.

The wing commander was not exactly sympathetic. He told John, 'I didn't ask you how fucking heavy you were, I asked you if you were going to be on target.' Even using maximum power the Chinook couldn't hover so it had to do a running takeoff like a plane. I was hanging out the front door watching the entire fuselage crinkling as the respective torques from the twin blades twisted against each other trying to hold the load in the air. The next few hours were extremely hairy. If the engines lost much power we would plummet to the ground. We were very vulnerable – not far off what's known as maximum continuous power just to keep the thing in the air. God knows what would have happened if we'd got locked on. If it was either a training or a nonoperational flight we wouldn't have done it.

Regulations get torn up in wartime. We knew that but the wing commander's attitude pissed us off. Steve French would at least have listened and suggested something helpful like 'I suggest you put more power on.' We could see he was fed up with having his toes trodden on by the wing commander who had appeared suddenly at Al Jouf.

Kim Ingles was OC of both 7 Squadron and the SF Flight but, because the squadron had teamed up with the Germany Squadron 18 and they were busy transporting ammunition behind the border, and with logistics and troop movements, he wasn't going to add to his medal collection. But if there was a nice job going he took it. There was one trip to Egypt to drop something off. A possible night out from the war for a crew who were risking their lives every day. So the wing commander took it.

Technically Ingles couldn't be in charge as we were under the direct command of the DSF. He had an input to the planning meetings but the main man on the job was still Steve French. Steve had just been promoted to squadron leader and was heavily involved in training and flying. In contrast he was a very good pilot and flight commander. He led from the front, flew the first mission behind enemy lines, dropped off Bravo Two Zero. Our only problem was if he got taken out.

During the war the SF Flight flew approximately twenty-five missions behind enemy lines. On average we'd fly a couple of resupply missions a week. Not all were routine. At one afternoon briefing the SAS ops officer, a WO2, briefed us that we were going to resupply with the usual water, food and ammunition. The only addition was that we had 'a NAAFI number to collect'.

'Collect a what?' asked John. Overseas a serviceman can sign against his NAAFI number like a credit card and will be billed later. But there wasn't much to buy in Iraq.

'One of our guys has been killed,' said the WO2. 'They've still got the body and we need it exfilled.' (That's military speak for 'exfiltrated', or taken out.) The dead corporal had been riding a motorbike during an attack on a Scud site. During the withdrawal he took three hits and was killed instantly. The team on the ground couldn't bury him for fear of leaving traces, and carrying his kit was slowing them down.

After we had offloaded the supplies four SAS troopers leaped on the ramp carrying a full Arctic sleeping bag, zipped all the way up so we couldn't see the body's face, and placed it on the floor by Wes's feet. A fifth man came on and dumped a large Bergen and a rubbish bag next to the body. Not one of them showed any emotion – they couldn't afford to. Wes strapped the body down.

'Why are you doing that?' I asked.

'I don't want the fucking thing getting up and walking around during the flight.'

When we returned to Al Jouf we landed on the other side of the airfield by the operations building, right next to a Hercules waiting there with engines running. As we lowered the ramp four SAS blokes ran in, picked up the body and a Bergen, and ran back to the Hercules. Wes was just about to raise the ramp when he shouted, 'The bastards have taken my kit.' He grabbed the dead man's Bergen, sprinted across the tarmac to the Hercules just as its ramp was rising, and managed to get the crew's attention.

One of the SAS desert teams had problems with its troop leader. Ops weren't happy with the officer, who kept questioning his orders, but on the ground the situation was worse. Messages were passed back by satellite to the effect that if he was going to stay in Iraq he too might be coming

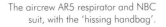

The aircrew AR5 respirator and NBC suit, with the 'hissing handbag'.

The night vision goggles that give you a two dimensional green and black world.

An American Chinook in Saudi. It hit the ground during a training exercise. This is what our Chinook would have looked like if I had not called 'Up, Up, Up'.

A Christmas Day formation flight in the Falklands.

Chinooks in line astern formation preparing for landing.

It's all work:
me monitoring the refuel with
engines and rotors still turning.

The Chinook carries a 'rain
maker'. The bucket contains
about 800 gallons of water and
is used to help put out fires, or
alternatively empty it over the
Phantom Squadron's crew room
in the Falklands.

The Chinook lifting an ISO-container
similar to the one that Royal Green
Jackets used as transport from the
mountain sites in the Falklands.

Another five tons of supplies
being delivered to a Falklands'
hillsite.

An abandoned car on the A74 with the burning crater to the left.

Part of the wreckage lies on the road with burning homes in the background.

A burning car on the A74 near where the Jumbo crashed.

The devastation caused to Lockerbie and its surrounding area by the crash of the Pan Am Flight 103 on 21 December 1988.

Me taking the helicopter down to the deck of HMS *Ark Royal* prior to our flight into Morocco on exercise transit.

Slowly accelerating away from the deck of a ship.

Note the effect of the down wash from the Chinook. This would cause the whole ship to rotate when hovering above it.

The Mull of Kintyre crash site of ZD 576.

The dead of ZD 576 are remembered.

All training over. I wonder what lies ahead?

ATR 72, one of the aeroplanes I fly today.

home in a bag – but that the fatal wound might not come from an Iraqi bullet. It was decided that he be replaced by a senior NCO. The changeover was also arranged to coincide with a resupply. The lieutenant didn't say much on the flight back to Al Jouf.

By the end of February it was clear that the main thrust of the SF war was over. Now we had to concentrate on taking Kuwait and the airport. Our mission was to go up and infil (infiltrate) the SBS into the British Embassy by way of Kuwait International Airport, where we were to set up a base. It was supposed to be timed with the American forces pushing the Iraqis out. The boss gave us our orders and as we came out of the briefing Stan, the chiefy, was there crowing again, 'You boys are for it now. We won't be seeing some of these faces again.'

The boss turned to him, and said very loudly and clearly, 'Oh, Chief, it looks like we'll be there for at least four days so I want an engineering team with us. I want you and three others to come.' Stan went white. He was very quiet sitting in the aircraft. Especially as we got closer to Kuwait.

Coming into Kuwait was horrendous. The Iraqis had set fire to all the oil wells. Whatever pollution was going that day we got it. The oil-well fires were billowing up thick, black, acrid smoke. We had zero visibility – and it stank. The heat from the ground was so immense I had to close the door to prevent overheating. The paint was bubbling on the outside of the aircraft. There was no radio communication with the ground troops and, since it was pitch-black, we couldn't maintain any visual contact.

As we flew overhead the Iraqi soldiers would run out and fire their guns in the air. You could see the tracer coming straight up but it was hundreds of yards away so I felt quite safe. However, there are some things I cannot resist. I turned to the chief and showed it to him. 'Look at that, Chiefy. They're firing at us.' He was petrified. I'm sure I smelled shit.

We circled round Kuwait International Airport, landed one behind the other, line astern, still in pitch-black darkness. I could see movement coming from the bushes. My thumb was twitching over the trigger on the minigun. Were they friendly? Do I push the button or don't I? Then the boss, whose ring was obviously twitching big time, came up with a classic question.

'Anybody got any ideas?'

A voice came over the radio, 'Yeah, let's fuck off.'

'Agreed. Lifting.'

We took off sharpish. The boss didn't need any encouragement.

A little later we re-established comms and discovered that they were our troops. So it was a good thing I hadn't hosed them down. We landed a bit further upfield and as we touched down I thought a nuclear explosion had gone off. The shock and pressure on my chest was incredible. An Iraqi Frog missile, which has a bigger warhead than a Scud, had landed about a mile away.

The airfield was a real mess. Half of the runway was unusable, studded with bomb craters. A British Airways Jumbo had been blown up and lay, like an eviscerated mammoth, across the tarmac. The others took photos. I didn't. It reminded me of Lockerbie.

It was still a very sensitive time. We weren't sure whether the enemy had been pushed back all the way. The SBS were worried that there might be some Iraqis lurking round the airfield perimeter so we were warned to be on our guard and to keep our weapons ready at all time. Just after nightfall Campbell-Smith decided it would be a good idea to take a photo of a helicopter sitting on the pan in the pitch-black.

He used a cheap camera with a built-in flash. He stood in the middle of the tarmac and suddenly there was this bright flash you could see for miles.

Using a flash gun in such a hostile environment – especially with no warning – sent everybody diving for cover. I thought for a moment he would get blown away. An SBS SC2 (swimmer/canoeist second-class – equivalent to corporal) rushed up, tackled him to the ground and then hurled spectacular abuse at his face. He did say 'sir' at the end. I don't think he meant it.

Later that night Wes and I were chatting with Rex, an SBS SC1 (equivalent to sergeant) and troop leader. Like all former Royal Marines he would fanatically sort and resort his kit before every mission, clean every bullet if he had a chance.

'You know something, Dave?' he said, squinting at me down the barrel of his Browning 9mm automatic. It was cleaner than Right Rupert's toecaps but he pulled another oily rag through it. Just in case. 'We were really worried about you lot before the balloon went up. Maybe the Hereford boys weren't but then everybody knows they haven't got the imagination. Training exercises are all very well but we'd never used you in anger before. The lads were relying on you and you came up with the goods. You've proved your worth now.' He grinned. 'In future, if we ditch together we won't have to kill you.'

Nothing, I thought to myself, bonds blokes together faster than having a few bits of lead thrown at them. The SF Flight had just been paid a hell of a compliment. Wes, however, had a somewhat different agenda.

'Does not killing us apply to all the crew?' he asked, with an absolutely straight face.

'What do you mean?' asked a puzzled Rex.

'Well, you know that officer who likes to set off camera

flashes in the middle of a warzone ...'

'There's always exceptions,' said Rex thoughtfully, slapping a full magazine into the butt of his Browning. I believe they were both joking. Well I think so.

The rest of the night was uneventful, though nobody slept much. We had four Chinooks up at Kuwait International Airport but only two were going to be used on the Embassy drop. Instead we had two Navy Sea Kings doing smaller drops on surrounding buildings to give us sniper cover.

It was very poor visibility – choking, acrid oil clouds – so we flew up the coast a while. Holding, waiting for the 'go' command to come over the satellite comm link. This was a daylight op with less perceived danger and we had fifteen of them, all armed to the teeth with tons of special gear. It was difficult holding in formation because the helicopters flew at different speeds. We couldn't relax. The message came through to us, 'Tell the guys not to kick the doors in. Somebody will have the key.' I passed the message to them. It was all intended as a good bit of publicity, a PR thing for the TV cameras.

We were going to fast-rope these blokes down but they also had other requirements and equipment, ladders, big Bergens full of explosives, all the standard kit. The access we had from the Chinook was the aft ramp – two ropes from that; we'd done more in the past but they tend to hit each other – the winch from the front door and the centre hatch. The problem was we had lots of blokes to get down and only two crewmen, Wes and me, to monitor it. Campbell-Smith had got the idea that he would be the third crewman doing the centre hole, which I wasn't happy with but John had said, OK. Anything to get the twat out the jump seat.

I gave him the briefing. 'The bloke will go down first and you just have to guide the stuff down to him on the roof,' I said. 'Get your intercom lead out of the way behind the soundproofing and plugged into this point here.'

'No,' he said, 'I'd prefer it down here.'

'No, you need to have the bloody lead over there or you'll be shagged.'

'I'm happy with this,' he insisted. 'I've done a dry run on the ground.'

Stuff you then, I thought to myself. After all, he was an officer.

We came over the target. Height position was good. We were in the hover. I gave the call: 'Five, four, three, two, one. Go!'

One minute we had fifteen blokes in the cabin. They kicked the ropes out, they whizzed down the ropes. All gone. I pushed their gear out of my door.

'Front rope clear.'

'Aft ropes clear,' called Wes.

We were both waiting for the third call of 'centre rope clear'. Nothing. I looked out and there was a set of ladders jammed halfway out the centre hatch. What had that stupid bastard done this time?

Campbell-Smith's intercom lead – which he had positioned himself – had wrapped around the abseil rope and jammed into the carabiner. The gear was stuck.

'I'll be all right in a minute,' flustered Campbell-Smith. Then he unplugged himself from the intercom but because he had wrapped it round the carabiner some of the wires had been cut and suddenly there was this howling loud squeal coming through all our helmets. All the pilots could hear was this squeal. They didn't know whether the blokes were down on the roof or wrapped around a wire halfway down. They couldn't see anything.

All I heard was John shouting, 'Get fucking Smith off the intercom now!' I stepped across, ignored Campbell-Smith struggling with his intercom lead, and pulled a T-pin. The ladders and ropes crashed straight down. Unfortunately he didn't go with them – it just disconnected his cord. He could have done that himself but he'd got flustered. John was absolutely furious with him. 'What was this stupid bastard doing?'

'What I briefed him not to.'

'Right, that's it.' (When we got back to the airfield he gave him a private roasting, officer to officer. I didn't hear the bollocking but I'd like to have done. OK, it was near the end of the war and it wasn't a hostile situation but it could have been. You can't afford to make mistakes like that in our job.)

Down on the ground the SBS promptly blew the doors down. When the key turned up the doors were already open – but minus their hinges. 'You can't be too careful – not with an ambassador,' Rex told me later. 'Besides, we had all this gear and it seemed a shame not to use it.'

Then we zipped back to Kuwait International Airport, spent ten minutes on the ground, picked up the ambassador. He was wearing this cream suit and I was half hoping there'd be a puddle of hydraulic fluid on the jump seat. There usually was. We took him back to the Embassy, except this time we landed just outside where the front door used to be and parked up.

Crowds and crowds of people came running over. Kuwaitis with their flags, waving and cheering: 'You are gods.' 'Brilliants!' 'We love you.' This businessman came over and started shaking my hand like he wanted to pull it off, saying, 'You are fantastic. Anything you want of mine is yours.' There was this beautiful black Mercedes saloon sitting there so I said – as a joke – 'I'll have the Mercedes.'

'It is yours,' he said and he started pushing the keys at me.

'I can't take it,' I protested.

'No it is a gift from me,' he insisted. I was sorely tempted, I can tell you. It was a beautiful car, but we had bloody long-range fuel tanks on board, so I couldn't get it in the back. I still wonder if there was any way I could have got it home.

Following the successful insertion of the ambassador into his embassy, we were then required to fly over Kuwait City dangling the Kuwaiti flag and the Union Jack under the helicopter. Our orders were to put a large Kuwaiti flag on to a long strop and a smaller Union Jack on a shorter strop. I acknowledged the order and promptly found the smallest Kuwaiti flag I could and attached it to the shortest strop, then found the largest Union Jack I could and attached it to the longest strop I could find. Nothing against Kuwait, but if I was having anything to do with it – and I was – the Union Jack was going to take pride of place.

A few days later we were going home for real, leaving somebody else to clear up the mess the Iraqis had made of Kuwait City. We were heading back to do the clear-up southbound from Kuwait into King Khalid Military City, flying down the motorway in formation. In daylight for a change. Suddenly I heard the flight commander saying, 'I'm only going to get one chance to do this boys.' The Chinook behind us peeled off, went down over the southbound carriageway until he was flying three feet off the tarmac.

Imagine. There was a Saudi driver driving happily along, minding his own business, secure in the knowledge that his country was safe from the Iraqis, heading home for tea and prayers. Suddenly all he could hear was this thundering noise and a bloody great Chinook came overhead, two feet from his windscreen. There sitting on the ramp with his legs dangling above the bonnet, waving his arms, screaming abuse, was Kev Hardie, enjoying every moment of it. I wondered if the car driver had shit himself – as it was, cars were careering off the side of the motorway. Steve French did it for five minutes, roaring with laughter all the way. I was begging John to join in the fun and have a go himself, but he wouldn't.

Maybe he'd had enough excitement for one war.

CHAPTER 15

POST-GULF DISORDER

With the war over everyone was desperate to get back to Britain as soon as possible. I had more reasons than most. While I might have escaped Saddam Hussein unscathed, my home back in Odiham had not. It had been destroyed.

The first I had heard of it had been two weeks before when Steve French, the flight commander, had called me over and said, 'Dave, I don't know what's been going on back home, but I think you'd better see this.' Then he handed me a letter from Danny Sharp, who'd been left behind at Odiham as cover in case of any domestic CT operations. It was full of the usual drivel, gossip and 'Wish I was with you' remarks, but then there was this ominous remark, 'Obviously, by now Dave will know about his house' – and nothing else.

'What the fuck is going on?' I yelled and stomped off to see the wing commander. He was his usual sympathetic self, telling me, 'Oh yes we knew all about that, but it was decided not to tell you.' Doubtless it was something to do with upsetting my morale. It took me about two days, with the time difference and 'communications problems', to cajole, threaten and blackmail a call to Odiham. I finally got through to Danny who casually told me, 'Oh, didn't you know? Your house has been destroyed.'

'Does Jill know?'

'Oh yes, she was down here a few weeks ago to inspect the damage. Didn't she tell you?' I could hear him giggling. Then after a muffled conversation with someone else in the room he came back on: 'Rick says she told the housing people that they weren't to tell you about it under any circumstances. She said something about you having enough to worry about being in the Gulf. Sorry.' The call ended in a crackle of static – unless it was Rick Cook and Danny pissing themselves laughing.

Next I called Jill, who was livid that I'd found out despite her instructions. Then she told me they'd tried to blame her for the accident. That put me in such a foul mood that for days afterwards even the Bedouins' camels gave me a wide berth.

After I'd left for the Gulf Jill had decided she didn't want to spend Christmas alone in married quarters with an eight-month-old baby. She'd headed off to stay with her mum up near Newcastle until my return. Being a practical girl, before she left she rang the housing people, who told her which taps to turn off. Unfortunately they forgot to tell her about one up in the loft. It was a cold winter and, naturally, the pipe froze, then it burst, and for ten weeks there was water pouring out into the loft. The bedroom and front-room ceilings had collapsed and had written off every piece of furniture we had. Tables, pictures, paintings, the TV and video. It was a semi-detached house and the only reason we found out was that the neighbour had damp patches on the wall and couldn't get rid of them. Eventually they broke open the door of our house. Apparently it was like Inspector Clouseau opening the shower. A torrent of water swept out through the front door taking half our belongings with it.

Jill drove the 200 miles back down to Odiham to sort out what was left. The place was such a wreck she knew we would have to move when I finally came back. She told them they couldn't contact me but it just goes to show that there are no secrets in the armed forces.

Despite all the promises that we'd be going home in a few days it took four weeks. Originally we were going to fly the aircraft home but instead we flew them down to the docks in the UAE, where the engineers dismantled them and put them on a ship. On the way down we stopped off at our old holiday camp in Victa, to hand in all the ammo.

We were pleased to get rid of the guns because it meant we didn't have to look after them any more. Usually you hand back a few rounds at a time but this time they had a huge bucket into which we just emptied our pockets. Some of the guys took big Iraqi shell cases – used ones! – and a few smuggled AK47s home but, as I'm not anoracked up on guns, I couldn't be bothered.

We had to stop off in Cyprus on the way back, which was really odd. For the majority of the war we had been wearing our standard olive-green flying suits – great camouflage on the desert, I don't think – and we'd waited well into hostilities before we got any desert kit. That never fitted anyway. Definitely one size fits all – from McMullons to midgets. Yet there on the base in Cyprus every single man and his bloody dog was strutting around wearing the most up-to-date Gucci desert warfare kit and a Gulf Medal badge. We joked that one of the powers that he had worked out was that if a Scud had gone off course and ricocheted off a satellite perhaps one hair on the fanny of the flea resting on its tail fin might have grazed the edge of Cyprus. Therefore everybody in Cyprus was in the warzone and entitled to all our kit – and a medal. Fair enough. But what pissed us off was that we weren't made to feel welcome. In the messes they all had this what-are-you-doing-here? attitude.

Eventually we got on a flight that was supposed to land at Lyneham but the whole of the south of the UK was fogged out, so we diverted up to Prestwick. We landed in the early hours of 3 April. It was wet and foggy and all I could think about was how nice it was to feel the cold British weather. Most of the blokes headed for a hotel but I just wanted to get home. Julian Mason and I jumped in a taxi to Newcastle, where he got a train south, and I went on to my parents' house. I arrived at six in the morning, dirty, unshaven, dressed in a flying suit with sand still stuck in every available zip and cranny. My father stumbled down to the door in his dressing gown.

My first words were, 'Hi, Dad. Have you got a tenner for the cab driver?'

Then I nicked my mum's car and hurtled down the motorway to see Jill, who was fifty miles away. Not being one for romantic surprises – like arriving and finding she'd gone out for the day – I asked my mother to phone and warn her I was on my way. In the movies when you see somebody again after such a long time it's all hugs and passion but in reality it's different. Although we were really happy to be together again we'd forgotten how we were with each other. She'd had to adjust her life to living by herself for four months while I'd had to adjust mine to killing ragheads. Suddenly we had to share again, and we were like lions circling the same camp site, eyeing each other up warily.

It took a day or two to relax with each other. Andrew helped. He didn't really recognise me but realised he was supposed to like me so he didn't cry. We had a week off, then headed back down south to sort the house out. I was worried that the housing people would decide that, since I was already used to living in a tent, we could sleep in the garden.

Two weeks later, I was back out in the Middle East. Feeding the Kurds in southern Turkey. It was a squadron duty but I was allowed out for only three days to do an aircraft changeover. I was one of the lucky ones.

When I got there I discovered I'd been taken in by all the hype. The TV crews had managed to find some dwindling old bugger in the corner somewhere and shown how starving he was. From what I saw the Kurds were generally better clothed, better housed and better fed than we were. I saw families throw out the rations we had to eat: they wouldn't touch them because they knew fresh food was coming. I saw a man with a torn jacket throw it away. Then he went to the nearest parcel, ripped it open and helped himself to a replacement.

On my first mission we had to go straight back into a hover as dozens of Kurds all tried to scramble on to the ramp. Just as we were transiting away they threw a package on board and ran away. It was a baby girl, no more than seven months old, wrapped in strips of grey rag and bawling her head off. We gave her back rather more gently. After that we'd stay in the hover at five to ten feet up and throw the boxes out the back. Some of the dumber Kurds used to hang on to the ramp and we'd have to stamp on their fingers or drop the box on their heads.

Helping the Kurds wasn't very popular with the Turks. Our base in Turkey was right next to a practice bombing range. They didn't close it down. We'd work all day and then try to sleep but because the bombing range was active there would be explosions rattling the sides of the tent all night. Dummy bombs are still bloody loud. Loads of aircrew went down with dysentery. They were living in shit, picking up every bug there was, sleeping and shitting at the same time, losing three stone in a month and a half. The only way to get away from the crap on the ground was to fly. I'd rather have been back out in the Gulf again, flying missions behind enemy lines.

The group captain in charge – who was staying in reasonable messing at another base – came over and was told by the pilots, 'Listen, we're flying ten hours a day, getting no sleep, the food is crap, we've got the runs. It's a flight-safety hazard. What are you going to do about it?'

He was a fast-jet man so his response was simple, if predictable. 'You're helicopter crews. Just fucking get on with it.'

When I left Turkey I left any post-Gulf euphoria behind in the mountains of Anatolia. I felt even flatter than I had after Lockerbie. Now that I had my commercial pilot's licence and my flying-instructor's rating, I just wanted to get the hell on with my life. The SF Flight were soon back into the routine of CT exercises, simulated oil-rig and car-ferry hijacks, but the thrill had gone.

In August I was posted to Northern Ireland for eight weeks. It was the next real thing to being in the Gulf. There was a threat there: every time you flew the aircraft had to be armed with flares and there were various tactical ways of flying.

The last time I'd been stationed over the water was back in 1986. That was a very sensitive time, just after a coachload of troops had been blown up going on leave. Most of them were killed and feelings were running high. To avoid endangering more lives it was decided that all troop movements should be made by Chinook. On the way over two aircraft deployed to Pontrailis and picked up some SAS there. En route the pilots were a bit concerned about a mechanical problem.

We decided that if we had to go down we'd make sure we had another aircraft with us and we'd try to land away from any inhabited buildings. Then this SAS bloke who'd been sitting in the jump seat all the way over suddenly piped up. 'What the fuck are you on about? We've got more weapons and ammunition in the back than the bloody *Bismarck* carried. If we go down nobody in the whole bloody world will come near us. More's the pity. We'd give those bastards a real surprise. If you have to go down in a field make a brew and just relax. We'd love to have somebody try.'

The first thing we learned if we were looking for anything was not to say 'contact'. That meant you were being fired at. Use that term on a military net in Northern Ireland and there will be a swarm of helicopters overhead in minutes. They didn't have a permanent Chinook presence in Northern Ireland then – now there is at least one aircraft and two and a half crews. Most of the helicopter landing sites were secure with huge walls round them, but they were built for the Wessexes and Pumas, way too small for the Chinook. When we landed a cordon of troops would come out and secure the area. A circle of guns pointing out looked like a highly dangerous hedgehog.

The danger was that if you were transiting back and forth to a place, the IRA could establish a routine and take you out. They knew where we came in. They'd sit and watch. We'd try to vary our routes in and out, but when you're doing thirty trips in a week to the same place there is only so much variation. Helicopters were fired at. One crewman even had a bullet through his bonedome. It went through his helmet but not through his head – not that it would have made any difference to that guy. I'm still amazed the Provisional IRA never really tried to take out a Chinook. (Perhaps it was because we had miniguns fitted. Every week we'd pop off to the ranges and blast off a few rounds. We'd fire them regularly so the blokes on the ground would think there was something meaty on the machine and they'd leave it alone.)

Because there was so much bad weather and helicopters have to fly low it doesn't take the brain of an Einstein to work out where the high points in the country are and position yourself there and wait. For safety we'd either fly low or above 3,000 feet – which is out of AK47 range.

In Belfast we were sharing the civilian airport, Aldergrove – the whole south side is military, the north side civilian. We had to interact with civil traffic. Taking off, we'd keep the aircraft as low as possible within the airport perimeter, then put in maximum power to get as much speed as possible. Come to the airport perimeter, pull back, zoom up as quickly as you can to get extra height on, then transit away. When you arrive at your destination you do tight spiralling turns to get down as soon as possible. Landing is very stressful. That's how I fucked my back up.

In Northern Ireland you have to wear extra body armour on top of the flying suit: flak jackets and chest protectors as well as weapons and helmets. It's a lot of extra weight to carry. Going down, you have to have the ramp cracked open and be looking out the back. To maintain that steep turn in an aeroplane you pull at least two Gs, which causes tremendous strain on the lower back. All the time you held a little grip so if you saw a missile launch you'd call it instantly and fire out a flare. At 300 feet the pilot dumped the collective lever so you came down in a very steep bank, tight spirals all the way down. That used to get my back every time.

For the first few days back in 1986 they wouldn't let us fly, terrified of what would happen if the bastards shot down a Chinook with fifty-four people on board. Then we were released to do it all at night, either at low or high level. The worst threat from small arms is in the mid-range. At low level you don't have time to draw a bead on the helicopter before it's flown past.

We never did much Special Forces stuff. Sometimes we were just tasked to go somewhere with the SAS and obey their orders. We obeyed. It was a vicious time. Some of our troops out there had been kneecapped, then beaten up and eventually had their throats slit. When you heard about that it made you tougher.

When we did get a Special Forces drop-off, at the most we got ten minutes' warning. We'd just rush out of the mess, spilling coffee everywhere, and sign out our bloody guns. Every time we took off we were issued with an SLR (self-loading rifle) and a Browning 9mm pistol. By 1991 we were given the SA80, which we dutifully carried round, though it was about as much use as farting.

On the mainland you were issued a green card, which was your authority to carry a weapon and give the fire-control orders. In Northern Ireland you got a white card, which told you when you were allowed to fire. The rules were pretty basic. You were not allowed to shoot anybody unless they shot at you first. You could return fire only when the bullet was entering your forehead.

The fines for losing a bullet were horrendous but all the lads used to have drawers of them. On my first trip I was logging out my weapons when this huge, unshaven, long-haired lout came and stood next to me. He might have looked and smelled like a hippy but he signed out a Heckler & Koch MP5, a pistol and enough ammo to start a small war. From the way he handled those guns he obviously knew what he was doing. Then he shoved them in a plastic supermarket shopping bag, got into a clapped-out M.o.D-issued Austin Allegro with its wing hanging off and drove off. I never saw him again.

After we checked out our weapons there would be a quick briefing on the task. We'd drop the blokes off, return to the base and wait on immediate standby. It was too high-risk to have a helicopter parked on site.

One thing I never understood was that I could go into the ops room at RAF Aldergrove and the wall there was covered with maps. Around them were photos of people and buildings with arrows going down to various locations and descriptions of Paddy So-and-So, suspected of murder, or Fergus O'Bloke, suspected of involvement in terrorist operations. There were notes for crews to report any movements of vehicles that they saw when flying over them. It was impossible to fly anywhere without flying over one of them. The security forces knew, still know, who all the terrorists are – and where they live. Yet they did nothing.

If it was me I'd arrest all the IRA bastards and have their balls strung up by barbed wire – but then I've always been lenient. The Iraqis were a bunch of bloody festering rings: they thought killing someone was like wiping their arse; they didn't give a fig for human life. I detested them both equally – I think I'd hate whoever my enemy was – but for different reasons. The IRA have committed so many atrocities, killed so many women and children. What can you say about somebody who blows up a bus with God knows how many people on board? I think the IRA are a bunch of tossers. If I could press a button and execute them all in one day I'd do it, but you can't do that. It isn't very politically sound.

While no terrorist activity should be tolerated, at the same time I have to be a realist. I know we can never win the battle with the IRA. The reasons for their doing what they are doing no longer matter. The only sensible option is to finish it.

POST-GULF DISORDER

It used to drive us crazy how they could just slip over the border into the Republic and we couldn't touch them. Once they were over the border there was nothing we could do. Once we landed half a kilometre over the border by mistake. We saw these Paddies running across the fields waving their arms at us. They were dressed in the wrong uniform. We took off at full pitch and disappeared back into the northern fog.

At least we never had to worry about any low-flying complaints. One time we flew over a house with an Irish tri-colour flag hanging up. The owner ran out into the garden, dropped his trousers and bared his arse. So we marked the house's grid reference and told everyone about the incident. For the next week every helicopter in the vicinity was blasting hell out of his flag pole at low level, day and night. Appropriately there was a full moon.

During my second trip to Northern Ireland our main task was troop movements. We also did a lot of transporting of families around, which made me really uncomfortable. We'd take families out only at night and always used the high option for them. Like anyone in the forces, I accept that if you are paid the Queen's shilling at some stage you have to earn it, but not wives and children. I wouldn't expose my family to that risk. There were little boys and girls in the aircraft having a great time – we always made it as much fun as possible – but they were being exposed to a danger. The Chinook is a military helicopter. How could the IRA know who was on it?

The most unpleasant task was moving big water tanks. We'd be on high hover, about 150 feet above the ground, within a quarter-mile of this huge housing estate in Crossmaglen. We are looking down at rows and rows of houses and windows any one of which could have housed somebody with a half-inch gun capable of blowing the shit out of us. In the hover with no speed up, we were a perfect target for a SAM 7.

The Provos do have SAM 7s. It is an easy weapon to get hold of, but so far they have used them to no avail. It is not a major threat because the terrorists need practice with it to be effective. The battery on the SAM has such a short life, only seconds. Switch it on and you have ten seconds to get lock-on and fire it or it's useless. If the target is in cloud it is useless. It has no look–down–shoot–down facilities. If they point the tube down and fire, the missile will just drop out of the end. It probably wouldn't blow up but it might break some Irish toes. The Stinger is much more dangerous but fortunately they've never laid hands on one. Or decided it would be bad PR to blow a Chinook out of the sky.

The real drag about ops in Northern Ireland was that they were always really early starts or late finishes, or both, so we ended up really shagged out. The day we had to do a dawn raid and a Lynx rescue sums it up pretty well.

I dragged myself out of bed at the ungodly hour of 0500 hours, pulled a flying suit on, and staggered off to the armoury with Graham Forbes to draw our weapons. The weather was, as usual, shite. We walked straight out into horizontal rain. Equipped with a 'club' (an SA80) and a rock (the pistol was only useful for throwing at people), we stumbled into the briefing room where the skipper, Rick Cook, had the details of the morning's tasking.

Rick, as usual, looked as though he had just come back from a six-week rest in the Bahamas and fresh as a daisy. Unfortunately he had also, while he waited for the rest of the crew, managed to concoct his version of coffee. The thought was there but, sadly, drinking it made our faces look as if we were sucking on a lemon. For some reason the plants in the briefing room never survived.

On the walls in the briefing room were Ordnance Survey maps of Northern Ireland, covered with writing and arrows and red circles (no-over-fly areas) plus any notes on exercises or any operations going on. The good news was that, for once, we were going to land on one of the IRA. Provided the weather let us fly.

Dave Prichard, the copilot, gave us the MATE brief (nothing sexual: it stands for Met Air-traffic Timing Execution).

'We have the standard zebra's arsehole coming in from the west,' he said, describing the tightly packed bunch of isobars on the weather chart, which meant wind, rain and low visibility. 'At the moment the cloud base here at Aldergrove is four hundred and fifty feet, the visibility is five thousand meters, and the wind is westerly at thirty knots. The forecast is no change – so basically a shitty day.'

A few minutes later we were on the tarmac going through all the preflight checks. I was Number One in charge of the ramp, Graham up by the door. Our passengers ready to arrest an IRA suspect were six RUC officers and six SAS in camouflage fatigues. The RUC were dressed in their dark-green uniform, with pale-green shirts, carrying Heckler & Koch MP5s. Tightly strapped on top of the uniform was their body armour: a square plate a foot square at front and back. Although it looked cumbersome it was quite light in weight. As it was pissing down at the time, they had a dark-green waterproof coat on top. Everyone had that familiar hearing aid connected to his secure radio, visible only by the tiny aerial sticking out the top of his waterproofs. Surprisingly they did not wear a Kevlar hat, just the standard-dress peak cap. The SAS weren't allowed to arrest a civilian. Officially they were there to provide armed support in case of any resistance to arrest or just in case the information turned out to be a set-up or an ambush.

We dumped them down on to the planned site. Outside it was freezing cold, pissing down with rain and blowing a howling gale. Rick kept the rotors turning while they kicked in the door and made a rapid arrest. Less than five minutes later they were back, dragging this half-dressed man with them. I couldn't see his eyes because he was blindfolded. His arms were tied behind his back with plasticuffs. He was thrown into the back and we were off into the hover. His face was chalky, drained of any colour, he was clammy with fear and shock. On the return trip nobody said an audible word to him, though one SAS bloke did whisper in his ear and he went completely rigid.

When we got back to base he was bundled off in a van. We'd learned never to ask what happened after that.

Our next mission was altogether less fun. We had to rescue a crashed Lynx, undersling it and bring it back

In case it a was a tandem load Graham and I had to do a full hook check, which meant lying on our backs on the ground in the rain checking the operation of the three hooks. It should have been an easy task, except that the weather was crap and the visibility was terrible. After we took off Rick had the speed up to 100 knots, and Dave, Graham and myself were really busy calling out all the obstructions, wires and pylons, as well as giving navigation information.

'We have rising ground closing from the eight o'clock,' I called as the ground got closer

'Rising ground closing from the right. You should have the gap ahead about three miles.' Graham confirmed my position check from the front door

'OK, thanks, guys. Looking for it. Speed coming back,' Rick replied. If you could not see ahead it was normal practice for helicopters to slow down to a safe speed and if necessary come to the hover or land. The rising ground continued to close on either side with no sight of any gap.

'Rising ground closing further on the right. Rick, there should be one-hundred-and-fifty-foot wires just under one mile ahead.' Whenever Graham was concerned his Scottish accent grew more pronounced. 'It does not look good at the moment.'

'Yes, OK, guys. I'm not happy with this either. Going for an abort.' The gearbox whine increased as power was poured in and the helicopter climbed like a Saturn rocket. We popped out of the top of the cloud like a cork coming to the top of a barrel of water, and levelled off in the smooth air above the clouds. A beautiful blue sky in contrast to the turbulent crap of a few moments earlier.

Rick was popular with his crews. He involved them in every decision. He wasn't a rip-arse or a frustrated fighter pilot. He was a great SF Flight pilot because he knew his own abilities and would never go beyond them. This mission wasn't important enough to risk our lives unnecessarily. The Lynx wasn't going anywhere.

Later that afternoon the weather cleared sufficiently for us to have another go. No one had been hurt in the Lynx crash – it was caused by mechanical failure, not enemy fire – the problem was getting the aircraft back to Aldergrove. The only way was to take the blades off and undersling the fuselage. We attached a large hook on top of the rotor shaft to carry it. The problem was that because the cargo was too light it would bounce about all over the place. We needed ballast.

There were twenty-five damp squaddies guarding the aircraft under the command of their sergeant major. He was a real Windsor Davies type: foghorn voice and a moustache with the wingspan of an albatross. Graham and I inspected the problem and then radioed back to Aldergrove for a

Wessex to bring out the ballast. Meanwhile those blokes were all itching to get going. I can't say I blamed them. They'd been guarding a lump of metal for six hours and they were soaked through.

'Everything all right, sir?' the sergeant major asked me. Like most soldiers he assumed that anybody in a flying suit must be an officer. 'What's the delay, then?'

'Oh nothing serious. We're just waiting for a Wessex to come in with some ballast. We need ballast before we can lift it.'

'Ballast, sir? How much will that weigh, then?'

'About four hundred pounds, I expect.'

'No problem, sir.' He bellowed over at a couple of soldiers. 'Jones, Smith, go sit in the helicopter while the officers lift it up.'

They rushed over and started to clamber in with me saying, 'No, no!'

'Don't worry, sir. They won't touch anything – or they'll have me to answer to.'

It took a long time to convince him we couldn't do that. His blokes wanted to go because they thought it was a quick trip back to barracks. The problem was that on a transport job like that I would be holding a pickle grip in my hand from the moment we took off to the moment we delivered the cargo. The first thing I would do if anything went wrong was pickle it off.

CHAPTER 16

TIME TO GO

That second trip to Northern Ireland finished it off for me. It was an interesting couple of months and I had a good time socialising with Rick, Graham Forbes, Kev Hardie and newer pilots like Jon Tapper, but when we came home I just needed to get out. Maybe it was because I was starting to get hangovers.

Nowadays I always get a headache after I've been drinking. I never used to. It's very strange. In the Falklands I can remember getting horrendously pissed and I was flying at six the next morning. There were two Navy petty officers waiting outside my door to see what I looked like. I just opened the door and I was perfectly fine. Now if I have six pints, the next day it's Endex.

The truth is I was never very good at the spit-and-polish side of service life. Flying was what I loved. Flying was what I was best at. I was always a scruffy bastard and if I'd stayed on I'd have had to smarten up. If I'd chosen to do pilot training I'd have had to reinvent myself as a gentleman of sorts. If I'd taken that promotion to flight sergeant for the extra money I'd have had to stay in four more years. Either way, I would have overdosed on the RAF and become a sour old bastard.

My official leaving date was 18 June 1992. I'd been

winding down for several months before and I'd fixed it so that I could go on leave for the last four weeks. Then this WO tried to screw up my leave, told me that I'd have to be on standby. Gary Mountjoy, who I'd never got on with, called me up and tried to tell me I wouldn't receive my gratuity unless I came back for the final two days. I told him to go away.

His attitude towards me pissed me off. So I got my own back in a disgusting way. Before I left I went to a pet shop and bought a rat. It must have been ill already because on the way back it died in the car. I stuffed it down the leg of his immersion suit in his locker. Then I went to a butcher's shop, bought four pounds of tripe and stuck that in the back of his locker. He never said a thing about it to the other crew as they'd have never let him forget it. I heard he eventually had the whole locker hauled away and dumped in a skip.

I've never missed the job. Occasionally I miss the idea of thrashing around and scaring the shit out of some old bastard driving his tractor up a field. Some of the people I miss, some I don't. If you didn't have a bunch of good mates and have a good time in the Air Force or you took it too seriously you'd end up putting a bullet in your head. I would never want to change my time there. I had a great time when I was in – some ups, some downs – and it changed me for the better. I saw a lot of the world. I saw death for the first time. I saw life in a different way for the first time. But having come out I certainly don't wish I was back in.

While I got out at the right time, my feeling on actually coming out was uncertainty. I'd left the cushioned life of the RAF to enter a hard outside world right in the middle of a recession. I might have got all my qualifications but suddenly all the jobs I'd set up for when I came out weren't there any more. Jill wasn't working and we had two small kids. Christopher was only three months old and Andrew just over two.

We still had a little bit of money left from the house sale and my gratuity so we weren't completely strapped. But with poor job prospects we couldn't afford to buy our own place. We lived with Jill's mother for a year. We'd been married six years and now I'd walked out on a safe salary of £25,000. We had nowt and my wife was back living with her mother. A lot of wives wouldn't have stood that, but she could see the point and supported me.

The reason our marriage survived the RAF – where so many of our friends' didn't – was because we were, still are, best friends. We saw so many other relationships where the couple didn't really know each other, where they had separate lives, where both partners played away from home. Neither of us are possessive but Jill trusted me and I trusted her. There was no jealousy and no recriminations. That's why we're still together and always will be. I can never phone up and say, 'Darling, I love you.' But I do love her – and Jill has always known that.

I travelled all over doing flying instructing, not making enough to get a house. I eventually got a full-time job teaching air cadets to fly at Carlisle Airfield. After twelve months, a job with Gill Airways came up and I jumped at that. I started in October 1993 and I've been there ever since.

A year after leaving the RAF everything had fallen into place. For the first time in my life I had a full-time job being paid to actually fly an aeroplane. We had just put a deposit down on a new house. We had two healthy baby boys. Jill was pregnant again and desperately hoping for a girl. We didn't realise how lucky we were.

Out of nowhere everything went horribly wrong. From very early on in the pregnancy nothing seemed to fit quite right. Jill went for a scan and was told she was only ten weeks pregnant. She knew she was further on than that. She was worried about this discrepancy between what she thought her dates were and the hospital scan. Then because she was older they did an amniocentesis. This is a sampling of the amniotic fluid to assess the condition of the foetus. I didn't think anything more about it.

Three weeks later a phone call woke us up at nine in the morning. I grunted and told Jill to answer it. It wouldn't be for me any longer. It wasn't.

It was the consultant telling us that the amnio had shown up a problem. 'Definitely not Down's, or anything like it,' she said, and we both breathed a sigh of relief, 'but the baby has the long arm of an X chromosome completely missing.' At the time that meant nothing to either of us. Then she said she wanted to check Jill's and my blood to check this was not a genetic fault.

I told Jill that everything would be OK. I might have believed it but I knew that deep down inside Jill didn't. At the hospital we were ushered into a room for the tests. I started joking with the nurses, trying to cover my concern. The bad feeling grew inside me. They promised to let us know the results within twenty-four hours.

The wait was agony. Far worse than the wait before we first crossed the Iraqi border. We lived in a state of suspended animation, minutes like hours, hours like days, going through the motions, playing with the kids, wandering through this fog of not knowing, but hoping. When the call finally came I wasn't there.

I needed a breath of fresh air so I'd just nipped to the shop. I was walking in through the back door when Jill just flew at me and fell into my arms sobbing. 'She called, David,' she cried. 'She said the baby has massive problems, but she can't discuss it on the phone. We must go to the hospital immediately.'

I was furious with myself. How could I have left her to take that call alone? I should have been the one to break the news. We left immediately. Jill was in a terrible state. Her mother and niece were crying too, but they were looking after the boys for us. Christopher was too young to understand what was happening but Andrew was getting very upset seeing his mum in tears and his dad trying to hold his emotions in check. The journey to the hospital was just a blur, Jill sobbing all the way. I kept quiet. For once.

The consultant was waiting for us. She didn't keep us in suspense. As we walked into the room, she just said, 'I'm very sorry. It's a girl and she's severely handicapped. Her head's much smaller than it should be. Her heart's not the correct size. This is so severe that there are only eight other known cases.'

'In this hospital?' I asked, half dazed by the news.

'In the world.' The consultant explained that because of the extent of the baby's deformities even if she survived the birth she would live only a few hours. She suggested Jill have a termination but this had to be carried out immediately as she was only a week away from the legal limit.

Then came the killer. 'I am afraid you'll have to give birth.' Both the boys were born by caesarean because Jill has such a narrow pelvis. She had always wanted to have a baby naturally and she had always wanted a girl. Now she would get both her wishes. But her child would be born dead.

I saw that news had finished her off completely. I just hugged her. There are some hurts words cannot assuage. After we agreed to the procedure Jill was given some pills to 'break things down' and we were told to come back two days later. That night as we lay in bed Jill felt the baby move for the first time. She woke me up and just sobbed the rest of the night, repeating, 'It's so cruel, it's so unfair,' until dawn came. I felt so helpless, wondering all the while if it was all my fault or whether we could have done anything to prevent it.

On 18 June – the first anniversary of my leaving the RAF – we arrived at the hospital and were shown to a room supposedly away from other women in labour. The nurses tried their best to be sympathetic but I knew Jill did not want me to leave her alone for one second. 'Hopefully it'll all be over by tonight,' one said, but Jill turned to me and said, 'No way. It'll all be over by lunchtime.'

They applied some vaginal gel and told Jill to lie back and wait. Almost immediately she got stomach cramps. All I could do was try to make her laugh. It might sound flippant but it's all I can ever do when others are in pain. I couldn't cry – it's never been in my nature. It hurt so much I wished I could.

Suddenly at eleven o'clock Jill said, 'Something's happening. Get a nurse.' When the nurse went to get assistance Jill looked at me and just cried. I just held her the whole time and I lied. I told her everything would be OK. The pain was awful to see, even though she was drugged up to the eyeballs. It took just over an hour. It ended suddenly in a few minutes of spine-wrenching contractions and one long drawn-out scream. The baby was already dead and for a while so were we. We held each other and gave in to grieving for the dead and for the living.

From the next room came the sound of a newborn baby crying.

We had been advised to see the baby, but we thought she was handicapped on the outside and would look awful. We preferred to think of her as she might have been. We named her Jenny. Two years later we were sent a picture of her. Only then did we learn that Jenny was perfect on the outside. Her problems were only internal. Now we deeply regret that we never held our little girl.

The memory never goes away but we blokes get on with life, laugh and joke our way through the pain. But whereas having a Down's child is an accident of chance, of fate, I couldn't ever quite believe that of Jenny. Only eight cases in the world? I kept wondering. Was it my fault?

It was. About four months after Jenny's birth Jill was watching a TV programme about Gulf War Syndrome, how it had affected returning servicemen, their wives and children. She wondered whether there was a connection. I remembered having my arm shot full of anthrax and hepatitis and everything else going, lying groaning on a camp bed in Victa. Of flying through the oil-well fires in Kuwait, absorbing black poison by the lungful.

We went back to see the consultant. 'I've been waiting for you to come back,' she said. 'I couldn't tell you at the time.' Girls have two X chromosomes and boys one X and one Y chromosome. Jenny had been missing one part of the X chromosome. She told us we were lucky that we'd had only boys because my chromosomes may have been damaged for good. The consultant was from a miliatry area and had dealt with a lot of mothers from that area. She had seen women having the menopause aged twenty-four. In her opinion the chromosome problem was caused by the drugs I'd taken in the Gulf. She can't say so publicly because she can't prove it. Jill and I don't need proof. We know.

We were horrified but in a way almost relieved. At least now we knew why it had happened. The Gulf War had not hurt me. But it had claimed a casualty from my family. It wasn't fair and it has made us both very bitter.

Jill got into contact with a solicitor who wanted us to make a claim against the M.o.D. I'd consider it. Jill won't. 'I can't put a price on my dead baby,' she says. 'It makes me very cross that they can think like that. I don't want money. I just want them to say sorry. It's morally wrong to put a price on my daughter's life. If they write us a letter saying "We are very sorry", I would feel better about it. I know now it's not my fault but part of me can never accept that.'

Jenny is missing from our lives and the reason she is missing is because in the Gulf men and women were given injections without anyone really knowing what the full consequences might be. If the tragedy hadn't happened we wouldn't have had our last little boy – but Jill still goes to bed every night thinking of her. We wake up in the morning and she's not there. Except in our memories. We talk about it but we will never get over it as long as we live.

There's nothing further I can say. I wish I could but it's impossible. I can never escape the legacy of my past.

CHAPTER 17

THE MULL OF KINTYRE

I knew it was a Chinook calling before I heard the pilot's voice. That telltale thud, thud, thudding in the background. The slap of the rotor blades is audible over the radio frequencies the moment they press the speak switch. Loud and clear.

'Aldergrove approach. Good afternoon. This is Foxtrot Four, Juliet Four Zero.'

'Foxtrot Four Zero, roger, call the zone boundary,' answered the controller.

A short time later the Chinook replied, 'Foxtrot Four Zero zone boundary to en-route frequency. Good day.'

Interesting, I thought, a Chinook coasting out to the north? Probably an SF Flight transiting to Prestwick out of RAF Aldergrove. I thought I recognised the pilot's voice but I couldn't put a face to the crackle. Now there was silence. That had been their last call on frequency 120.00.

I'd been out nearly two years but I still knew most of the blokes on the Flight. I wondered how they were getting on with the new Mark 2s and all those Gucci computerised controls. The weather forecast was fog up in Scotland so tonight was a guaranteed layover. They'd be out on the piss up in Prestwick. For a moment I envied them. If I'd stayed in the RAF I could have been flying it myself. Hell, I'd been at the controls flying those beasts for almost 100 hours. With my commercial fixed-wing licence I required only a few more hours to qualify for a helicopter licence.

Instead my attention turned back to the task in hand. My real job. Flying GILL 732 Bravo from Belfast City Airport to Newcastle. The ATR 72 twin-engine turboprop aeroplane was climbing up to 20,000 feet. We crossed the coast at West Fraugh. After twenty minutes tracking along the southern Scottish coast I glanced out of the left-hand cockpit window. I saw a small town fifteen miles to the north. At that height it had the clear clean lines of a model village. Lockerbie looked serene and peaceful.

It was just after 6 p.m. on Thursday, 2 June 1994.

Ninety minutes later, as I was in the pilots' lounge getting ready for my final flight of the day, my mobile rang. It was Jill. Strange time to call, I thought. Usually at this stage she'd have been relaxing in front of *EastEnders* with the boys in bed. She was pregnant again, shattered most of the time. We knew she was carrying a healthy baby boy but the memory of Jenny was still fresh. Jill wasn't taking any chances.

'David,' she said, 'a Chinook's gone down in Scotland. There was a news flash on the TV.'

'Who was on it?'

'They didn't say.'

My immediate reaction was to find out if there was anybody I knew on board. I flicked on Ceefax to see if they had released any names but there was nothing there. Just the bare facts. An RAF Chinook had crashed on the Mull of Kintyre. No information about survivors. I didn't expect any but you still hope. And when hope fails all you can do is pray that you don't know anybody on board.

Being out of the RAF I was also out of the loop. I was in a dilemma. Did I phone up the squadron and say 'Dave McMullon here, just phoning for a quick chat,' when it would be blatantly obvious why I was calling. I had another problem. My flight to Aberdeen was taking off in ten minutes.

Instead I yelled at Jill, who had been patiently hanging on all the time. 'For Christ's sake, phone somebody and find out what's going on. Try Debbie Scullen. Or any of the other wives. I've got to go.'

Waiting to hear was the hardest part. Every minute I felt the worst had already happened. At least flying concentrated my mind. For a while. I'd hardly been back on the ground a minute when the phone rang. Jill.

'David,' she said. 'You had better stand by for this.'

'Who was it?' I slumped on to a chair.

'Rick Cook …'

Silence. Somewhere in my head I counted. One thousand and one. One thousand and two.

'Kev Hardie …'

One thousand and one. One thousand and two.

'Graham Forbes …'

One thousand and one. One thousand and two.

'Jon Tapper.'

The names hit me one after another, punching home hard, driving into my stomach. I mumbled something to Jill and switched the phone off.

I just sat there, knuckles clenched tight and white around the phone. I was shocked, perhaps in shock for a few minutes. Then through the fog I began to remember. My immediate reaction on hearing somebody has died has always been to think of the last time I saw them, to recall what I was doing.

The last time I had spoken to Graham was on the phone

a couple of months before. I had Christopher in my arms. He'd been wriggling and squirming, chattering so much rubbish I had to cut the conversation short. Graham, always the gentleman, always laid back, always smoking a cigar. Jon Tapper, wishing me the very best of luck in my civvy career and shaking my hand outside the crewroom just before I left. Kev, getting pissed at Steve French's party, standing there with a glass of beer in his right hand, his left running back through his strawberry-blond hair, his chest all puffed out to show his muscles, pecs flexing, trying to chat up all the birds – Jill included – while his wife laughed in the corner. Kev never relaxed. He was always holding a pose. He'd probably held it as they hit the ground. At that thought I tried a smile but nothing moved

I'd spoken to Rick a lot on the phone and my mate Andy Fairfield – Rick's best man, and his daughter's godfather – kept me up to date with his movements. But the last time I'd seen him was at one of the squadron parties in Belfast. No, hang on, the last time I saw Rick I was flying him. We were coming back into RAF Aldergrove with Rick and Dominic Potts in the cockpit. 'Right, Dave, it's your turn.' Rick leaped out of his seat to let me in, and I flew back to RAF Aldergrove with Rick in the jump seat.

I landed it, too. Christ, Graham Forbes was in the back too, taking the piss out of me because I didn't have a steady hover. 'Come on, Dave, bring the fucking tail round, man,' he said in his soft Scottish accent. 'Sod off, I can hardly keep it straight.' Rick was pissing himself with laughter.

That was the last time I actually flew a Chinook, I thought. That was when I knew I wouldn't ever be going back. They have taken too many of my friends.

I drove home, the memories tumbling around my brain. I called Andy Fairfield, who'd been speaking to Rick's brother Chris on the phone. They were still waiting for information. They hadn't said officially that everyone was dead. They didn't need to. When a helicopter crashes you don't think about survivors. Twenty-three tons of spinning metal doesn't do anybody any good.

I couldn't get any information out of Odiham and I was left there with the phone dangling in my hand asking all the unanswerable questions. Why? How? What if? Then all the news bulletins came through and I saw the sections of the aircraft broken up and all I could do was keep imagining where my friends had been. Kev was Number One, back left; Graham was Two sitting at the door; Rick in the right-hand seat, Jon in the left.

My wife's thoughts were very different. Jill imagined a woman sitting snug in her married quarters at Odiham, switching on the radio or the TV and hearing about a Chinook crash in Scotland. She imagined the station commander's black car pulling up outside the house and looking out of the window to see the Number One uniform and the padre walking slowly up the garden path, to her front door. I had never thought of it that way before. In the past I was always the one going away. Only now can I imagine the pain. To live with that must be horrendous.

It hit Jill hard. She knew Kev and particularly Graham well. We'd been to mess dinners and parties together. Graham had always been charming company. Now he was gone, leaving a fiancée, an ex-wife and children. Kev was married. The two pilots had kids. Jon's wife was pregnant too. Fucking helicopters.

It took six months for the Board of Inquiry to report. The papers were rife with their usual bollocks suggesting mobile phones might have upset the control system. I kept hearing some pretty disturbing rumours from mates on the squadron about the new Mark 2 Chinooks. Then a few weeks before the findings were made public the whispers started: they were going to blame the pilots. I couldn't believe it. The RAF's own publication on Flight Safety – AP3207 – states that: 'Only in cases in which there is no doubt whatsoever shall deceased aircrew be found negligent.'

Yet there it was in the conclusions of the AOC (Air Officer Commanding) to the forty-three-page Board of Inquiry report. In black and white. 'For not exercising appropriate care and judgment the pilots were negligent to a gross degree.' Aside from slaying the pilots' good names without sufficient evidence the Board findings were a slap across my face. I took it personally and I still do. That might seem strange. After all, I wasn't in the RAF any more and I'd been a crewman, not a pilot.

All they talked about on the Board of Inquiry was the pilots. They failed to even consider any input from the crewmen. The Board treated it as if the loadmasters had nothing to do with the flight except look after the passengers. Indeed the AOC's remarks on the Board findings showed how much use he thought the crewmen would be on the flight: 'They were not in a position to offer much useful navigational information to the pilots', and 'they would have been occupied with the passengers'.

That is bollocks. The implication is that they would be busy with the VIPs, pouring out tea into china cups from a silver teapot. Once a passenger is in his seat and strapped in, then he or she is just self-moving cargo. The crewmen would then continue with their job of helping the pilots in whatever way they could. Clearly with these comments the AOC has no idea of the calibre of crews he has working for him. He is selling them far short of their worth. All the crewmen knew exactly the workload in the cockpit of the helicopter, knew what the pilots required and when they needed assistance.

I can say that both through the eyes of a former crewman

and of a pilot. Today I am a training captain, and an examiner for the airline I work for, so I can see both sides of the crew's problems. I know that Graham and Kev would not be sitting there with their thumbs up their arses looking good for the passengers.

To the AOC they were just stewards in uniform and so they were generously absolved of any blame. But in my book if it was crew error (which is far from proven as far as I am concerned) all the crew should be held responsible. That was what we had been trained for in the SF Flight – one for all, all for one. If I was in the back and there was a crash I would be responsible. You are all part of the crew. You are all going to die in the same crash. It is the job of the whole crew to get the aircraft through its appointed task. Not just the pilot.

Unfortunately Chinooks do not carry flight recorders so the absolute truth about the crash will never be known. It is difficult to formulate an opinion without all the facts, but the facts that I have learned have made me angry. Very angry. The greatest irony is that while I, a former crewman, feel that the crew are either all or none of them responsible for the crash, those in the higher echelons of the RAF seem only concerned with hiding their own failures. Of pinning the blame on dead men who can't answer back.

Flight Zulu Delta 576 was carrying twenty-five of the top security men in the country. The crew were naturally aware of the passengers' importance – and not just because they were all issued with prawn sandwiches. Both Jon Tapper, the skipper, and Rick were renowned for being very cautious. If any member of the crew wasn't happy the first thing the pilot would do was head for a safe altitude.

I know that Graham had prepared maps for the flight the night before (that fact was brought out by witnesses to the Board of Inquiry). He had been briefed and he'd then gone through the route on his own. So there was another set of maps in the cabin. All the crew knew from studying the maps that there was high ground and where it was. This was a well-flown route and the Chinook had more navigation kit on board than the commercial airliner I fly now. Nobody is going to deliberately kill themselves. Even if they suddenly flew into cloud they wouldn't crash straight into the hill they saw five seconds before. It would be as logical as my driving the wrong way up the M1 in rush-hour traffic at ninety miles an hour.

One inescapable fact to me is that this was an SF Flight. To be considered for it pilots have to be above the average and most are well above that mark. These were guys who after eleven hours' solid flying could pull an LDV out of a gorge in the pitch-black with inches of clearance on either side. I'm not saying that mistakes don't happen – because they do – but as soon as the weather started to get worse all four of the crew would have been alert and looking out for things.

The last sighting of the Chinook was from Mark Holbrook, an instrument maker who was sailing off the Mull of Kintyre. Sailors are generally very good judges of weather conditions – they have to be – and he reported he was two miles away from the Mull lighthouse, which he could see. He could also see the high ground but cloud was covering the top of it. When the Chinook flew overhead he estimated its height as between 200 and 400 feet. Visibility like that is Ray-Bans weather for a helicopter. When it's really shitty is when the cloud base is fifty feet and you are trying to hover-taxi to find where the wires are. At the Fatal Accident Inquiry in Scotland, Holbrook stated that he thought the pilots could see the Mull when they flew over him.

Throughout the flight Graham would have been studying his map, and been in intercom contact with the pilots. At the first sign of bad weather he would have raised the front door to look out and see if anything was there. I'd have been moving between the door and the pilots, constantly checking and supporting them while Kev would have been looking out of his perspex bubble. If either of them had called a 'low-level abort' Rick would have reacted as he had a thousand times before. Immediately. Straight up.

The standard low-level abort in a helicopter is to roll the wings level and pull maximum power. If you do that in a Chinook the rate of ascent virtually goes off the clock. As Zulu Delta 576 was carrying only people it was as light as a feather. At full power it can climb 200 feet in less than three seconds. Even if they went into cloud at 100 feet knowing there was high ground ahead, if Rick had just pulled the power on they would have cleared the summit with no effort at all. It wasn't a big hill.

They had the power available to them, the crew available and they knew where they were. So why didn't they climb?

Instead the back of the aircraft hit the hill first. That first impact ripped the rear half of the fuselage off. Kev Hardie was killed instantly. The Chinook, at an angle of thirty degrees up, trying to climb, bounced off the hillside and came down 200 yards over the brow of the hill disintegrating into thousands of pieces. They know Rick was flying because of the lacerations on his body. The front door was destroyed by the crash impact but Graham was thrown clear. Sometimes I wonder what his final thoughts were. I know what mine would have been. Fucking Mark 2.

Twenty-nine people died on the Mull of Kintyre that day. Why? I do not know. I will not come to a conclusion (as the AOC did) without any evidence to support it. I do feel that the RAF have not supported the people who so eagerly supported them. I feel that the AOC was too eager to loose the arrows of guilt when there was not enough evidence to attribute human failings. Why did the AOC want this 'negligent to a gross degree' result from the inquiry? Against all other evidence, and against the RAF's own Flight Safety AP3207? I support the families of the deceased crews, who have shown great determination in clearing the names of some excellent men and fighting the unjust verdict of the M.o.D. They are hanging on like a terrier dog and will not let go until it is resolved.

Chris Scullen, the best helicopter pilot I have ever flown with, told me that it took him six months before he felt comfortable flying the Mark 2 Chinook. It took most pilots on the squadron twelve months and some are still not happy with it today.

On 2 June 1994, Jon Tapper and Rick Cook had precisely three hours' flying time on the Mark 2. Between them. On the morning of 2 June the same crew had carried out an earlier duty in the accident aircraft, and returned to Aldergrove to prepare for its last flight.

Rick Cook was barely in currency on the Mark 2. He had completed his conversion four months earlier on 7 March 1994, amassed only one hour fifty minutes of nonhandling time, and two hours of dual. Less than two hours' actual handling time. Jon Tapper was not current on the Mark 2. The QHI (qualified helicopter instructor) who delivered the aircraft the day before flew with him for twenty minutes.

With the restrictions laid out below I am interested to know how engine-failure emergencies were practised on the conversion (i.e. if one engine's power was reduced to simulate failure as was the normal in training on the Mark 1, what would have happened if the good engine had failed?). If there were concerns over the reliability of the engines and they did not have any single-engine practice what happens if one does go?

Although from the outside the Mark 2 looked identical to the Mark 1 the only thing that was the same was the number on the side. The old models were shipped back to Boeing in the States and completely stripped down – even the shell was peeled back – and the insides changed. Lots of new high-tech electronic gizmos were fitted. One major modification was putting in a new engine–control management system, called FADEC (Full Authority Digital Electronic Control). This was designed to make the engines more responsive to the pilots' power demands, and removed the need for the engines to be 'beeped'. FADEC controlled fuel management to the engines, so now a computer decided – after comparing the amount of power the pilot requires – how much fuel went to the engines. Too much fuel, and the engines, followed by the rotors and the gearboxes, would overspeed. Too little and the engine would stop.

Whenever an aircraft is modified it is sent to Boscombe Down, where the RAF test pilots put it through its paces. Their job is to fly the helicopter to the limit of its abilities and then to write the crew manual, which tells the pilot the limitations of the aircraft: its maximum speed, maximum angle of bank, flight envelope. All of this helps them handle any emergencies. Less than halfway through the testing of the Mark 2 the new engine–control management system kept on doing all sorts of weird things – either shutting down the engines or making them overrun for no apparent reason. In the old mechanical system the pilots could solve the problem manually but the new electronic black box could not be overridden by a mere mortal.

The test pilots stopped flying the Mark 2s for six weeks and requested that Boeing and Lycoming came across to sort the problems out. When they resumed flying, five weeks of regular malfunctions from the FADEC caused them to suspend any further tests. They refused to fly the Chinook

Mark 2 any more on 1 June. The day before the crash.

The ZD576 (and all other Mark 2 Chinooks) had a restricted release to service, which gave them a maximum takeoff weight of 18,000 kg. This was the weight at which the helicopter was able to hover on one engine. Due to the number of failures it was considered a reasonable possibility that a failure could occur. An icing restriction was placed on it – no flight in cloud below a temperature of four degrees Celsius – because in order to do an icing test the test pilots had to partially block one of the engine intakes to simulate ice build-up and see if this put any limitations on the engine. This test was not done because of the unreliability of the engines. The pilots feared the good engine might fail, leaving them with a partially blocked-off intake on the untested engine.

ZD576 was delivered as a Mark 2 on 21 April 1994. On landing at Odiham it had an engine problem with the Number 1 (left-hand) engine, which resulted in the complete engine being changed. After a flight on 10 May the collective lever was found to be stiff and have a restriction. After an inspection a mounting bracket was found to have come away from its mounting point on the flying-control pallet. This caused the collective lever to pull to the floor and was very stiff.

The engineers sent out a 'Serious Fault Signal' and informed all the other Chinook squadrons and Boscombe Down of the find. On 17 May an emergency power caption illuminated three times, indicating an engine problem. The whole engine was rejected again. On 25 May there was a master warning indicating that the Number 2 engine was about to fail.

Just over a week later Zulu Delta 576 crashed killing everyone on board. In just under six weeks, from delivery to crash, the helicopter had been through two engines, a string of engine-failure captions and a serious flying-control fault. This was not considered relevant by the Board of Inquiry.

Tony Cables, the Senior Investigator of Aircraft Accidents for the AAIB, said that 'the possibility of a control-system jam could not be fully determined'. The part that had become detached on the collective run on 10 May was found to be detached in the crash wreckage. He wrote, 'There had been little evidence available to eliminate the possibility of pre-impact detachment.' He also said after inspecting the wreckage, 'The method of attaching components to the pallet appeared less positive and less verifiable than would normally be expected for a flight control system application.'

The method used to see if there was a fault with the FADEC was a device known as DECU (Digital Engine Control Unit). This was too badly damaged in the crash to ascertain the serviceability of the Number 1 engine system.

At the time of the crash the M.o.D was suing the engine manufacturer, Textron Lycoming, for $3 million over problems with the FADEC engine-control system, which had caused serious damage to ZA718 – the first Chinook to be modified. These problems included engines overspeeding, causing rotor r.p.m. to go up to 140 per cent. Luckily this was on the ground, otherwise the results might have been lethal. This case has now been settled. The M.o.D has been paid. I think that is relevant too. The M.o.D disagrees.

The AOC did not like the delays very much, as the aircraft had constant commitments. The squadrons continued flying the Mark 2s while flying under certain restrictions, even though the test pilots were unhappy. I have never heard of that happening in peacetime. If it was a fast jet, or anything with wings, there wouldn't be a cat in hell's chance of pilots being asked to fly it. In a Tornado if something goes wrong you have a yellow handle and you can eject out of it. But helicopters are the shit end of the RAF.

The Chinook Mark 2 had been put into operational service with no manuals and little or no training of the crews. The pilots were not happy because they had not had enough flying time. Instead of pages of different limitations they had a blank sheet of white paper with the comprehensive and reassuring information 'to be issued'. The Flight Reference Cards, which were kept in the flying-suit pockets – and detail emergency procedures – were based on the Chinook D Model, which did not have FADEC fitted. The pilots were worried and had even communicated their concerns to their families. Rick Cook had taken out extra life insurance.

Rick's last words on the ground were that he was unhappy with the machine he was flying that day. Flight Lieutenant Geoffrey Young spoke to Rick just before he left Aldergrove on the afternoon of 2 June. He asked him how he was getting on with the Mark 2. 'He replied,' Young told the Board of Inquiry, 'with words to the effect that the Mark 2 was OK but there were some concerns over the reliability of the engines. He then qualified that, as not being concern for the engines but for their control units.'

If there had been any doubt, the helicopter would have pulled up to safe altitude. In the Board findings they suggested they would have been reluctant to climb to a safe altitude because the machine hadn't been cleared under icing conditions below four Celsius. Apart from asking what the hell it was doing on a sensitive flight without having its icing conditions cleared, that is simply ludicrous. If there is high ground approaching at 150 m.p.h. you don't crash into it because you're more worried about busting your icing clearance. Grow up. That doesn't happen.

Then there was the transponder code which identifies

every aircraft on a radar sweep. There are three universal emergency codes used worldwide. If you have a mechanical problem and put 7700 on the transponder every single radar screen for miles around will flash up with red lights; 7600 is the code for a radio failure and there is another one for a hijacking. Crash investigators discovered the transponder was reading 7760, two digits out from 7700. It shouldn't have been anywhere near that as the Chinook code is a dozen digits out. That difference could not have been caused by crash impact because you need a sledgehammer to move them.

Were the pilots trying to change the transponder codes to an emergency frequency as they hit the hill?

Because there was no flight data recorder the Board of Inquiry used information from the TANS (Tactical Air Navigation System) to determine the sequence of events leading up to the crash. Yet pilots, the RAF, and Racal, the makers of the system, all acknowledge that it cannot be viewed as accurate. Except in this one case.

There are too many ifs and buts to stamp 'Pilots negligent to a gross degree' on Rick Cook and Jon Tapper. If a Jaguar or a Phantom manages a 'controlled flight into terrain' they usually manage to blame it on bad weather. The President of the Board of Inquiry could not bring himself to blame the pilots for human failure. However the AOC took the findings and overruled them. Day, a former helicopter pilot, had not been out on the Mull himself to look at the evidence.

That would never happen in the civilian world. Indeed, a fatal-accident inquiry in Scotland chaired by Sheriff Sir Stephen Young deemed there was insufficient evidence to allocate blame. The RAF have refused to change their findings, perhaps because they are in shock that anyone has dared to challenge the findings of a Board of Inquiry. If there was indeed negligence my opinion is that it lies much further up the chain of command. The pilots were made the scapegoats.

When a new aircraft crashed into the Mull of Kintyre with twenty-five of the nation's top antiterrorist and security experts on board it was very embarrassing. Especially for any high-ranking officer who might have ordered that machine into service against the advice of his own test pilots. Once sabotage was ruled out it was in the interests of the hierarchy for the cause of the crash to be crew negligence.

Talking to my friends in the SF Flight I heard another story that concerned Jon Tapper. In Belfast there was an incident in which a Chinook had dropped a bunch of troops off. As usual a crowd had gathered. The downwash had picked up a piece of netting, which hit someone on the ground. Only a minor incident causing a minor injury. However, there was a unit inquiry over it. In a telephone discussion with one of the Squadron Leaders at Odiham Jon was informed that if he was involved in an incident in which the CA (Certificate of airworthiness release) was broken then the captain would be held personally liable for any civil litigation. Apparently, the RAF doesn't have any liability.

That stinks. It is immoral. I was always taught that loyalty was a two-way street. But if the RAF cannot support one of their own in so minor a matter why should it surprise me that they should crucify his good name, particularly if he is dead? More than ever the behaviour of the RAF over the Mull crash made me certain that my decision to leave the service was the right one.

Nearly every week high in the skies above the Irish Sea I hear the familiar slap of the Chinook rotor blades over the radio. I used to wish I was back with the boys. Not any more. The Mull killed that desire as dead as it killed my friends. Flying in a Chinook is like wrestling with a force of nature. You have to treat it with constant respect. Or one day it will catch you unawares and tear you apart. It has never suffered fools gladly and I no longer wish to be a fool.

I have lost twelve friends in Chinook crashes. I nearly died myself more times than I care to tell my wife. That is more than enough.

But I still love to fly.

GLOSSARY

AFCS	automatic flight-control system: makes the helicopter more stable in flight
AI	attitude indicators: tells a pilot about the attitude of his craft in relation to specified directions, especially when the natural horizon is not visible
APU	Auxiliary Power Unit
ASI	airspeed indicator
AWACS	airborne warning-and-control system
Bergen	rucksack
Bluntys	administrative staff
bonedome	flying helmet
BV	small tracked vehicle for carrying personnel
CA release	airworthiness release to service, listing any limitations on aircraft use
CAP	crew-alerting panel: alerts the pilots to problems
CGI	cruise guide indicator: measures stress on fore and aft gearboxes
collective	a lever with a large hand grip that comes out of the floor to the left of each seat; on top of the collective are various 'BEEP'

	switches used to fine-tune the engine controls
coolie hat	a control device shaped as its name suggests – part of the cyclic stick – which controls the fine trimming of a helicopter's flight
crabs	RAF personnel
CT	counter-terrorist
cyclic stick	held in the pilot's right hand, used to control altitude
DASH	differential airspeed hold
DS	drill sergeant
DSF	Director of Special Forces
ECL	engine condition lever
Endex	end of exercise
EW	electronic warfare
FEBA	forward edge of battle area
GPS	global positioning system
HSI	horizontal-situation indicator: provides navigation information to the pilot
Jesus Nut	large nut holding helicopter rotors on to gearbox shaft
LDV	two-seater vehicle for desert use – like a beach buggy with guns
minging	dirty and smelly
MSR	main supply route
NAPs	nerve-agent poisoning tablets, for protection against biological weapons
NBC	Nuclear Biological Chemical warfare: protective clothing used for protection against nuclear, biological or chemical weapons is an NBC suit
NVGs	night-vision goggles
OCU	Operational Conversion Unit – a course for aircrew

oggin	sea
PATA	Pontrailis Army Training Area near Hereford, UK
pickle grip	used by crewman to control rescue hoist or jettison underslung loads
PNGs	passive night goggles, similar to NVGs (q.v.)
PPL	private pilot's licence
PTI	physical-training instructor
PVR	premature voluntary retirement: given to recruits who are not up to it or are difficult to discipline
radalt	radar altimeter: gives the height of a helicopter from the ground
RV	rendezvous point
RWR	radar warning receiver
SA80	British armed forces standard-issue rifle
SAM	surface-to-air missile
SAS	Special Air Service
SBS	Special Boat Service, the nautical equivalent of the SAS (q.v.)
SF Flight	Special Forces Flight
SQMS	Squadron Quartermaster Sergeant
VSI	vertical-speed indicator: shows how fast the craft is climbing
WO	warrant officer
XMSN chip	a warning that indicates that a chip of metal is lodged in one of the gearboxes
X-rays	terrorists
Yankees	hostages
yaw pedal	rudder pedals that, by controlling the rudder, also control the craft's yaw – or its tendency not to hold a straight course

CHINOOK!

Zero Doppler Notch   refers to the Doppler shift in radar signals when a craft is coming towards or moving away from the radar system; can be eliminated by special manoeuvring of the craft

PICTURE PERMISSIONS

All photographs are the property of David McMullon except where mentioned below. Where we have been unable to ascertain copyright, we will be pleased to correct the copyright details in any future editions of this book.

Copyright on other pictures used as follows:

In bi-plane © George Taylor
Chinook stuffing © Boeing photo C105497
Chinook controlled by FADEC © Boeing photo C110345
Carrying three loads © Boeing photo C63280
Building tower © Boeing photo C114927
Cross-section of Chinook © Quadrant Picture Library
Chinook 13 course © Crown Copyright/M.o.D.
Reproduced with the permission of the Controller of Her Britannic Majesty's Stationery Office
Landing on to carrier ship © Crown Copyright/M.o.D
Reproduced with the permission of the Controller of Her Britannic Majesty's Stationery Office
Piece of plane wreckage in front of burning homes © Robin Bryden
Burning car © Robin Bryden
An abandoned car on the A74 with the burning crate to

INDEX

aircrew respirator 69
aircrew selection 18
aircrew training 20
Airman Aircrew Initial
    Training Course 25
Ark Royal 139

body armour 214

Cessna 10, 12, 15
Chinook crash, Mull of
    Kintyre 232–47
  Board of Inquiry
      235–36
  pilots blamed 236
Chinook helicopters
    39–58
  auxiliary power unit
      48–49
  control system 43,
      46–47, 51–52, 54,
      57–58
  crew 44, 55

  grounding fears after
      crash 100
  hydraulics 47–48
  instruments 44–45
  refits 145–46
Civil Aviation Authority
    134
combat survival course
    99, 101–2
  interrogation 102
counterterrorist unit 71
Cyprus 33

de la Billière, General Peter
    156
desert camouflage 158

Falklands 43, 56, 101,
    103–8, 196
fast-roping 68
flying lessons 11–14
  first solo 13–14
Frog missiles 200

Full Authority Digital
  Electronic Control
  (FADEC)   241, 243

Gatling miniguns   167–68
Gazelle helicopters   33, 34
Germany   146–48, 151–52
glossary   249–52
Gulf War   155–69,
    171–89, 191–207
  American deaths   176
  end of   207
  Frog missiles   200
  Iraq bombing   168
  kit   167
  Patriot missiles   176
  Scud missiles   161, 169,
    175–76
  Special Forces (SF) Flight
    missions   197
  see also Iraq and Kuwait
Gulf War Syndrome   229

Harriers   138
helicopters
  Army   63
  Chinook   39–58, 43,
    44–45, 46–48, 51–52,
    54, 57–58, 100,
    145–46
  Chinook crash, Mull of
    Kintyre   232–47
  Gazelle   33, 34
  Huey   64

Lynx   71–72
Puma   33, 36–37, 64
Sea King   33
Sikorsky   62
Wessex   33, 34
Huey helicopters   64

IRA   213, 216–18
  surface-to-air missiles
    218
Iraq   161–62, 171
  Frog missiles   200
  main supply route   174
  military targets bombed
    168
  Patriot missiles   176
  poison fears   164
  Scud missiles   161, 169,
    175–76
  see also Gulf War and
    Kuwait

Kurds   211
Kuwait   199–205
  oil-well fires   199
  see also Gulf War and Iraq

Larnaca, Cyprus: hijack
    108
Lightnings   8
Lockerbie   3, 111–27, 130
  media vultures   120
Lynx helicopters   71–72

marriage 61
McMullon, Jill 226–30
  birth problems 226–28
  Gulf War Syndrome
    worries 229
  house disaster 208
  marriage 61
Morocco 140–41

nerve gas 164
night-vision goggles
  64–68
Northern Ireland 33,
  212–22, 246
  body armour 214
  IRA 213, 216–18
  terrorists known to
    security forces 216
Norway 131–32
nuclear/biological/chemical
  warfare kit 68–69,
  163

oil rigs 131

Patriot missiles 176
Piper Vagabond 134
promotion turned down
  135
Puma helicopters 33,
  36–37, 64

RAF
  aircrew selection 18, 19

aircrew training 20
Airman Aircrew Initial
  Training Course 25
career choice 17–18
Chinook crash 245–46
combat survival course
  99, 101–2
first-aid training 30
parachute training
  31–32
Special Forces (SF) Flight
  59, 62–64, 102–3

Saddam Hussein 155
SAS 62, 63–64, 70, 75,
  77–83
  desert tactics 74
  desert vehicle 173
  Gulf War 161, 169,
    174–75, 185–86
  Northern Ireland 213,
    219–20
SBS 62, 63–64, 75
  Gulf War 161, 199,
    204
Scud missiles 161, 169,
  175–76
Sea King helicopters 33
Secombe, Harry 156–57
SF Flight See Special
  Forces
Sikorsky helicopters 62
snow hazards 131–32
Special Air Services See

SAS

Special Boat Services *See*
   SBS

Special Forces (SF) Flight
   59–60, 62–64
   enemy missions   197
   Jordan   73–74
   officer–NCO
      relationships   102–3
surface-to-air missiles
   (SAMs)   136–37
   IRA   218

teaching post   225
Thatcher, Margaret   106
Turkey   211–12
Turner, Chris   14
Turner Special   14–17

United Arab Emirates   157

Wessex helicopters   33, 34
white-out conditions
   131–32

**SIMON &
SCHUSTER**

THE TOMBSTONE
IMPERATIVE
THE TRUTH ABOUT AIRCRAFT SAFETY
Andrew Weir

'We regulate by counting tombstones'
US FEDERAL AVIATION OFFICIAL

This book is a thorough and meticulously
researched investigation into the important
issue of passenger aircraft safety. It
concludes that not enough is being done to
improve flight safety and that improvements
are only made when enough passengers die
in a crash to force the issue into the public
eye. It is a fallacy to believe that flying is the
safest way to travel.
This is a serious ground-breaking,
campaigning book which is bound to cause
enormous controversy.

PRICE £16.99
ISBN 0 684 81993 7

POCKET
B O O K S

This book and other **Pocket** titles are available from your book shop or can be ordered direct from the publisher.

0 671 01603 2	**White Lie**	John Templeton Smith	£6.99
0 671 01048 4	**Goldfinder**	Keith Jessop	£6.99
0 671 85292 2	**The Ten Thousand**	Harold Coyle	£5.99
0 671 85266 3	**Code of Honour**	Harold Coyle	£5.99
0 671 85564 6	**Shock Wave**	Clive Cussler	£5.99
0 671 85563 8	**Flood Tide**	Clive Cussler	£5.99

Please send cheque or postal order for the value of the book, and add the following for postage and packing: UK inc. BFPO 75p per book; OVERSEAS inc. EIRE £1 per book.
OR: Please debit this amount from my:

VISA/ACCESS/MASTERCARD...
CARD NO...
EXPIRY DATE..
AMOUNT £...
NAME...
ADDRESS...
....
SIGNATURE...

Send orders to:
Book Service By Post,
PO Box 29, Douglas, Isle of Man, IM99 1BQ
Tel: 01624 675137, Fax 01624 670923
http://www.bookpost.co.uk
e-mail: bookshop@enterprise.net for details
Please allow 28 days for delivery.
Prices and availability subject to change without notice.